Portraits, Passion, and Other Pastimes

ART OF LOVE
BOOK ONE

CHARLIE LANE

First Edition

Editing by Krista Dapkey / Chris Hall

Cover art by Anna Volkin

❀ Created with Vellum

To Brian, who, like Raph, claims to have no imagination. (Yes, he does.) But even if he didn't, I'd still love him.

Prologue

A*pril 1806*

Some days brought childhood back, screaming in on horse-fast legs with greedy fingers. Today, so far, proved such a day—perfect blue sky above spring-green grass, and a breeze trailing invisible fingertips over the lake's mirrored surface. Miss Matilda Bellvue tipped her face to the sun and held the spring day to her tightly. A perfect day for a picnic, and one never knew when joys would sink to sorrows.

Matilda smoothed her lavender skirts and pulled her mother's cream-colored shawl close despite the day's warmth. She pulled it more to ward against a shiver of the soul. She'd stopped wearing black on the outside only.

Too heavy thoughts for a day like this, so she shook them away, let her shawl drop, and opened her ears to the chatter of her companions. Twelve-year-old Maggie beside her made observations about the clouds. They looked like ladies' hats.

1

And little Theodore, not quite ten years of age, argued with her. They looked like horses, not hats.

Across the soft expanse of blankets on which they all sat, the Marquess and Marchioness of Waneborough whispered lovely things to one another, low and sweet as the tarts they'd all shared moments before. Only bits and pieces of their conversation floated to Matilda on the wind, but each one made her blush.

A soft, warm swish bothered her skirts, but she did not open her eyes. She knew what it was—the boot at the bottom of a gentleman's extended leg, swaying mindlessly back and forth. Viscount Stillman, the marquess's heir, laid out long and lean along one side of the blankets, arms folded behind his head, ankles crossed, face lifted to the sun.

She opened her eyes, just a bit, to peek at him. In all her nineteen years, she'd never seen so fine a man—dark hair, strong jaw, and when he opened his eyes, bluer than blue. Laid out as he was now, he made her breath catch. A governess should not find air difficult to breathe when in the presence of her charge's older brother.

But the air *would* thicken, and her heart *would* race, and with parents gone and half brother decidedly uninterested in her well-being, one must take pleasure where it came, whether that be in a sunny spring day or the fine form of a dozing man. Especially since, as a governess, she'd likely never have what she'd always expected to have as Baron Cowperly's daughter— a husband, a home.

She squeezed her eyes shut once more. She'd left her home almost a year ago, had watched it shrink as the coach had taken her farther away toward a family she'd never met before, away from being a daughter to being in service, a governess of no importance. She'd not known what to expect of the marquess and his family, had heard they were more than odd, outcasts of the ton for their bohemian ways. But her half brother, Gerald, had not even said goodbye or waved from the front door as she'd left, while the Marchioness of Waneborough and her two youngest children had been waiting for her when she'd arrived at their home, Briarcliff Manor. Gerald had treated her like a stranger, and they'd treated her like family from the start, and no matter what the ton whispered, Matilda liked them. Likely too much. Governesses were not family, after all. Merely temporary employees. They did *not* get attached.

She had no family now. Best to remember that.

"Matilda, my dear, do have another tart. You look positively wraithlike. Still. I've been trying to plump you up, but you do tend toward the slender." The marchioness puffed the last word into a pout.

Matilda opened her eyes and found the viscount staring holes into her, those blue eyes like the hottest of flames. "I think you look perfectly well, Miss Bellvue. Mama, it's not quite the thing to comment on another lady's looks in a negative way."

Matilda chuckled, and the viscount caught her gaze, glowered a bit before his face softened, the wind picked up a lock of his hair to tousle it, and his full mouth hinted at a smile. Just for her. But his eyes seemed removed from mirth, seemed to see things beyond a picnic blanket and spring day. What ills plagued a man like him?

His mother threw an arm out wide. "But I'm worried, you see!"

The viscount pushed to sitting, his large hands splayed wide in the grass. "I don't see. There are more worrisome matters than a perfectly healthy young woman."

"You mean a perfectly *pretty* young woman." The marchioness grinned, winked.

Oh heavens. A blush ripped through Matilda to rival the sun, and she looked away.

"I should like to focus," the viscount said, "for a moment,

3

if you please." He likely could sniff out a matchmaking mama as well as—better than—Matilda herself. "Father, I have just spoken with the farmer Mr. Tweedle, and he says the fence along the eastern border is broken. Has been for months."

"That's what's painted a storm cloud on your brow?" his father said. "Wash it away this instant. It will be taken care of."

"But when and how?"

The marquess shrugged. "The Lord will provide. He always does."

"*You* are the lord of this estate, Father."

But his father's hands continued their unbothered fluttering. "*Or* Mr. Howards will provide. It's what a steward's for, after all." He tucked a strand of hair behind his wife's ear. "If you are so concerned, speak with him. He'll know exactly what to do. It's why I hired him."

A kingdom for her knitting right now, or her current book, or perhaps the ability to turn invisible and flee a family squabble she had no part in.

The marchioness smoothed the hair off of her husband's brow, smoothed his lapel, and tried to soothe his mood no doubt. "You are not meant for such practical tasks, love."

"I should never have had them." With the large, soulful eyes of a puppy dog, the marquess flopped onto his back, his hand entwined with his wife's. "Do you know, Miss Bellvue, how I came to be in my position?"

Blast. Not invisible.

She put on a cheery smile. "You inherited the title, I'm sure." Perhaps others would find her response a bit too teasing, but this family encouraged such feeling, and they laughed at her small joke. The viscount rolled his eyes.

As usual, the marquess showed greater bonhomie than his son with a belly-shaking laugh. "To be sure. The usual way. But ... an unexpected inheritance. Meant for my older brother. I was supposed to attend the Royal Academy of Arts. It is the

4

future Franny and I had planned for. But I was never able to contribute to the world of art what I wished to, what I hoped to. Those hopes died with my brother."

"Not true, my dear!" The marchioness shot to her feet. "You have contributed so very much. Think of all the artists in London you support so they can focus on painting and creating. Think of the party we hold here every year and how many new brilliant works of genius come out of it. Think of all the ideas our guests share with one another. You advance the community through your patronage."

"It's good to hear you say so." But the marquess still drooped like a branch under the weight of a spring rainstorm.

"Father." The storm brewing on the viscount's brow became a thunderclap in his voice. "The fence is not the only problem. I've heard in the village that there are some who have not seen payment from you in months. *Months*."

"Things will ... sort themselves out, my boy. They always do."

Matilda picked at a bit of grass beyond the edge of the blanket. Were there troubles here? She did not like to think so. Briarcliff and its people had seemed to her an Eden after so much grief, after being thrown from the only home she'd known all her life.

The marquess sat upright with a grunt. "I'm sure it's all easy to take care of. Speak with Mr. Howards. He'll know. I am proud of you, Raph. I've always been proud of you, even though you've not a delicate sensibility in your body."

"Father," the viscount warned. "Not being able to paint is not a sin. I have other talents. And I've discovered in the last few months that I have a talent for the work I do here. I love Briarcliff, its people." A red stained his cheeks, and he jumped to his feet to pace away from the blanket and back.

Matilda almost clutched her heart to keep it from beating out between her ribs. Impossible to deny. Nothing more attractive than a man impassioned by his responsibilities. Not what the debutantes the year of her come-out had swooned over, but she did. Or would. Swoon. If it were proper for a governess to do so. And it was not.

The marquess found his feet and clapped a hand on his son's shoulder. "You are a true heir, and you will be a better marquess than I ever have been."

The viscount's shoulder's straightened, and he seemed to grow taller. He glanced at her. But why? She was a baron's daughter, yes, or had been. She was no one now, certainly not to a young, handsome viscount. She gave him a smile, though, prim and proper as she'd learned to be, then she looked to Maggie to see how the familial drama sat with the girl.

It sat not at all. The girl had rolled to her belly and turned her attention to a book. Her younger brother had wandered off to the lake to skip rocks across its surface.

Matilda did not look back at the viscount until she heard him clear his throat.

"Well, then," he said, "I'd best talk with Howards."

"That's a good son." The marquess stooped to gather the picnic basket. "We'll return to the house with you."

It did not take long to gather the hamper and the blankets and the children, and soon they entered the wide double doors of the old manor. It was a castle really, drafty but cozy at the same time. The viscount had strode forward, leading them like a man who had been born to do so. But now and then, she'd caught glimpses of a pale cheek, an uncertain eye. As loving as they were, his parents did not offer much comfort. He shared his concerns, and they waved them away.

When her father had grown ill a year and a half ago, she'd tried to speak to him of Gerald, and he'd waved her fears away, too; told her her brother would take care of her if the worst happened.

He had not. If her father had listened to her, perhaps she'd not have been pressed into service, bereft of home and everything she'd ever known.

The viscount disappeared toward the study, and his parents simply disappeared, as they were wont to do, so Matilda took the children upstairs to the nursery and found herself wandering back toward the study. She couldn't settle until she'd offered the viscount an ear, a sympathetic heart. It made her ache to think of others aching as she did.

She stood before the slightly open study door and raised her arm to knock.

"What do you mean you're leaving?" The viscount's voice rang high, raging with the clear reverberations of shock. She let her arm drop and stepped back. "You're done for the day?"

"Done for good." Another man's voice. This one she recognized as belonging to the steward, Mr. Howards.

"Is this a joke?"

"No. I quit."

"But why would you do that? We've fences to mend, and there are people in the village who have not been paid in months."

"Take that up with your father. There's nothing I can do about it."

"You mean there's nothing you have done about it. These would not be problems had you not—"

Mr. Howards laughed, hard and mirthless, a sound that shoved Matilda into the wall opposite the door. "I've done everything a man in my position could possibly do, my lord. And your father has done absolutely everything a man in his position can do to financially ruin his family and impoverish his estate." Footsteps hastened toward the door then stopped. "Take a look at the books. While you've spent your time after graduation getting to know your tenants and getting to know your lands, I've come to one conclusion: you are out of money. You are out of money, and there will be no getting more because your father has spent it all on paintings, on statues, on artists in London, on the house party every single year. There's nothing left, and you will have to sell everything off."

"It can't be true." The viscount's deep rumble came low and hollow.

Heaven and hell, she should not be eavesdropping. She must move, and she had two directions to escape in—left or right—but her feet had determined to turn stone, and her heart, well it bled a little bit for the viscount. And maybe if she stayed right here, he would not have to suffer this alone because she understood what he did not yet seem to—the steward told the truth about the marquess. She had no real reason to believe it, but it felt heavy and sharp at the same time, as truth always did.

"You are a good man," Mr. Howards said, "and you are going to be a good marquess, and you do not deserve the legacy that you have been given. But I have had no hand in it. I have tried to stop it—the spending—on multiple occasions, and it never stops, and I leave it now to *you* to stop, to fix. If he listens to anyone, perhaps it will be you, whom he so admires and so loves."

Silence seemed to charge the air, then the door flew open and Mr. Howards stepped into the hall, hat on head, leather satchel in hand. He didn't even notice her as he put distance between himself and the wreck of a viscount in the study.

For he *was* wrecked, his mouth half open, his eyes wide and blank.

She should flee. She'd intruded, and she should run.

She did run. To him. She wrapped her arm around his waist and led him to a chair, and he let her, though he did not spare her a single glance. It was as if the wind had moved him, settled him, as if the wind had a head that reached his shoulder and a too-weak arm to hold his weight. She managed it—him

8

—though, and knelt before him, chafing his bare ice-cold hands in her own.

"Shall I ring for tea?" she asked. She did it, not waiting for an answer, and when she knelt before him again, she did not touch him, but said, "I am sorry. I did not intend to eavesdrop. I came to offer some sympathy. For the conversation by the lake. And I ... I could not seem to move away once you and Mr. Howards began to talk. I am terribly sorry. I will tell no one what I heard."

His gaze snapped to her, and life seemed to rush into his body like a flood rushing through a dry river bed after a heavy rain. "Do not apologize. I am ... grateful to have someone here right now."

Relief almost knocked her backward, but she rose to her feet and pulled a chair near him, sat and knitted her hands in her lap. "I am here, and I will help in whatever way I can. Tea will arrive shortly."

He nodded slow and steady, a movement that somehow melted into a shake, from yes to no with the oozing slowness of honey. "Bollocks." He dropped his head into his palms. "Bollocks, bollocks, bollocks." When he lifted his face once more, the pale chill had departed, replaced by a mottled red. "What do I do, Miss Bellvue? Where do I start?"

"Speak with your father, I would think."

"Yes, yes. You're correct. And then ... and then ..." He looked at her with the lost eyes of a young boy, not with the confidence of a strapping man of two and twenty.

"Perhaps you can sell some of the art collection?" she suggested.

He jumped to his feet and strode to the desk, opened a large book laying in the middle. He dropped into the brown leather chair behind the desk. Should she stay? Go? The tea came, and she busied herself with pouring him a cup and setting it steaming before him, then backed toward the door to leave.

"No. Please stay." His voice fell empty yet pleading at the same time, twisting his lips into a grimace. "I find I need a bit of moral support at the moment."

"Yes. Of course." She left the door open and poured herself a cup, filled it partly with milk, and scalded her mouth with the first sip. He leaned an elbow on the table next to the files he studied, shading his eyes with a hand cupped over his brows. Her heart cried for him. She'd stay here, silent, as long as he needed. Or until the children needed her. She musn't forget her place.

"Bollocks," he hissed. Then, "Apologies. I should not curse. Apologies." He slammed the book closed and rejoined her in the chairs placed much too close together.

Her skirts kissed his boots, and the flash of muddy brown and lavender together seemed ... right. No, no. Not that. Not that.

When he spoke, he startled her. "Thank you, Miss Bellvue. You are paid to teach Maggie, not comfort me."

"I am happy to do what I can. For any member of your family. I do not have one anymore. A family, that is. And your mother and father have welcomed me with open arms. I owe them so very much. If I can pay that back in kindness to you, I am happy to do so."

For one moment—in which her heart felt like it might crack in two—the viscount's eyes glittered raindrops. Then he pressed them closed, and when he next opened them, he'd tamed the floods, a victory hard won that left him with eyes like stones—hard and dull.

"It is worse than I imagined." He looked away from her. "I do not know how my father will react to the suggestion we sell his art collection. And I cannot sell it as it is not mine to sell. I do not know if we will be able to pay your wages much longer."

Had her heart been close to breaking before? Now it seemed blackened ash, consumed in an inferno, gone in a breath. "I understand." Simple words, but difficult to say. A buzzing in her ears, a tingling in her toes that swept numbness up her limbs. The world dulled and fuzzed a bit around the edges. Like the day she'd learned of her mother's death, her father's too. The day Gerald had told her he wanted her gone since she wasn't really his sister, because her mother had been a plain miss before marrying a baron while his mother had been an earl's daughter. The Marquess of Waneborough and his family had not cared about that. They'd treated their governess like family, as unimaginable as it was.

She'd have to leave here too. She'd have to leave *them*.

"Miss Bellvue?"

That had always been part of the position, of course. But so soon? She'd thought she'd had a few years. Until Maggie made her come out.

"Miss Bellvue?"

Another loss to count among her many, and this one just as painful.

"Matilda!" A big hand settled at her waist, a warm, rough palm rested against her cheek. "Matilda, look at me."

Somehow, she did, blinking back the fuzzy gray at her vision's edge, focusing instead on the parts of her body where he supported her, tethered her to the solid world.

The solid, cold world.

She pulled out of his arms and pushed him away. Gently, but away nonetheless. "Thank you, my lord. I am well. I will not succumb to swooning. I promise." She'd have to be made of sterner stuff from here on out. No more pampered baron's daughter. No position would last, and no matter how much it felt like home, she must remember it never was. This first posi-

11

tion had offered an illusion of home only. There was no more home for her, only a series of temporary residences and employers, a parade of people, not a life lived with loved ones.

He stood slowly, his gaze trained on her, those stone eyes now turned to cutting diamonds. "And *I promise you* ..." She looked away. She could not bare to see him lie merely to comfort her. "I will not let you suffer more than you already have. You do not deserve it. I will find you a good position. I swear." It is my family's fault you are let go too soon. I will make up for it." His fingers appeared beneath her chin, and he tilted it up until their gazes locked. "I will protect you, Miss Bellvue. *I swear it.*"

And, between warm fingers and glittering blue eyes, between wind-tousled hair and a jaw lightly stubbled, she lost the ability to breathe again, but she gained something just as good—hope. Because she believed him. Believed he would help her find a position, a steady footing in life, even if he could never (because no one could) find her a home.

One

～

F ebruary 1821

The portrait, tall and wide as the wall it adorned, hung in pride of place at the end of the gallery and caught that twinkle in the old marquess's eyes. The one Raph, former Viscount Stillman, used to love. The very same one he'd dreaded now for fifteen years ever since the steward had quit but not before he'd told Raph the truth—that twinkle meant trouble. It revealed his father's intentions to buy something expensive. It was a prelude to more difficulty.

But the marquess was dead, and there would be no more expensive purchases. The difficulty, though—the debt that remained—had been passed on from one Marquess of Waneborough to another, from father to Raph, as surely as the title itself.

His four brothers shifted uneasily from foot to foot beside him, and Maggie, heavy with child, perched on a nearby window seat with her husband, Mr. Tobias Blake. They all wore black even though their father had told them not to. He'd wanted bright colors. He'd wanted celebration in death as he'd always wanted it in life.

"The lawyer will be here shortly," Maggie said.

Raph didn't look at her. He kept eye contact with the painting, counting the brush strokes in the irises. The thing was massive. Raph knew its price in every way a thing could have a price. And in all ways, it cost too much.

But his father hadn't been able to understand money. He'd died with a cry of forgiveness in his eyes and the words "the Lord will provide" on his lips.

"Doesn't look a bit like him," Atlas grumbled, hands deep in pockets, large shoulders hunched forward. He'd dropped his pin-straight military bearing in the last few years, curving in on himself since Waterloo.

Drew snorted. "Whoever painted it likely saw our dear papa as a god of the arts, not a bit of him soft." He leaned toward the portrait, his too-long brown hair, lighter than the other brothers', falling over narrowed eyes. "Can't even recognize him. Do we have a more faithful likeness?"

Lysander left their line and joined Maggie and Tobias at the window, crossing his arms over his chest and leaning his hip against the wall. His dark curls looked black with the sun shining on them. "'Whoever painted it'? Thomas Lawrence painted it. It's damn near priceless." Zander would know too. He knew everything about art. From a profitable point of view.

If only their father had viewed art the same way—a commodity to be sold as well as bought. Maybe then his obsession would have done them some good.

Drew shrugged. "I do not rightly care who painted it as long as there's someone who wants to buy it."

Silence.

They all knew what they should say—we cannot sell Papa's portrait!

They all knew the truth—they had to or eventually the debt collector would catch up to them.

Theo stepped farther from the painting, tilting his head before turning and walking down the length of the portrait gallery. Long strides, long arms, scruff on his jaw, and dirty-blond hair a tangle over his messy cravat. "Sell all the others first. Then ..."

Then maybe they wouldn't have to sell this one. Raph scratched his jaw, also scratchy with stubble, and looked toward Zander. "Well?"

"Don't know why we'd do that. Lawrence has painted kings. He has all the credentials"—he rolled his hand at the wrist—"Royal Academy, Dilettanti Society, etcetera, etcetera. I know cits who would sell their firstborn for it."

"Find a buyer, then." Raph turned his back on the painting. He couldn't stare down the portrait one more day. He wanted to hate his father, but those twinkling eyes poured grief into his calcified heart.

"Ahem." The housekeeper, Mrs. Counts, hovered in the doorway. One of their few remaining servants. Plump with frizzled gray hair, she stood tall, hands folded neatly together. "Lord Waneborough, the solicitor has arrived. He's waiting in the parlor with your mother."

Raph strode forward, and his siblings followed, filing out of the portrait gallery like a queue of black-clad ducklings. He'd thought his father had no will. Had only found out recently such a thing existed. And it, apparently, was legal. Had a witness and everything. Shocking that his father could do something other than run them into the ground and produce talented, starving artists out of thin air.

The day was still young, though, and the contents of the will a mystery. Perhaps his father had come to his senses before he'd taken his last breath, realized that, no, everything did not in fact turn out well enough in the end for the patient and hopeful. Perhaps he'd concluded that all the meaningless platitudes he'd used to spout, used to *believe*, were actually nothing more than a heaping pile of horse dung.

His mother sat like a queen of death, veiled from head to toe in black lace and bombazine, at the top of the parlor. A man in a black suit stood beside her, his bald pate gleaming in the candlelight. He held papers before him.

At least Raph thought he did. Too dark to tell rightly.

"It's the middle of the day," Raph said, as his siblings searched for chairs around the mostly dark room. "Can't we open some drapes?"

A wail pierced the layers of veils hiding his mother. "And dishonor your father?"

"If you'll allow me to point out, madam"—Tobias Blake strolled across the room and knelt beside Raph's mother as if he were her knight. Maggie's husband had a flare for the dramatics, which meant he knew how to speak Raph's mother's language—"we are here for a reading of your dear husband's will, but ... that may be difficult if we have no light."

Veil-smothered sniffles. "Very well. To do Edward's bidding, we will draw back the curtains. But only for as long as it takes to read the will."

Atlas, already sitting nearest the windows, jumped up and pulled worn drapes back. A flood of sunlight swamped all.

Tobias, blinking as he rose, joined Maggie, who held her arm over her eyes.

Raph would thank the man later. He'd not had the patience to find a sensible argument, but Tobias had, and he'd been able to couch it in the sort of chivalric language his mother preferred. That, Raph had never been able to do.

Everyone sat, scattered about, but for the solicitor and Raph. The solicitor waved at a chair. An invitation Raph could not take. He felt caged. He'd been living the life of the marquess in all but name the last fifteen years, and this was a distraction from his daily duties keeping the estate, its lands, everything, falling to creditors.

"No." Raph paced across the meager space of the room. "I'll remain standing."

"As it pleases you, my lord," the solicitor, a Mr. Grant, said. He snapped the papers up, hiding half his face, and read. "I will spare you the florid language, and I will leave a copy here for all of you to peruse if you so wish. Does that meet with your approval, my lord?"

Good God, how had his father found a practical sort of solicitor when he'd been anything but? "Yes."

"Very well." They could not see his lips moving, and his voice floated up, wove them all together tight in the dusty yellow light of morning. "The estate and all lands go to the new Lord Waneborough, naturally. As I'm sure you all are aware, there is no"—he cleared his throat—"money to settle on anyone. There are, however, items of great worth in your father's art collection, and he wished to disperse those accordingly and fairly between his children and those who will care for them most."

Lysander snorted. "Hear that distinction? There are those who will care for his art collection most. And then there are his *children*. The old man knew us well."

"Lysander!" The sound of the *a* in Lysander's name had taken on a life of its own, and was snaking about the room, a grief-powered wail.

Theo cringed, Atlas hunched into himself, Maggie pulled at her earlobe, Drew tugged at his cravat, and Raph pinched the bridge of his nose.

"Sorry, Mama," Zander said, flinching. "I care about the collection."

"You care very much about it," Theo drawled, crossing

and uncrossing his legs from where he sat in the shadows on a low settee. "if there's someone who wishes to buy it."

Zander opened his arms out wide. "Precisely."

Their mother continued keening, a sound now likely making every dog in the county bark and howl. The wailing burrowed deep in Raph's ears. He stopped pacing and rubbed at his chest.

"Continue, Mr. Grant." He barely raised his voice, but the keening and the bickering ceased, and Raph continued his pacing.

Mr. Grant cleared his throat, pulled the paper back up to cover the bottom half of his face. "As I was saying, your father's last thoughts were of fairness. Each of you has been willed a painting of great worth."

"Which ones?" Zander demanded.

"Only your mother knows," Mr. Grant said, snapping the paper tight.

"And I'm not telling," their mother said.

"Mother?" Raph's voice rumbled in his chest. "What are they worth?"

"Quite a bit." A prevarication.

"The paintings," Mr. Grant said, "were appraised for several of thousands of pounds all together."

Zander whistled. "A small fortune. You'll get your improvements, brother." His lively air hid some shadow, though. Raph searched for its meaning as his brother searched his mother's veiled form. Finding no meaning—and apparently Zander found no answers either—he snapped his gaze toward the window.

Atlas shook his head. "I cannot countenance it. Father never did a practical thing with money or art in his life. Why now?"

"Ah." Mr. Grant waved a tentative hand in the air. "I'm not done yet."

"Here we go." Theo slumped farther into his chair. "The *impractical* bit."

"The drop of the guillotine's blade," Drew added.

Raph rooted his feet to the floor. Whatever it was, he'd weather it, as he had all these years.

"There are stipulations," Mr. Grant said.

Raph grunted. "Of course there are."

The black veil rose to its shaky height, and his mother said from within, "They are *necessary* stipulations that I helped your father conceive. Your father knew ..." Her voice trembled, the veil too. "He knew he'd ruined his legacy, and he wanted to ensure that he'd left something of value behind in his children. For them. That is, in the end, the only way we achieve immortality. Through our children. And our art. He wished to know something of himself lived on in you. The best part of him. For he knew his faults." A sniffle, muffled and low, and then her pale, skeletal hands disappeared beneath the veil and her head bowed, her body shook.

Maggie crossed the room and wrapped their mother in soothing arms.

Raph looked to the solicitor. Surely the man would convey greater sense than his mother did.

Mr. Grant looked to Raph's mother then back to the will. "Each child must, individually, earn their inheritance by producing a work of art themselves."

Raph's arms went numb first, all the way to his fingertips. Then his legs at the hip to his toes. And as his limbs lost feeling, his gut churned, and his brothers found their very best, or worst, language to make their disapproval known.

"Bloody hell." Atlas looked like he'd like to snap Mr. Grant in two.

A long, low whistle from Lysander.

Drew threw his arms into the air. "I'm a tutor. Not a bloody *artist*."

Theo offered a relatively tame, "Damn."

But Theo actually *was* an artist. Not a respectable one, and not a well-known one, but the man's hands had talent. Could earn money with that talent, too, by selling his work to *Ackermann's Repository* and any other periodical that relished political gossip through garish caricatures.

His mother, standing all the while for Mr. Grant's news, threw her veil back and pushed out of Maggie's embrace. Her auburn hair, silvered with gray, hung limp and tangled around her ashen face. Everything about her drawn with the charcoal pencil of sorrow, thick lines and smudges.

She pointed a finger at them all, letting it draw a line around the room from brother to brother. "That is why the stipulation is in place. None of you learned a thing your father tried diligently and"—her hands fluttered to her breast— "heroically to teach you. If you would not learn the meaning of art and its importance while he breathed, you must learn it now once—" She crumpled into her chair, hands gripping the rounded oak arms. "Once he'll never breathe *agaaain*." The last word a wail.

Maggie hugged her and whispered soothing words, but the sobbing had started and would not soon stop.

Feeling returned to Raph's arms and legs. If he didn't regain control, the entire reading would never refocus.

"I have a question, Mr. Grant." He spoke loud enough to be heard over his mother's grief. "As anyone who grew up in this house knows, whether they appreciate artistic endeavors or not, what a work of art is often changes according to the viewer. Who is to ascertain that we have, indeed, produced works of art?"

"Excellent question," Mr. Grant said, "and your father has considered that difficulty. It is very easily solved. Your—"

"Me." The single word dropped from his mother's lips like a stone at the end of a final wail.

Damn, indeed. Looked like he wouldn't be sketching out a rose and being done with it. She'd want passion. She'd want originality. She'd want a message and meaning.

Raph just wanted to figure out the best dung to fertilize the fields.

"When you have produced a work of art"—his mother stood tall, losing her grief for a heartbeat in her purpose—"you will bring it to me, and I will judge its merit. If it meets my approval, you will have your inheritance, and you may do with it what you'd like." She sniffed. "Even if you choose to sell it."

Raph stood before her, trying to soften his gaze though he did nothing to soften his stance. "We have managed to pay off all father's creditors. But you do realize we're barely paying the few servants we have, yes? You realize we've closed off a wing of the house because its roof makes it unlivable."

"I offered to pay for that," Tobias said from somewhere behind Raph.

"Thank you, Tobias, but you have paid for much more. We are not your burden."

"Not a burden, and I have the funds."

"You have a child due in three months or so. I'll not let you pay for what we should be able to pay for ourselves. Not any longer."

"Raphael." His mother's face had pinked, anger putting color in her cheeks, bringing her to life. "Life is not all about money and things. It's about ideas and—"

He turned his back on her, paced to Mr. Grant. "We can sell them, the paintings. Can't we? There are no stipulations against it?"

He shook his head. "But there is another stipulation."

A collective groan rumbled across the room as all six Bromley children hung their heads forward or flung them backward.

"What?" Raph demanded.

The solicitor swallowed. "You are aware that your father has been supporting a handful of young artists."

"Yes, he was a patron to many," Raph said.

"He was a saint to many," his mother added.

"Yes, well ..." Mr. Grant shifted from foot to foot. "Your father, Lord Waneborough, has stipulated that you cannot stop the flow of funds to three of the artists until you have found them patrons to replace him."

Another round of cursing.

Zander whistled. "When the old man had time to screw us all over so thoroughly while dying, I'll never—"

"Lysander!" His mother was on her feet once more. "Those artists need to eat. More importantly, they need to work. And they cannot do that without food, so if we can provide the food—"

"We can keep the art alive," Theo finished for her. "Yes, Mother, we know. Nourish beauty and all that."

She beat a fist to her chest. "Nourish the *soul*. It's what your father wanted. He wanted to nourish *your* souls." She sailed back to her chair to collapse, weeping into Maggie's arms.

"What of the other art?" Raph asked.

"Anything in his lordship's personal collection, bought and curated by him, is to be donated to the Royal Academy."

Anything and everything of significant value, then. "Is this will valid?" Raph crossed his arms over his chest.

"Yes, my lord, it is."

Raph nodded, turned to this brothers. "This is nothing more than we've become used to throughout the years. We have persisted, and we will continue to do so."

They all stood, nodding.

Raph met each of their gazes in turn. "Let us get to work."

Zander left first, waving an arm as he slunk through the

door into the hall. "I've ... things to look into. I'll return later this year." Back to London with him, or to parts unknown. In his work as an art curator, many sought out his opinion on building their collections and thus their social status. Atlas departed without a word, likely headed toward the stables. Theo and Drew left together.

"I'll start looking for patrons for those artists," Theo said.

Drew pushed a long sigh through clenched teeth so it sounded more like a whistle. "I would stay to help with Mother, but I must return to Manchester. I've left my secretary in charge of things. She's competent. But some clients will only deal with me."

"I understand." Raph clapped his brother on his back. Drew's work brought in the most steady income. His agency for tutors and governesses was well-respected. And Raph despised asking him for funds. Didn't keep him from needing them, though. He turned to his sister and her husband. "I think I might need a wife."

His mother perked up from her black bombazine puddle. "Someone you've never met? Raph, you can't. You must only marry for—"

"There is no love for those who cannot afford it, Mother. You and Father had love, but I cannot. Maggie, will you help me find a suitable woman?" And by *suitable* he meant wealthy.

She nodded, their mother howled, and Maggie and Tobias gathered her up and ushered her hopefully to her bedroom. The howls diminished. In volume at least.

Raph finally dropped into a chair, as heavy as a dead body covered in rain-soaked earth.

"Thank you, Father," he said, tugging at his cravat and stretching his long legs out.

He'd worked to rebuild the estate and refill the family coffers for fifteen years, and he'd barely succeeded. If he found a wealthy enough wife quick enough, perhaps his worry would end soon.

Hopefully Theo would come through. Or Maggie. The sole artists among them.

Because one certainty rang like a death knell over Raph's numb brain—no matter how hard he tried, his clumsy fingers could produce nothing of beauty, and even if he served his best attempts up to his mother on a golden platter (pilfered from another estate because they certainly could not afford anything of true gold), she'd say no. His inheritance would remain barred from him. Art had never saved him. Only the back-breaking work of the body and the taxing work of the mind.

He'd put his faith in those.

Beauty? Art?

Bah.

Two

August 1821

The parlor had become a purgatory since Raph had commandeered it for his own purposes. Painting. Attempting to. A hell, truly, despite the large windows the sun streamed through. The open space with old, cozy furniture scattered around, boasted worn rugs and a large fireplace stretching across one wall that sat empty now in the summer heat. It once had been a little heaven, the room he, his brothers, and Maggie had crowded into on cold winter days to play in the sunbeams before the fire, their mother looking on with a small, fond smile. Their father falling to his hands and knees to let the smallest of them have a ride across the room. A chaos. A lovely one.

Now?

A Purgatorial Painting Parlor. A Territory of Tempera Torment.

Raph contemplated the muddy canvas on the paint-stained easel, leaning forward till his nose almost touched it, studying, in particular, the smear of yellow near the top. Should look like sunshine, the deep yellow of dawn right as the pink begins to fade.

It looked like piss.

And what was that dark-brown speck in the corner? Mud? He leaned closer. Sniffed. Jerked away. Not mud. He should have taken a bath after working in the stables. He rocked back on his heels and sighed.

And a wail rent the air, loud and keening. He held his breath for a moment, waiting. Would it stop?

It got louder. Bollocks.

He snapped the fallen paintbrush up and threw it into a jar of murky water, then left the room and marched a path toward his mother. No idea where she was. Didn't matter. The wailing would tell him.

He tried, he truly did, not to diminish the gravity of her pain, her loss. But sometimes he did so wish she could mourn a little quieter.

He knocked on her door, wincing. Her wails made shreds of the air and his eardrums. "Mother?" An abrupt cessation of sound. "May I come in?"

Sniffles. "You may. It's unlocked."

Raph strode through.

She lay on the floor in a puddle of black bombazine, and he joined her, splaying the entire length of his body out beside her and turning his head to look at her. "What did it this time?"

She sniffled again and wiped her eyes. "You do not understand. You have never loved as I do. You are going to marry a woman you do not love."

"True." He couldn't deny it. He'd been in London all season, trying to find the perfect bride. He had it down to two very wealthy choices and could not decide. "But I am trying to understand nonetheless."

"Very unexpected of you." She reached out, patted his wrist. "It's all the art you've been doing. Softens the heart and soul." She began weeping again, her shoulders shaking as she raised her palms to hide her mottled face.

He wrapped her up snug, held her close, and held tight to his patience until she sniffled and moved away.

"It's the little framed sketch over there." She pointed near the window where several framed sketches ornamented the wall in a long vertical row between windows. "He drew all of those. For every one of my birthdays. For the anniversary of our marriage. For the births of each of our children. And they usually bring me joy, but today I realized I ... I will n-never have"—she closed her eyes tight, deepening the wrinkles at their corners—"another in all my *daaays*." The last word, predictably, became a wail.

"Paper and ink and the thoughtless intentions of a man who'd pulled his family down low."

She swatted his arm and stormed to her feet. "How can you say that? Your father was not thoughtless! He loved me. And you. But you see only money."

"And tell me what you see, Mother."

She turned, and her back curved like an eggshell, so frail. "I was ruined when he met me. No one wanted me. He didn't care. He could have had an heiress after his brother died. His father tried to convince him to have one." A tremor racked her body and stopped her words.

He'd heard the story. What did it matter?

"He wouldn't have an heiress, though." His mother straightened, strode across the room to stand right before the sketches. "He was loyal. More loyal than any man on earth. I owe him everything, but he never made me feel it. Never showed me anything but love." She traced the frame of one of his father's sketches as if it were her husband's cheek, then she turned to face Raph, eyes clearer, more determined than before. "I owe him the exact same loyalty."

That came as no surprise. She'd always loved her children, showered them in affection, but her deepest love had belonged to her husband, her only loyalty had belonged to him, even when his actions—yes, his thoughtlessness—hurt those children. She loved her children, but she could never deny her husband.

Not when he wanted a painting.

Or a statue.

Or to support another artist.

Or to hold another house party.

Raph sat cross-legged on the floor. He looked at his palms turned upward and resting on his knees. In one hand he seemed to hold a pure, blue rage. In the other, affection, grief, patience. The latter gained from a childhood with parents who seemed to love him dearly. The former gained through an adult's greater understanding.

He clenched his hands into fists and stood. "I'll draw you something for your birthday." And hope the wailing soon stopped. Several of their few remaining housemaids had quit because of it, and his own ears were close to bleeding. The dower house was infested with mice, among other things. Entirely unlivable. Even if the dower house were habitable, Raph couldn't kick his mother out. She was lonely enough in the main house, living with him and Atlas, their siblings coming in and out month by month for visits. She would die of loneliness in a house with no family. Even if it was updated and nicely furnished. If he moved her there *now,* the plague would get her before loneliness did.

He patted her shoulder, and she turned and curled herself into the side of his body, wetting his waistcoat with her tears.

He needed a solution.

Because his mother needed comfort, but he needed to run the estate. He couldn't afford to hire an estate manager, and while Atlas worked alongside him, negating the need for such a paid position, Raph had his hands in every aspect of the work.

Her sobs quieted into small hiccups.

"Are you well now?" he asked

Her eyes widened. "No! How can you even ask that? I'll never be *well* again."

"Well, are you all out of tears for the moment, then? Wails, really. You can cry all you like as long as it's quiet."

"Raphael."

He blinked.

She shook her head and stood, smoothing her skirts. "I will keep in mind that while you speak heartless nonsense, you recently held me when I cried." She wandered across the room and stopped before the fireplace, whirled and halfway lifted her arm. "Ra-aph—"

"Whatever it is you're about to say—no." He stood, groaning.

"It's just that the time of the annual house party is quickly upon us—October, you know—and your father would not have wanted us to cancel it for the sake of grieving him."

Raph took several breaths, trying to simmer down the rage building like a forest fire. He would not speak until he could do so calmly. But every muscle clenched and every part of his brain screamed to scream at her.

Finally, he said, "No. There will be no house party this year, and I'll not hear another word about it." He strode for the door. He needed a good ride, fast as Oak would take him, then perhaps a dip in the lake. He needed to move, no matter how, long and fast and hard.

Soft steps rushed after him. "But, Raph! Think of how

disappointed our friends will all be! Think of how disappointed I will be." That tremor again.

He rolled his lips between his teeth, softened his features, and turned around. "No house party, Mother. We can barely fill our own bellies, and the bellies of those who depend upon us. We will not add the bellies of thirty well-to-do *artists*."

"You say the word like it disgusts you."

"Because it does. I would sell every damn statue and portrait in this house if I could. I would make sure the three artists in London assured of two hundred pounds a year from us knew they would no longer receive it. But as in life, in death Father has tied my hands." He held up his own hands, smeared in pinks and purples and that damn piss yellow. "I do this only because I must." He swallowed, found a softer tone. He hoped. "I am sorry, Mother. But no party. Not this year. Not ever again."

He left.

And she did not wail with his leaving. He preferred her anger to her sorrow. Let her hate him. He had been hated for years, and he could withstand it longer if it meant bringing prosperity back to the estate.

He breathed a world-clearing breath as soon as he set foot under the robin's-egg blue sky and shook the emotion from his muscles and bones. He found the stables quick enough, where he found Atlas, too.

His brother grunted a greeting. If there was anyone less loquacious than Raph, it was Atlas. He groomed a mare's gleaming coat in smooth, gentle strokes. They did not have much horseflesh anymore, but Atlas cared for what remained with a surprising ferocity and keen intelligence. They'd no need to pay a stablemaster with Atlas willing to do the job.

"Care to join me for a ride?" Raph asked.

Atlas looked up, nodded, and soon he'd saddled a bay for

himself. Raph saddled his draft horse, Oak, and they cantered out of the stable yard and into the sun soaking the fields.

Raph glanced at his brother sitting loose and confident in his seat, every inch the soldier he'd once been. "Do you think Mother's any better?"

Atlas snorted. "Worse. The usual time for the house party fast approaches."

"She mentioned that just now. I'd hoped she'd forget."

"She's more likely to forget her own name."

"We can't, Atlas."

"I know. She's not going to like it, though." He clicked his tongue against his teeth and pushed his bay into a faster pace.

Raph followed, and their horses climbed a small rise. At the top of the hill, a view opened up, revealing the estate. From this far away and this far up, it looked like perfection—a house more castle than manor with gardens on three sides, a long, green lawn sloping down to a lake, and farther back the stables and militaristic rows of trees that bloomed apples in autumn.

He'd run there as a boy, his father running with him, Atlas on his shoulders. They'd carried wooden swords and pretended to be theives, stealing golden apples from the gods.

Such dreamy memories were deceptive, lulled him into a forgiving mood. Better to think on the bad, to consider the failure of the orchard instead of childhood memories, to remember when he'd tried, years ago, to make cider and sell it. A long-standing tradition at Briarcliff Manor, one that had gone the way of the money when whoever had been brewing the stuff had failed to receive payment for their services and left. Rightly so. Raph had rolled up his sleeves, tried it himself. But no one had particularly liked the brew. And he hadn't the funds to pay an expert. He'd given it up.

"Deceptive, isn't it?" he said.

Atlas nodded.

"I told Mother today that we couldn't host the house party this year."

His brother raised a single brow. "And how'd that go over?"

"As well as you can imagine."

"She needs something, though, Raph. She can't languish alone forever."

"She's not alone. She has us."

"And we don't share any of her interests. I've been thinking ... money is tight, but—"

"Ha! Tight? Excellent understatement. I could laugh all day."

"But surely we can find a way to afford, oh, I don't know, a companion? Do we have any spinster cousins? Someone to offer Mother company."

"A companion." Not a bad idea. But Raph shook his head. "We can afford only necessities and what is required for improving the estate, making it profitable once more."

"Mother's happiness is a necessity."

Raph opened his mouth to argue but could not. He did not agree with her on most things in life, but she was his mother. She'd given her loyalty to his father, but she'd given love in her own way to her children. He wanted her happy, but he could not give her the house party happiness she desired, so he'd have to make her miserable.

"And think," Atlas said, "of how much silence we'll have once she's happier. How often have you lately complained that you cannot think or complete any of your tasks with all the wailing and the consoling you do. And you are needed to complete those tasks because you do not consider it a necessity to hire others to complete tasks for you."

"I cannot hire others."

"I know. The best, most direct, strategy to victory in this particular situation is a companion, someone to keep Mother happy and occupied. Someone to do the consoling when you are busy doing other things."

He rubbed his jaw. "The cost—"

"Ask Maggie. You've let Maggie take care of expenses for Mother since her marriage. Let her continue to do so."

He bristled. He hated it. But Atlas was right.

"Fine. I'll find a companion for Mother. I might know someone who will do, too."

"Really? You are fine friends with the spinsters of the ton, then?"

Just one. The corner of his lips tugged up. And he wrenched it back down. "I wouldn't call us fine friends. Acquaintances. You know her too." Atlas tilted his head in question. "Miss Bellvue."

Atlas scowled, then his face brightened with recognition. "Maggie's old governess?"

"Just so. She owes me."

"Not sure I want to know about that."

"It's nothing nefarious. I helped find her a position after she left our employ." Because she'd comforted him as no one ever had at the worst moment in his life, and he'd let her go. Without remuneration. He'd paid her what they'd owed her slowly throughout the years, though, and made sure she always had a new position to go to when the old one ended. As a governess at first, but then she'd requested companion positions, and he'd done what he could to please her, to keep the promise he'd made to her that day. Perhaps she'd think kindly enough of him to help now.

"I leave for London tomorrow," Raph said.

Atlas laughed, a short snort of a sound that broke the sweet silence of the view. "Will you make a proposal?"

Raph nodded and turned Oak around, headed down the hill and into the woods at the bottom. Two women with rich fathers and inheritances but little to no social standing.

Women who were his perfect match, who wanted a title as much as he wanted their money. He'd not been able to propose, though, or even to ask formal permission to court either of them. Some force like a chain bound tight around his chest restrained him, and he'd returned home instead. Running, hiding, picking up a paintbrush to see if some heretofore hidden artistic impulse would ignite along his veins. To see if he could produce a work of art good enough to please his mother and thus good enough to save him from a loveless marriage.

But his fate crowded in on him like the trees—prison bars, stout and eternal. London called. His future beckoned.

Miss Bellvue was in London, though.

Perhaps he'd visit her, ask her in person instead of through an epistle to join his mother at Briarcliff. She'd always seemed a ray of sunshine, a fresh breeze even on rainy days. And he needed a final glimpse of the sun before the walls closed in entirely.

Three

The Viscountess Pratsby started snoring, and Matilda peeked over the edge of her book. Lady Pratsby slumped in her large, rose-pink chair, sleeping. Thank the heavens. The woman had been suffering a horrid bout of insomnia. Nothing seemed to work to help her sleep, and she despised being coddled. But she did like Matilda to read to her, and it had been Matilda's turn to choose the book. *Evelina*, one of Matilda's least-favorite books, had proved a blessing, and after a warm cup of tea and a chapter or two of Francis Burney's novel, Lady Pratsby snored contentedly as Matilda had hoped she would.

And Matilda could stop reading. Thank the heavens. Her tongue had gone numb from reading aloud. She stretched her jaw up and down, side to side, and curled and uncurled her tongue. She stopped short of wagging it and slowly, oh-so-slowly as to avoid even the merest shush of skin against paper, she closed the book and stood. She'd been reading ... how long now? She looked to the tall clock ticking away across the room, its patterned rhythm adding an odd percussive to the soft patter of the light rain that had washed London all morning long, hitting the windows. She squinted, read the clock. She'd read for over an hour. No wonder her legs were stiff, her back ached, and more unmentionable areas of the body had gone numb. Besides her mouth.

She pressed her hands into her lower back and arched, stretching, praying no crack of bone and spine would echo across the room and wake the viscountess. Ah. Better.

Now she just needed tea like a pup needed a scratch behind the ears. Imperative.

She poured the now lukewarm beverage into her cup and swallowed it down in four large gulps, then retook her seat and opened the book once more.

"The die is thrown," she read in her most moderate, sleep-inducing tones, "and I attend the event in trembling." What event? The events of *Evelina* always quite slipped from her mind as soon as she'd read them. She could never remember from one chapter to the next what had happened. Quite perfect book for inspiring slumber.

In a fortnight, she'd never have to read *Evelina* again if she did not want to. For the first time in ... well, perhaps ever ... her time would be her own to do with as she pleased. In her own home. She grinned and heard a happier tone in her usually monotonous recitation.

Lady Pratsby shifted a bit, made a face, and snorted more than snored. Just one. Perhaps it did not herald a waking.

"Lady Pratsby!"

Matilda stood, whirled around, and glared at the butler in the doorway who'd called out. She held a finger to her lips. "Shhh!"

He shrank back, his wide eyes flashing to the sleeping woman. "Apologies," he mouthed.

Matilda turned to the viscountess, her breath held tight in her chest, hoping, hoping ...

The viscountess's eyes shot open. "He's mine, wench!"

Blast.

Mr. Johns took a step farther into the room, collecting his dignity about him with a shove of his sharp nose into the air. "Apologies for waking you, my lady, but a Marquess of Waneborough is here to speak with Miss Bellvue. Are you at home?"

Lady Pratsby pulled herself more upright, patted her hair, and said, "No, we're not. I'm tired."

Mr. Johns turned to leave.

"Lady Pratsby," Matilda said, "the marquess has come to see me. You are still weary, and I would like you to retreat to your rooms and nap if possible. While you are resting, I'll visit with the marquess."

"I wonder if others' companions order them about as you do me."

"If I order you about, it's because I care for you."

"*Humph*. Well, you can't visit with the man alone, and— oh—" She shook a finger at Mr. Johns. "Isn't Lord Waneborough the funny chap who has that outrageous house party every year. Only for artists?"

"Yes, that's him." Matilda folded her book and put it to the side. "And I rather think I should speak to him. I worked for him for a year." A long time ago. "As governess to his daughter." But why he would be here now, asking to speak to her, she could not say.

"Show him in, Johns." The viscountess straightened her shoulders and smoothed her skirts. "I've always been curious about that house party."

Mr. Johns left, and Matilda rang for more tea.

"I think you should leave me to speak with him alone, my lady."

"Poppycock. You're an unmarried girl."

"I'm a companion, four and thirty years of age. He is a

married man and father. He could be *my* father. I believe we can be allowed some privacy." She bustled to Lady Pratsby's side. "Do you need help rising?"

"I'm five and sixty, not dead, my dear."

"But your knees, Lady Pratsby." Matilda held out a hand.

"*Bah.*" But she took the proffered help and they stood together, facing the door, smoothing their skirts. Lady Pratsby sliced her a sideways glance. "What's a marquess doing here to speak with *you*?"

As if Matilda hadn't been born a baron's daughter, hadn't taken her bows and had two seasons. After a certain amount of servitude, the life you were born into no longer mattered.

Lady Pratsby's elbow dug into Matlida's ribs. "He likely wishes to marry you."

Matilda laughed and moved away from the bony assault. "It is not that, I assure you. It's been, oh, it must be fifteen years since I've seen him."

"Randy men don't forget pretty faces. Or figures."

"He's horribly in love with his wife. Who is, as far as I know, yet living. If you'd seen them together, you'd understand. He has no intentions of straying from his marriage bed."

"*Humph.* What then? Come, now, don't hide anything from me. You're my companion, and it's your job to keep me informed and entertained. Especially with gossip."

"I've no clue, my lady." The truth, that. She'd barely said a word to him even when she'd resided in his house. The day of the picnic had been her most interaction with the man. And with his son.

Footsteps down the hall, the heavy fall of thick-soled boots alongside Mr. Johns's softer patter.

Mr. Johns swept into the room. "The Marquess of Waneborough."

But the man standing awkward by his side, turning the brim of his sodden hat round and round in thick, long, increasingly wet gloved fingers was not the Marquess of Waneborough. The ends of his hair curled at his nape, stark and dark, damp and thick against the crisp white of his cravat. The rest of his hair—mahogany, a slight wave to it—was dry. The hat's doing, likely. Mr. Johns must have taken his great-coat because the rest of him was dry as well but for his boots, which boasted a dull layer of mud. His stubbled jaw and a straight, strong nose seemed carved from marble, and the nose, a little bump on it up high, must have been broken once.

His eyes were the pale blue of a hot summer sky.

He was not the marquess she knew, but she did know him. Though the boy she'd known back then had been, it seemed, carved away entirely, any soft points he'd had honed to rough hardness.

She took several stumbling steps toward him. "Viscount Stillman ... I'd not expected ... but Mr. Johns said—"

"My father died. I am the Marquess of Waneborough now."

She rocked back on her heels, the breath leaving her. "Oh. I do apologize. I had no idea. My condolences, my lord."

He scratched a hand through his hair, dividing it into dark sections. "Boll—blast. I should have broken the news in a less startling way. I did not think."

Perhaps, but she did not remember him as a particularly eloquent or smooth sort of man. If a woman ever took it upon herself to polish him up, she'd fail miserably. But some men needed no polish. They were fine the way they were—rough-hewn and of the elements.

"My lord?" Mr. Johns stepped forward. "May I take your hat now?"

"Pardon?" Lord Waneborough looked at the butler, star-

39

tled. "Oh, yes, of course. Boll"—he jerked a wary glance toward Matilda and Lady Pratsby—"blast. Apologies. I remain in the country as much as possible, and I'm afraid there's not much need to hold my tongue there."

"Don't mind me, lad," Lady Pratsby said. "I'm no stranger to an impolite word or two. I bet I could shock you."

Lord Waneborough looked to Matilda, mouth slightly open. Did he seek help? He'd find none from her. It suited Matilda, most hours of the day, to let her employer do and say as she pleased. It kept the woman happy, gave her pleasure, and Matilda would never deny that, especially not to the woman she'd met in the middle of earth-swallowing grief. Lady Pratsby had healed quite nicely from losing her husband in the three years they'd been together.

"Oh, she would shock you," Matilda said. "Terribly."

"Yes. Delightful." The marquess scratched the back of his neck. "Miss Bellvue, may I speak with you?"

To the point, then. Yes, she remembered that about him. An admirable quality. She'd long admired him.

"Yes, of course," she said with a nod just as Lady Pratsby said, "No, of course not."

Matilda turned, stiff, to her employer. "My lady, you need not remain here. His lordship and I are old acquaintances."

Lady Pratsby only narrowed her eyes at the marquess. "You can say what you have to say to her before me."

"Very well then." He held his chin high. "I am in need of a companion for my mother. She has suffered much since the loss of my father, and she needs distraction. A friend."

Lady Pratsby huffed. "A *paid* friend."

"Is that not what you have, my lady?" Lord Waneborough's tone could snap through wood.

The viscountess chuckled. "But I won't for long if you have your way. Isn't that right? You're trying to steal her from me."

Matilda frowned. The two thought they could march right over her. Matilda preferred to do the marching herself once she understood the rhythm. She stepped between them. "Do you intend to ask me to be a companion to your mother, my lord?"

"I do." A stiff nod. His toe had started tapping on the floor.

She pulled in a deep breath. "I am sorry to disappoint you, my lord, and I am honored you have thought of me, but—"

"Who else would I think of, Miss Bellvue? You were the only person who kept Maggie from going feral all those years ago. You're the only reason she has a thimbleful of understanding of the social world she moves through. And you did it all without ... snuffing her out." He waved a hand toward Lady Pratsby. "And look at the viscountess. She clearly does not wish to lose you. And I have seen you through each and every new position you've taken, and each family, each house, has looked on you with pride. I ask again, Miss Bellvue, who would I choose, if not you?"

"Huh." Lady Pratsby sank down into her pink chair to the creak of angry knees. "Keep talking. I like it when a young man knows truth."

Matilda gathered her skirts and swept toward the study door at the other end of the room. "We will have that private audience now, my lord. Please follow me." She did not look to the viscountess for confirmation. She was no green girl.

Lady Pratsby wagged her finger at them. "Don't take too long, or I'll come in after you. And Miss Bellvue?"

Matilda stopped at the door, Lord Waneborough almost bumping into her. "Yes, my lady?"

"Do let him down gently."

"I'm closing the door."

Lady Pratsby waved a hand at them, and Matilda slipped into the small, dark study. She swept across the room and threw open the curtains, letting the gray light of the rainy day turn dark shadows into slightly brighter ones.

When she turned to him, he stood in the center of the room, hands clasped behind his back, a lock of damp, curling hair falling over one eye. A handsome man in an unrefined way. He should intimidate her. But she'd known him when he was still quite young, when he was seeing, for the first time, the breaks and fractures in the world, same as she was. They'd learned bitter truths side by side, and she saw in him not a gruff marquess demanding her help but a man trying his best to keep his world afloat, same as she.

"My lord," she said, "I am so very sorry to hear of your loss. Is it ... recent?"

"January. Thank you for your condolences. But what I truly need is your help."

She nodded. "That is what I understand, but I am afraid I cannot help you."

"I cannot pay you well, which you know, of course. I assume that colors your refusal."

"Not at all. And I am valiantly succeeding in not being insulted by your implication. You have done much for me through the years. Always a supporter from afar, and I do appreciate that. I am quite, *quite* grateful." Her breath hitched and she spoke in lower tones. "You've kept all your promises to me."

"What, then, puts a refusal on your tongue?"

"I am afraid— No, I am *pleased* to tell you I am a free woman. In a fortnight, that is. Then you will be free of me, of the burden of promises made long ago."

His brows lowered, drew together like two storm clouds about to strike lightning. The London rain had coalesced on his forehead.

"I've inherited a house," she explained. *A home.* "In

Cumbria. A small cottage. A small—very small—annuity. From an aunt. When Lady Pratsby's daughter returns to London in a fortnight, I will leave her employ and head to Cumbria to live a life of solitude and ease."

"I see. You should have told me."

"I had planned to write you once I was settled. My lord, I have served others for fifteen years, and now I shall serve myself. I hope you are pleased for me."

"Blast it, Miss Bellvue, of course I am."

"You do not sound pleased."

His palms found his face, scrubbed up and down. "My mother ..." He heaved a sigh as his arms dropped heavy to his sides. "It is not your worry."

"Please do give her my good wishes. She was always kind to me, and I hope she heals from her loss."

"Of course. And I do understand. If I suddenly inherited ... Well, if fifteen years of struggle came to an end ..." Another sigh, this one rough as a brick. "I understand, Miss Bellvue. And I wish you well, even if selfishly I wish your aunt had left someone else her cottage in Cumbria."

She laughed just enough to slide a bit of easiness between them.

He bowed, a stiff board bent in two. "Good day, Miss Bellvue."

"Good day, my lord." She pointed to a second door across the room. "If you escape out that door, you will not have to face the viscountess again."

He grinned, the first one she'd seen from him since he'd arrived muddy-booted minutes before, and heavens, but her heart raced *again*. Not from fear this time, though she was startled; startled by how handsome his chiseled, grinning face was, how tempting and soft his full lips looked curved round a moment of humor. Her heart skipped because in that grin was the young, unsure man who'd also pulled the air from her lungs with such ease.

"Thank you," he said. "At least you've saved me in this way. And, Miss Bellvue ... you were never a burden."

She returned his smile and tried not to watch his legs and other lower anatomy move in his buckskins as he crossed the room and passed through the door. Tried and failed. No reason not to enjoy a peek, though, when she'd never see him again. He'd always had a lovely lower half.

"Now that man knows how to fill out a pair of pants."

Caught. She turned to her employer, who leaned against the frame of the other door. "Filling out breeches is not something someone can know how to do. It is just something they do."

"Precisely, girl, and that fellow *does*."

"If anything, we should be praising his tailor, and—oh." She closed her eyes and found the right path of conversation. "Shall we finish another chapter of *Evelina*, my lady?" Matilda joined her in the doorway.

"No. But we can talk about that man's offer."

Matilda sailed into the other room. "You told me to refuse him gently. I did so. Ah. I see Miss Hoskins brought more tea in my absence. Lovely."

"I only have you, my dear companion, for another fortnight. I'll not send you away sooner than that."

"Just so."

It had been ... interesting to see him again, to see the man he'd become. No more gangly youth. But something else was missing from him too—a vulnerability. He used to wear his smiles easily, and that no-nonsense way of speaking he'd had, that used to be his delivery of compliments and easy conversation. Now, she feared he did not speak unless accomplishing something, did not move unless he had a purpose.

A pity, that. She'd lived the last fifteen years of her life with purpose and had thus learned the value of leisure.

That life of labor would soon be done. The home she'd always longed for so very near. There were plenty of women in England in need of a position as companion. Let the marquess find someone else to work for him.

Four

R aph hated unfinished tasks. They were like low-hanging clouds, gray and heavy and promising muddy inconvenience. He'd failed at yesterday's task of securing a companion, and today's task seemed no closer to fruition, either. In fact, the closer he came to proposing to Miss Sawyer, the less he wanted to.

Hyde Park at the popular hour proved less crowded than it did during the season, but it still buzzed with gossip and watchful eyes. The late summer sun above sizzled Raph's skin, and the lady walking next to him—her mother strolling with a younger sister and Maggie right behind—offered a slight upward tilt of her lip at any observation he made.

A slight upward tilt was all she ever offered, no matter what Raph said, a welcome sign of emotion in her cold blue eyes. Unfortunately, Raph had run out of things to say some time toward the end of the season. They walked, this afternoon, mostly in silence.

Would he truly marry a woman to whom he had nothing to say?

Yes, he would.

So he might as well try his best to find something to say to her.

"Miss Sawyer."

"Yes?" She kept her gaze trained on the path before them.

"Do you enjoy London when the ton has left for their country lives?"

"I do not notice much of a difference. Anyone who matters to me is still here."

Her father owned a cotton factory and had more money than half the ton combined. So it was said. He'd not met her in a ballroom, he'd met her at a dinner party at Tobias's father's house. Tobias's father, too, was a master of textiles, a tradesman, and an earl's youngest son.

She peeked up at him, that corner tilting up. Just a bit. No more than useful.

Could he say anything, anything at all, to get her lips to spread wide into a full smile? Like Miss Bellvue's had so easily?

Perhaps a proposal of marriage.

To Miss Sawyer, not Miss Bellvue.

He focused on the woman beside him, found another path of conversation. "Miss Sawyer, do you enjoy the theater?"

A pause. Then, "It is fine."

Just fine? "Do not you think it rather splendid? A world created within our own, a few hours where the realities of life give way to a—"

"Falsehood."

"Pardon? Falsehood?"

She nodded. "Theatrical productions are not true, so I do not see their purpose."

He could see that point. He'd often thought the same of painting and sculpture, but theater was different. It was alive whereas other forms of art were not.

He swallowed, found the words, opened his mouth—

"Ah, Miss Delaney," Miss Sawyer's voice called out, startling him into silence. "Have you met Lord Waneborough?"

He looked up to where Miss Sawyer gazed. Two women walked toward them, an elder and a younger. Mrs. and Miss Delaney.

Bollocks. Yes, he'd met them both. He'd walked with them here a few times, too. The daughter was on his list of matrimonial candidates.

Miss Delaney paled, her long, dark eyelashes fluttering like a hummingbird's wings.

"Is there something in your eye, Miss Delaney?" he asked.

"N-no," she stuttered and looked to her mama.

The older woman pulled herself up tall. "Yes, his lordship and my daughter are well acquainted, Miss Sawyer."

Well she didn't have to say it like that, as if they were *well acquainted*. A few walks and a dinner party with several other men at her father's house did not count toward being *well* anything.

"I did not know his lordship had returned to town," Mrs. Delaney said. "Did you, Petunia?" She looked down at her daughter who only shook her head and hid her face behind her large straw bonnet. Mrs. Delaney frowned at Miss Sawyer. "I see you knew of his return."

Miss Sawyer shrugged.

Mrs. Delaney's gaze whipped to Raph like a sword point. "You've been in town how many days, my lord?"

Had he angered her by not visiting her daughter first?

"Two days, I suppose," he said. "I had hoped to run into you soon."

She pursed her lips together. "Unfortunate you ran into Miss Sawyer first."

Miss Sawyer did not seem to care one way or another. Was she even attending the conversation anymore? Her attention had wandered to a copse of trees in the distance.

Mrs. Delaney's message, meanwhile, was clear. She thought she owned his attentions, or rather, her daughter did. But he'd made no such declaration.

He stepped back to put space between them. "Actually, my first social visit was yesterday. To the Viscountess Pratsby and a Miss Bellvue."

"Miss Bellvue?" Mrs. Delaney turned the name over like an foreign dish with too much spice. She clearly did not like it. "*Humph.*" She tossed her nose in the air and pulled her daughter down the path. "Come along, Petunia. We will go where you are appreciated."

Hell, but he hated that woman. Would he truly have her as a mother-in-law? He glanced at the daughter. Pretty but pale. Timid. Miss Sawyer seemed to have some color in her. She did not blush so easily, and she could speak for herself, but she did not seem inclined to do so. He should cross them both off his list of matrimonial candidates. But that left him with one other name he couldn't even remember. Bollocks. He couldn't cross them off. He'd have to choose the lesser of two evils.

Maggie and Mrs. Sawyer caught up with them, and Maggie rested a hand on Raph's arm. "Was that Miss Delaney?"

He nodded.

"A lovely woman," Mrs. Sawyer cooed.

Raph didn't believe she believed that a bit.

The woman moved to her daughter's side and linked their arms. "Laticia, my love, have you invited Lord Waneborough over for tea tomorrow?"

"No, Mama." She turned to Raph and lifted emotionless eyes to him. "Will you come to tea tomorrow?" A mechanical offer.

"Yes, of course." An equally rote response.

"Excellent." Maggie sounded much too cheerful for the lot of them.

49

If Miss Sawyer and Miss Delaney were his best options, and if he didn't have a companion to pull his mother from the doldrums, it might be the last and only cheer Raph would know again.

~

If she could order the sun to shine a bit less brightly, Matilda would do so. She was practically sweating beneath her light spencer and muslin gown, and though the wide brim of her bonnet offered a bit of shade, it also made her head feel hot, stuffy. And Bond Street should be less crowded. The season was over, the ton fled to their country roosts. It was why she'd waited to do her shopping until after the season's end. Yet the crowds remained, as did her list of items she'd need for her new home.

It was fully furnished, thanks to Great-Aunt Gladys, whom she'd only met once. But it would need those little touches that would make it Matilda's home.

And Lady Pratsby needed to exhaust herself to fall asleep later tonight. Perhaps there was some perfect combination of exercise and *Evelina* that would act as a sedative.

"This way, Lady Pratsby," Matilda said, pulling her toward a drapers. She'd seen a lovely blue velvet last month. Hopefully it was still there.

The viscountess tugged her in the opposite direction. "Curtains? *Bah*. Let's go to the bookshop."

"We will, my lady, but first—"

"I want to buy something." Lady Pratsby became a statue in the road.

Matilda counted to ten and breathed steady. "You already have. Woolen shifts and night rails; thick, lumpy hats; pelisses made of the stoutest materials. Those brown shawls, too." Matilda shivered.

Lady Pratsby chuckled. "Ugly, aren't they? But when it's cold and you're alone, what use have you for lace and pretty things?"

"The cold? Does that also explain the bed warmers and eyeglasses? Neither of us wear spectacles, my lady. The purchase I wish to make, however, is logical. Curtains for my cottage."

"My purchases make perfect sense. It may be warm in London now, but it will be cold enough to freeze a witch's tit in Cumbria come winter. I'm making sure you've got the necessities, girl."

"Those are for *me*?" Wool and bed warmers. All things to keep her warm. Surely it would not be *that* terribly cold. "What about the spectacles?"

The viscountess shrugged. "You're sure to lose your eyesight soon."

"I don't see why you would assume that. My eyesight is perfectly fine." She suppressed a tiny growl and tugged at Lady Pratsby. "Come along. Curtains."

"Books. Then curtains."

What harm in letting her have her way? And no reason not to switch up the order of things. It would harm nothing.

"Very well," Matilda said, letting the viscountess drag her down Bond Street. A short walk brought them to a storefront with a wooden sign swinging above the door. Hopkins Bookshop. A bell jingled over the door as they entered. The shop was tiny and cluttered, and a man popped up from behind a counter, his white hair sticking out on all sides. Except for the top, where no hair ranged at all.

"Good afternoon," he said. "May I help you?"

Lady Pratsby bustled closer. "I am looking for very specific books." She leaned low over the counter the man stood behind and held a palm to her mouth. "The kind meant to keep a body warm. At night. When alone."

The man's face turned beet red. "Madam!" His voice rang out like a thunderclap across the empty shop. "What sort of establishment do you think I run?"

Lady Pratsby rocked back as if slapped, and the little man shuffled backward from the counter, gesturing for them to follow. He pressed a finger to his lips.

Matilda stood her ground. Naughty books in the backrooms of bookshops? No. "Lady Pratsby, I am aware you are trying to make a point, but—"

The viscountess grabbed Matilda's arm and dragged her forward. "Quit being an old lady."

Matilda sighed but allowed herself to be ushered into a back room and shown a stack of books with shocking illustrations.

Lady Pratsby barely glanced at them. "We'll take them all."

The white-haired man rubbed his hands together. "Excellent. Bestsellers. Every one of them. You won't be disappointed."

"*She* won't be disappointed." Lady Pratsby scowled. "Don't act so high in the instep, girl. I know you've devoured my own copies of these texts. I'd give you my own if I didn't wish to keep them myself. Consider it a spinster present."

The man wrapped their books in brown paper, and they found themselves on the street once more, this time ambling toward the waiting carriage.

When they were inside and settled, Matilda found the patience to ask, "A spinster present? What is that?"

"Like a wedding gift, but for when you've wed yourself to loneliness and obscurity instead of a strapping man."

Matilda dropped her head into her hands with a groan. "I should not have asked."

"You're in a foul mood."

"And whose fault is that? We'll procure material for

curtains now. Beautiful ones." Ones that would make the cottage feel like a home.

Lady Pratsby grinned. "I was hoping you'd be in a better mood after my display of generosity, but as I see you're not, I'll have to delay my question for later today."

"What question? Have out with it, my lady." She'd surely heard the worst of it already. Spinster present, indeed.

"Don't worry yourself. I'd be a grump, too, if I had to think all day of the sacrifices I'm making by moving to a tiny mountain cottage."

"I'm not a grump. And I've been given to understand that tiny cottage has four bedchambers. You're welcome to come visit. Your question?"

Lady Pratsby cleared her throat. "After further consideration, I am of the opinion you should accept Lord Waneborough's offer. You must be his mother's companion."

"First, that is not a question. Second—"

"But! I want to go with you." No mirth remained in the lines of Lady Pratsby's face. Matilda had never seen the woman so serious before.

"And why would you wish to do that?" Matilda asked. "It's a house of mourning, and you have only lately found your own peace. When your daughter arrives in a fortnight to reprieve me of my duty, she will be garbed in black, grieving her own husband's death. Surely you wish a rest from grief until then."

"Let us set aside the fact that I wish to see what the house and the marchioness are like. Rumors abound, and I will not deny curiosity. But more importantly, grief is precisely why we should go. You pulled me out of mine like no one else could with your books and your walks and your letting me cry. With your ordering me about and making me do and think things other than how sad I was. All that woman has is a deliciously handsome son who looks like he'd rather stomp through manure than talk about the holes in his heart. Or his mother's. She needs our help, Miss Bellvue."

"Our?"

A tight nod. "You're a youthful ray of light, and I'm a lady who's been where she is—lost in darkness. Together, we will guide her out."

Matilda watched the London world roll by—gray and dingy yellow, brick-brown and foggy outlines, even in the hot, unforgiving sun. "Good points, my lady." Other good points —Lord Waneborough had always been so solicitous of her, keeping abreast of her positions, helping her find them. A far-off benefactor who offered support through means other than the financial. She was indebted to him. The thought had been on repeat in her mind since his visit yesterday, rubbing the inside of her skin raw. She owed him.

"A fortnight, Miss Bellvue, helping that handsome pup and his mother. Then you may hie off to Cumbria and your cottage and be done with old women. Hire your own young companion and become an old woman yourself."

That did not sound so appealing. Itchy wool and metal bed warmers to heat her body. Naughty books to warm her imagination. No one else for miles. She only just managed not to scrunch her nose. Not at all what she'd pictured for herself. She had pictured a young poet roaming the waterfalls, writing verse on daisies, wandering next to her cottage, knocking upon her door, falling in love. With her, of course. She'd planned days and months of rearranging furniture and hanging new curtains, laying new rugs, welcoming visitors in pretty, muslin gowns.

Was Lady Pratsby's vision much more likely? She shivered despite the day's warmth and wrapped her arms tight about her.

"A fortnight only, Miss Bellvue. Help a grieving woman and offer me a bit of fun before you leave. And we both know the ... *view* ... promises to be grand." She chuckled, leaned back into the squabs, and closed her eyes. "And by *view* I mean that young man's backside."

"Lady Pratsby! Do have some decorum."

The viscountess chuckled. "Think on it, Miss Bellvue. Think on *all* the reasons."

Think on it. She could do that, but it likely would do no good. The cottage was her future, her home. But Briarcliff Manor was her past, her most vulnerable past. Thrown from her home by a heartless half brother, forced to find a paying position when she'd learned few useful skills in her days as a debutante. She'd known French, thankfully, and the Marchioness of Waneborough had liked her "fairy eyes" and wanted her daughter to learn the rules of polite society so she could break them if she so chose. The woman had been an oddity. Neither she nor her husband had cared for the ton's dictates. But they'd been kind, offering security to a girl standing on shattered ground.

She shook her head. So close to her own future, she did not wish to relive that past.

But it would make Lady Pratsby happy, and her joy had been hard earned.

Too, it might help Lord Waneborough's mother find some peace.

Finally, she could not forget Lord Waneborough himself. He'd kept his promises to Matilda. Promises he'd made at his lowest point, tears pooling in his eyes, his worry on her and not himself. He had her gratitude, yes. She'd never denied him that. And now he deserved her help.

Three excellent reasons to relent.

Not necessary to consider a fourth, no matter how grand it might be.

Five

R aph was in no mood for this brother-in-law's teasing jests. But as the man had given more to Raph's family than Raph's own father ever had, he sank lower on the settee—careful to keep his muddy boots off the upholstery —and tried to close his ears and just let the man ramble.

Tobias paced before the empty fireplace, pink silk waistcoat blinding. "I think you should throw them all in an empty ballroom and see which one makes it out alive. The victor shall be your bride, my friend. But Maggie thinks you should offer for Miss Delaney."

"I can say what I think myself, Tobias. Thank you." Maggie sat at a nearby desk, perusing a sliver of paper that held two names. Why she had to write them down, Raph could not say. They could remember two names, especially when he'd spent significant time with both women last season.

"Of course you can, Maggie darling. Only you weren't saying. You were *considering*. Without words. And your poor brother is languishing, his heart as of yet untouched. We must quick tell him who to love so he can get about the business of loving her."

Enough. Raph sat upright and braced his elbows on his knees. "Love has nothing to do with it, Tobias. And the list we should truly make, Maggie, is one with names for companions." Miss Bellvue had said no. A surprise, that, and now he felt ... lost. Who but Miss Bellvue was right for the position?

She'd been so very confident and steady two mornings ago, the exact sort of presence his mother needed. The viscountess she currently worked for clearly did not wish to lose her. Understandable, and another mark in Miss Bellvue's favor. But Raph's need was greater. His mother's need was greater.

"Don't you have a spinster sister or cousin or some such, Tobias," Raph asked, "who we can sweep off to Briarcliff?"

"Only got the one sister, and she's married."

Raph looked to Maggie. "Do you have friends, acquaintances in need of a position?"

She shook her head. "I think we should focus on finding you a wife, Raph. Consider this. A wife will fix many of your woes. The financial and the maternal. A wife can offer Mother company, after all."

"Hm. Excellent point." Raph tapped his toes. "Which of the women on your list best suits Mother?"

"No." Maggie stood and strode around the desk she'd been sitting at. "Absolutely the wrong question. We must ask who best suits *you*, and then she will also suit Mother."

"No, she'll be frustrated with Mother if she suits me."

Maggie sat next to him. "I do not wish you to blindly choose a wealthy woman to wed, the first who says yes." She laid her hand on his arm and squeezed. "I'd like you to enter into a marriage where there is, at least, the possibility of forming the happiness Tobias and I share."

Raph offered a weak grin. "The man's a nodcock, but he makes you happy."

"The man is standing right here."

They ignored Tobias.

"I'd like it if my eldest brother could be happy. You've not been in many years."

"I'll be happy once I have a wife." Raph snatched Maggie's list from the desk. "Miss Delaney is nice enough. I should offer for her."

"She's a bit ... pale," Tobias said. He leaned against the fireplace mantel, tapping one arm with a finger.

"What does her coloring have to do with it?" Raph demanded.

"Nothing. I mean pale of spirit. She'll disappear into the mist at Briarcliff. There one day and"—he wiggled his fingers in the air—"gone the next. You'll forget she exists, and your mother will eat her alive. Atlas will likely terrify her."

Raph turned to Maggie. "Do you think it's true?"

Maggie bit her lip. "I ... am not sure. Her sweet and biddable personality is the opposite of everything you are, and I thought it a good thing. You will not butt heads."

"Precisely," Raph said.

"But ... it's possible you need a *stronger* woman."

Raph popped a hip against the desk, crossed his arms, and closed his eyes, picturing the women on his list, testing them for strength. But the remaining two did not step up.

Instead, Miss Bellvue stood politely, calmly, stoutly before him. Chin held high, shoulders wide, face implacable. Now there was a strong woman. She knew her mind, her wants, and she would set about getting them.

Admired that, he did.

There was much to admire about her. Last he'd seen her, she'd been nineteen and a bit lost. She'd done well as Maggie's governess, but doubt had draped heavy about her like a cloak she could not divest herself of. She'd had the look of a wren in the shadow of a storm—brown feathers soaked, frail and scared. But determined.

Now she looked like a ... well, like a woman. All curves and steel spine and looking nothing like someone paid to give company then blend in and disappear when necessary. She looked like the sort of woman who took charge.

Strong, yes.

Sensual, too. The curve of her hip, her lip, the slight wave of her hair that made him think of a candle-shadowed bedchamber and soft white sheets. He couldn't lie to himself. He'd conjured her image before. Often when they'd slept under the same roof.

His eyes popped open.

Miss Bellvue was *not* on the list.

Miss Bellvue had a cottage in Cumbria.

He snapped the list up, pretending to read it before tossing it back on the desk. "Miss Sawyer should do." A bit cold. It would be a frosty sort of marriage. But ice had strength if it was thick enough, tempered in cold enough weather.

"Hm." Maggie stood and paced the room. "Miss Sawyer. Yes. Perhaps. But she seems too ... I'm not sure how to phrase it."

Tobias joined her. "She the one with icicles for eyes?"

"Tobias!" Maggie admonished.

He shrugged. "What use does a marquess have for a woman who won't care what happens one way or the other? You're trying to save your family, Raph. You need a woman with passion. And Miss Sawyer is a limp cravat."

Maggie glared.

Tobias held his arms out wide, inviting argument. "Am I wrong, Mags?"

She sauntered up to him, pressed close as she wrapped a hand around his neck. "Be nice. She may soon be my sister."

Tobias's eyes softened. "If Maggie says so, I'll do it, I suppose." He lowered his face to his wife's.

A kiss was coming. Raph groaned and turned from the

sight. The sound of a voice clearing in the doorway broke the pre-kiss calm.

Tobias and Maggie jerked away from one another, Tobias wearing a wicked grin.

The butler stood in the doorway. "A Miss Bellvue is here to speak with Lord Waneborough."

Maggie clapped her hands. "How lovely. Do send her in. I've not seen her in years." She turned to Raph, a smile stretched wide across her face. "Perhaps she's come to accept after all!"

What else could it be? Why else would she—

Then there she was. Her impossibly thick dark hair hidden beneath a straw bonnet, a navy spencer over a brown gown with little suede half boots peeking out. He took her in all at once then focused on each and every detail because ... because.

Hell, he could not say what the because was. But he could not stop, either.

Miss Bellvue curtsied, wove her gloved fingers together.

Maggie ran to her, swept her into a hug that made Miss Bellvue's eyes open wide, made a grin split her lips.

"Oh, Miss Bellvue," Maggie said, "you look exactly as I remember you! Stern and soft at the same time."

Stern and soft. The perfect descriptor.

Maggie dragged the companion toward her husband. "Tobias, you must meet my first and only governess, Miss Matilda Bellvue. She taught me all I know about behaving correctly in polite society. Miss Bellvue, this is my husband, Mr. Tobias Blake."

Tobias bowed. "You could have taught her a bit more. She's an unpredictable little sprite."

Raph strode forward. "He's teasing, Miss Bellvue." He needed her to know that. What if the odd man's jokes ran her off? "And you will not have to worry about him at Briarcliff.

He runs a silk business here and does not often visit us in the country."

Miss Bellvue turned her stern attention to him. "You are assuming something about my visit this morning, my lord."

"Why else would you be here?"

Tobias and Maggie took a step back.

"I could be here for a social visit with your sister," Miss Bellvue said.

"You told my sister's butler you were here for me."

Heat spread like freckles across her cheeks, and her tongue darted to roll against her bottom lip, and damn, his body wound tight as a gear in a clock she alone had the key to. He turned, strode to the window, and watched the stream of London traffic pass by. To unwind.

She chuckled. "I am here to speak with you. And, though it ... irritates me, you have guessed right. I have come to accept your offer. If you've not already found someone to replace me."

He swung around. "No, I have not."

Maggie and Tobias had backed up all the way against the silent, empty fireplace, and only their eyes moved, darting back and forth between himself and Miss Bellvue.

"Should you like us to give you some privacy?" Maggie asked.

"Yes," Raph said.

At the same time Miss Bellvue said, "It's not necessary."

Silence no one seemed pressed to break. Hell. Silence achieved nothing.

"What, precisely changed your mind, Miss Bellvue?" Raph asked.

"My conscience. And my employer. She—I—*we* have a request. If I travel to Briarcliff to act as companion for your mother, Lady Pratsby must come with me."

"As a chaperone?" he asked.

Miss Bellvue blinked. "Chaperone? No, of course not."

No, of course not. Why had he thought that? It was only that she'd been standing there, looking stern and soft at the same time, speaking of traveling to his house to stay, and he'd only been able to think of the need for a chaperone because ... because ...

Why did the *becauses* elude him so today?

"You're right," he finally said. "A joke."

Tobias barked a laugh. "You? Joking? You don't even know how, Raph."

Raph sliced his brother-in-law the sort of look that said, *Would you kindly stuff it?* Then he returned his attention to Miss Bellvue. "Of course she may come. As our guest." If he must have Lady Pratsby to have Miss Bellvue, he'd take her.

Miss Bellvue inhaled deeply, held his gaze with eyes that made him want a closer look. Brown but with something else dancing about the edges. What? Green? Gold? A tangle of both? And how close would he need to be to find out?

"Lady Pratsby has also asked," Miss Bellvue said, "that she continue to pay my salary while we're at Briarcliff."

"Ho, ho!" Tobias rubbed his hands together. "Economy. Now you're speaking that man's language."

Maggie held a finger to her husband's mouth. "Tobias, *shh*. Let them speak to one another."

"There is no need for that, Miss Bellvue," Raph said. "You may tell the viscountess we are strapped but not without resources."

Tobias raised a hand. "I am resources."

Agitation rumbled into noise in Raph's throat. He disliked accepting more help, but in truth, Lady Pratsby's offer was tempting. Her presence would double the number of new mouths Briarcliff would be need to feed. And if the viscountess paid Miss Bellvue's salary, Tobias would not have to.

But no. He shook his head. She'd have twice the trouble with two ladies to act the companion to. "Lady Pratsby may do as she pleases, but you will receive a salary from my family." He glared at Tobias, daring him to once more specify from which branch of the family her salary would stem from.

He did not. The man had some sense of self preservation, then.

Miss Bellvue gave a sharp nod. "As you please."

"What of the length of your stay?" Raph inquired, folding his arms behind his back.

"As long as it takes, or until Lady Pratsby bores."

"Then we shall endeavor to keep her entertained."

Miss Bellvue didn't smile, but she wanted to. Easy to tell. The corners of her lips flinched, and her eyes lit up like candle flames. She kept it tightly hidden, though. "We shall leave tomorrow?"

He heard the question, but he did not believe it, though. She'd wrapped up a strong suggestion with the upward lilt of her tone to make it appear less of an order. Did the woman think to control his travel schedule? He opened his mouth to tell her the truth of the matter—she did not control a damn thing—but snapped it shut. Tomorrow the roads might have dried from yesterday's rain. And if they did not take advantage of a break in the clouds, they could end up traveling muddy. Which meant traveling slowly.

"Yes, tomorrow," he said. "Early. I'll arrive no later than eight to escort you. If we travel swiftly and without trouble, we should arrive at Briarcliff before nightfall."

Her eyes narrowed then cleared. "Yes. That plan aligns suitably with my own. I am happy to offer my help, my lord. As you know, I have worked as a companion to four widows over the last fifteen years. I have learned much about the process of grieving. I am confident that with time and love and occupation, your mother will heal. Do not worry."

"I'm not worried. Not now that you've taken hold of the problem."

"Just so." She turned to Maggie. "I am delighted to see you so happy, but I am sorry for the loss of your father."

"Thank you. And thank you for what you're about to endure. My mother has not been easy."

"I remember her being a tad ... dramatic. But terribly lovely all the same. I did not say at the time, but her warm welcome of me into her home was a most-needed gift when I least expected one."

Maggie dashed toward her, hugged her again. "Tell her that. She'll love to hear it."

"Yes, well." Miss Bellvue dislodged herself from the embrace. "I certainly will." She curtsied. "I will see you tomorrow morning, my lord."

"I'll escort you to the door." He stepped toward her.

"Oh, no need. Thank you, but I'll see myself out." Then she left, not leaving even a whisper of a moment for him to argue with her about it.

Tobias whistled. "She's going to run right over you, isn't she?"

Raph grunted. "She may do as she pleases as long as she stops Mother from wailing."

"Oh?" Tobias raised an eyebrow. "*Anything* she pleases?"

Maggie left her husband's side and picked up the list of possible brides from its forgotten grave on the desk. "Now that the issue of Mother's companion is settled, let us turn our thoughts to more matrimonial matters."

"No." Raph strode for the door. "I think we should ensure Mother is on the path to healing before we bring another woman into the situation." Besides, after his walk in the park yesterday with Miss Sawyer and Miss Delaney, he felt in no rush to bring either of them home.

"Miss Bellvue is another woman," Tobias pointed out.

"She's a companion who will not usurp mother's place as the marchioness. It is better to let Miss Bellvue do her work and then choose a bride."

"Or," Maggie said, waving her paper before his face, "you can choose now and begin the process—bans, planning. It takes time, brother. And during that time, your Miss Bellvue can work her magic."

"No. I've not decided on a wife yet, and I will not propose until I am certain the proposal is what is best for Briarcliff and the Waneborough line. You wish for my happiness, Maggie?"

"Of course."

"Then I need more time." Time, potentially, to use the silence Miss Bellvue might procure for him to paint something his mother might approve of. Time to win his inheritance. "I'll return in a month and revisit the list."

Maggie dropped into a chair. "You may find the ladies otherwise engaged by that point."

He shrugged. "There are other dowries."

Maggie flinched. "Do not be so hard-hearted, brother."

He wrapped a hand around the doorframe and squeezed. "I have to be." But he gave her a smile, to show her it did not bother him, the necessary stone of his heart. "I'm off to prepare for our early departure tomorrow." He left without waiting for a reply.

He'd accomplished only one of the tasks he'd set for himself in London, arguably the least important of the two when it came to finally—*finally*—steadying the family's financial footing.

He felt lighter nonetheless. Miss Bellvue had the perfect sort of shoulders to share a burden with—stern and soft. She would ensure a quiet, calm home so he could focus on what was most important—filling the family coffers. Everything, soon, would be perfect. No longer hindered by his father's excesses, Raph would right everything in no time.

Six

〇〜〇

The moon hid behind thin, dark clouds, casting striations of light on Briarcliff Manor. Big. That was all Matilda could determine, stretching her neck left and right, up and down after the long journey. It had taken them longer than the marquess had estimated, and he did not seem pleased about it. They might have moved more quickly had he not had something to say about every tiny detail of the journey. She had not told him that.

He strode toward the front door. "Follow me."

Lady Pratsby took Matilda's arm and pulled her after Lord Waneborough. "Looks like a regular house to me. Nothing odd about it yet."

"It's not so much the house that is odd, my lady, but what happens inside of it each autumn. The artist's party is ... fascinating."

Exhilarating. Matilda did not possess a single artistic bone, but she admired those who did, and to see them all gathered, sharing techniques, developing new ones, arguing about others. It had felt like life painted with the brightest colors.

All that light gone now in the evening gloom. Even the moon hid.

It was cold inside, and the marquess's footsteps echoed.

"Welcome." A voice in the dark, a ghost's greeting. Shadows swept down the stairs toward them and took shape. Then the darkness lifted like fingers parting a veil, and a pale face peered at them from the shadows. "I did not expect two guests, but I am delighted nonetheless." The woman, the marchioness, curtsied as if she were meeting the queen, not a viscountess and her companion.

"Good evening, Mother. I apologize for the late hour of our arrival."

She waved away his concern and took the rest of the stairs at a run. Her steps made muffled slaps against the marble floor before she threw her arms around Matilda. "Welcome home, dear girl." She held her at arm's length. "Welcome *home*."

That word—home. Like a knife in her gut. The same hearty welcome she'd receive fifteen years ago. Should she accept it, sink into it? Or keep her distance?

Matilda looked at Lady Pratsby for some insight.

Lady Pratsby only chuckled. No help there.

She looked to Lord Waneborough, but he'd already turned toward the door.

"I must see to the horses," he said, disappearing into the moon-shadowed dark outside.

Nothing for it but to follow suit. "I am so pleased to have finally returned to Briarcliff, my lady. And may I introduce the Viscountess Pratsby?"

The two women eyed one another. There was likely a decade between them in age, with Lady Waneborough being the younger. Hopefully their personalities would not clash too terribly. She remembered little about the marchioness other than her bright spirit and open heart, which she'd already demonstrated this evening.

Lady Waneborough offered the viscountess an equally warm smile, and a slight sheen caused her eyes to glimmer in the weak, flickering candlelight. "I am perfectly pleased to have another guest. It has been lonely the last six months."

Matilda nodded. "I am sorry for your loss, my lady."

The marchioness turned and glided down a dark hallway. She lifted a hand and gestured for them to follow. "Are you parched? Or hungry? I'll have Clarkson provide … something." She led them to a small parlor lit only by a low fire that bathed the room in a stifling, rolling heat. A few candles, nearing their end, stood weary on wall sconces. A dark room to match the form dressed head to toe in unrelieved black.

Six months was not time enough to mourn the loss of a beloved spouse. The marquess's mother did not grieve unnaturally. Lord Waneborough perhaps misunderstood.

The marchioness stood before the fire and turned to them, outlining her dark skirts with a deep orange flicker of low flames. "How was the journey?"

"Uneventful, my lady," Matilda said.

"Oh, you must call me Franny. I'm determined to be nothing but that once Raph marries, and Grandmama once he has children. The two of you may help me become accustomed to it." She turned to the fire. From behind, she was a pillar of black, straight and cold. But her request to be called by her first name held a note of hope. She looked forward to the future, planned for it. All was not lost.

Lady Pratsby shuffled forward. "Let us all be informal, then, Franny. You must call me Jane. And the young one we'll call Matilda."

The marchioness peered at them from over her shoulder. "Excellent."

Lines radiated from the marchioness's eyes and bracketed her mouth. Six months was not too long to mourn so heavily, but that did not mean Matilda and Lady Pratsby could not help the woman find relief from her oppressive loneliness.

Excellent. Unconventional to call two ladies not of her relation by their given names, but if it would speed along the marchioness's healing, Matilda would do it gladly. Though it would take some getting used to, certainly. A sense of purpose settled over her, and she bustled to the marchioness's side, moved her from the fireplace, and sat her in a chair some distance away, motioning for Lady Pratsby to join them.

She glanced at the door. Would the marquess return? She could not feel surprised that he'd slipped out to see to the horses. He had taken an active role in every detail of their journey, had a word for every man who approached their conveyance in the coaching yards. Likely a word that suggested he knew better, too. He'd told their footmen exactly how to pack up the trunks and made sure she and the viscountess knew exactly the route they planned to take, how long they would be traveling, and what the almanac suggested the weather would be like. He'd also let them know he might disagree with the almanac.

She chuckled softly, found the bell pull and, hopefully, summoned someone who could provide a bit of nourishment before bed.

"You find something amusing, Miss Bellvue?" Lord Waneborough's voice so low and so near.

She startled and turned to find him leaning against the doorframe, the very portrait of a powerful peer. He should pose just so for his own portrait when the day came.

"I do," she said. "How did you guess?"

"The corner of your lip is tilted up. As it used to do when you watched Maggie do something silly."

"Ah. You've discovered my secret."

"When you were still too young to hide it well."

She shook her head. "I am no longer that girl. And I see not an inch of that boy you used to be in you."

"We meet as strangers, then."

"Mm. Are there candles? There are too few lit here, and it is too hot for such a fire in the grate."

He scowled and joined her as she pulled open a drawer in a nearby table.

"We use them sparingly. You will find this house not prone to excesses. Tell me what you found amusing."

"You." Ah, there, in the very back of the third drawer she pulled open—a tallow candle. She carried it to a sconce, lit it with the current, dwindling flame, and fixed it steady to the partner sconce before the mirror. The reflection sent light rippling throughout the room. "There. Much better."

He scowled, whether from her blatant use of a new candle or because of her admission, she could not say. "Me? I'm the very opposite of amusing."

"You are amusing in that you poke your nose into every detail surrounding you."

He stopped, boots rooting to the ground. "I beg your pardon. I poke my nose into *nothing*."

"You do. That nose of yours, its beak and all, have been in my trunks, Lady Pratsby's trunk—"

"Trunks of a certain weight must be secured in a precise way, and—"

"My sewing basket and book—"

"I needed to know if you were carrying valuables a high-wayman might find tempting."

She began counting on her fingers. "Harnesses, the bottom of the horses' feet, the coachman's history—"

"It's important to know if a fellow has the proper qualifications to drive ladies a long distance."

She lifted a brow. "Is it?" Her gaze narrowed to his nose.

His jaw twitched. "I like everything done *right*. If I have a say in everything, it is only to ensure nothing falls apart. You, for instance. Sit down already. I hear a tea cart rattling down the hall."

She allowed him to shepherd her toward his mother and Lady Pratsby.

"Will you join us?" she asked.

"I must see if my brother is awake."

"Which one?"

"Atlas. Did you meet him when you were last here?"

She nodded, and he bowed and left as she took a seat with the other women.

Lady Pratsby cocked her head and stared. "Strolling with that young man so long, I thought he'd ravished you. Don't look ravished, though. Don't worry, girl. There's still next time."

Lady Waneborough flinched, her bombazine rustling. "What a lovely notion, Jane. Do you think he will ravish her? I know him better than you do, I dare say, and I find it highly unlikely."

Heavens no. She'd been worried the two women would not suit temperamentally. But it seemed they suited all too well.

The tea cart appeared, and Matilda took control of it with a soft *thank you*. "Please retire for the evening. I'll take care of everything here."

The maid yawned and disappeared.

Matilda rattled the cart to her two charges and poured them cups. "There is to be no ravishing. We were in plain sight in the same room as the both of you the entire time. My, what healthy imaginations you both have."

"Naughty imaginations," Lady Pratsby said, elbowing the marchioness.

Lady Waneborough tittered. "A ravishment might be just what this house needs."

"Then find another house to ravish this one," Matilda answered. "I'll take no part."

The viscountess cackled. "You're a spitfire sometimes. Why I like you." She sipped her tea and settled it with a hard clink on the saucer. "Will you truly say no to a man built like a bull who answers to marquess? Who sought you out in particular to bring home with him."

Lady Waneborough put her cup down entirely. "Do you think he sought her out for a particular *reason*? I thought it was merely ... convenient."

"And it was," Matilda assured them.

The marchioness stripped off her gloves. "My, it's hot. Let's have done with these. There." Her hands glowed against her skirts, and she smiled at her fingers as if she hadn't seen them in some time. "Now, to return to the subject of ravishment."

Matilda rolled her eyes. "Do not build castles in the air, my lady. My ladies. No castles from either of you."

Lady Pratsby snorted. "Don't be too high in the instep for a good tupping, Matilda."

"My lady." Matlida's voice held a warning she hoped the older woman would heed.

"You'll need memories to keep you warm in your Cumbrian cottage. No shame in it for a woman of your years. I'm not going to tell a soul and neither is the titled bull with the glorious backside."

"A cottage in Cumbria?" Lady Waneborough blinked at her. "No! How beastly."

"I think it rather lovely," Matilda said. "And I remind you not to speak ill of my future home." She had plans for it. Lovely, delightful plans.

The marchioness seemed not to have heard Matilda speak. She turned promptly to Lady Pratsby, her brows pulling together in a frown. "While I admit my son is well-built, may I request we not refer to his backside so casually? As if ... as if commenting on the quality of a roast?"

Lady Pratsby chuckled. "I'll do my best."

Hm. This friendship promised to be trying. But the quick strip of Lady Waneborough's gloves gave Matilda hope. Her stay here would not be long. The lady merely needed distraction, companionship.

"Let us be direct and firm in our understanding of one another now, Lady Waneborough, Lady Pratsby."

"Franny, my dear," the marchioness said.

"I believe we've moved on to Jane," the viscountess added.

Matilda stayed strong. "In no situation would Lord Waneborough solicit my attentions. And if he did, there is not a jewel in any crown that would convince me to let him have his way. No offense to you, or him, my lady." The boy she'd known long ago had been solicitous and kind. This man, though ... "He's the sort who thinks he knows best, and that is not the sort I wish to dally with, marry, or pursue any other sort of relationship with—scandalous or otherwise."

Lady Pratsby chuckled. "Is it like looking in a mirror, then, Matilda?"

"Is Matilda high-handed, too?" Lady Waneborough asked.

An echo of footsteps down the hall grew louder, and Lord Waneborough appeared. He dropped into chair between his mother and the tea cart. "Atlas sends his regards, Miss Bellvue, and looks forward to greeting you in the morning."

She nodded, sipped her tea, thanked God for good timing. "I look forward to renewing our acquaintance." Hopefully he couldn't see the wash of heat across her cheeks. She'd have to temper his mother's imagination, and Lady Pratsby's, if she wished to face him with any sort of dignified composure.

"Tell me, my lord"—Lady Pratsby leaned back in her chair and eyed the marquess—"why have you not wed before now? Young, strapping man like you. You need a wife."

"I am in the process of choosing one. I had hoped not to have to make a choice based on mercenary reasons but ... I suppose you'll see, so there is no use hiding it ... my father almost ruined us."

A small gasp from his mother that didn't even trip up the march of his words from his tongue.

He continued without pause. "My brothers and I have been paying off his debts as well as we can, and we have mostly caught up, but it has left everything else in disrepair."

"Honorable," Lady Pratsby said. "You staved off marriage because you hoped to keep a lady out of such a situation."

He nodded.

His mother picked up a glove, played with the fingers of it, stroking and stretching.

Did he not realize how insensitive his words were to her?

Lady Pratsby said, "But surely you can put things right soon enough and take a wife to make a little pleasure in this world for yourself."

"There are complications I will not bore you with. But I am on the hunt for a wife."

His mother's skirts rustled once more. "How was London, Raphael? Are you engaged yet?"

"No," Lord Waneborough said. "I have not yet made a decision."

Lady Pratsby waggled her eyebrows. "Failed to bring home a wife, yet you brought home a companion. Such a good son."

Something pointed in the viscountess's speech turned the heat in the room higher. Matilda finished the rest of her drink and turned her attention to the cart. "Ah. It appears we have bread and cheese here. It looks divine." She took a large slice of the bread.

Just as Lord Waneborough did the same. Their hands tangled but neither moved.

"I am interested in eating that, my lord," Matilda said.

"It's too large. Let me cut a chunk off for you." His other hand reached for the knife.

"It is fine. I'll take small bites."

"You'll choke."

"I'm not a babe, my lord. I've been competently chewing my own food for over three decades."

Still, his hand did not move. In fact, it tightened, and not only on the bread but on her hand, a warm vice of rough skin and hard muscle. Could palms have muscle? His did anyway.

Lady Pratsby cackled. "You two offer more entertainment than a book. Or even a Drury Lane theatrical. Don't you think, Franny?"

"Quite right," his mother said. "I'm all aflutter. What *will* happen next?"

Their hands flew away from the bread. He attempted to shove his through his hair only to find it occupied by a knife, which he dropped to the table before threading his hands behind his neck. She clutched hers against her belly, trying to squash the tingling along her fingers.

Raph stood. "I am exhausted. I believe I'll retire for the evening. You ladies should as well. Good night, Mother, Miss Bellvue, Lady Pratsby." He bowed low and left.

Lady Pratsby watched him leave. "That boy needs a bit of fun." She swung her gaze to Matilda with a wide smile.

Lady Waneborough nodded, her veil bouncing around her face.

"*I* am not going to give him fun."

"Hm," both ladies said at the same time.

"I'm not! Lady Waneborough, you are his mother. This behavior is beyond the pale."

"A lovely lecture, my dear. I do remember you being expert at them." She chuckled. "I'm sure Maggie remembers, too. But you'll find me unlike other marchionesses. Much I do is beyond the pale. I quite *live* in the pale."

"Well, I intend to live in a cottage in Cumbria, and—"

Lady Pratsby let her head fall back on her chair and pretended to snore.

"I choose to ignore that," Matilda said.

Her head snapped back up, her eyes bright. "Some things you can't ignore, girl. Like the body. Or *someone else's* body."

"Jane," Lady Waneborough warned, "I may live in a very pale place, but I have my limits as they regard the appreciation of my son's form. Please do remember that."

"I'll try."

Matilda bit into the bread. Still warm from where her hand, and his, had covered it. She chewed with vigor, gnawing the little remembrances of his touch into nothing. "This is an entirely inappropriate conversation. It is highly unlikely we will ever see one another in the coming weeks. I assume, my lady"—she looked to the marchioness—"your son is not one to be kept in your pocket, seeing to your every need and comfort."

"Are you blind?" Lady Pratsby barked. "All he's done today is fuss over our comfort."

Lady Waneborough sighed. "He is a thoughtful lad. Though vexing."

Matilda snorted. "He's only made sure to tell us exactly how to do everything."

"So we are comfortable and safe," Lady Pratsby offered.

"So he can show off his competence," Matilda countered.

Lady Waneborough grinned, the first true grin she'd shown since they'd arrived. "You think he's competent. It *is* nice to hear one's offspring praised."

Matilda put the bread aside and stood. "Of course I recognize his competence. But he is also insufferable. Apologies, Lady Waneborough. I've been terribly impolite." But every bit of the conversation since she'd arrived had seemed tailored toward aggravating her. She did not wish to be ravished or paired off with a marquess, no matter how glorious his back-side or competent his person in general.

The marchioness waved her apology away. "You're quite correct. He can be insufferable. I've no argument there."

Matlida wished to retire as the marquess had, but she was a companion and must keep the hours the ladies required of her. So she pretended to explore the room, each piece of furniture, knickknack, the many paintings dotting the walls. Even in the dim light, she could tell each was exquisite. Each created a mood or story that begged the eye to look closer, that churned the heart to emotion.

Lovely. She must procure a painting or two for her cottage.

But until she could acquire those and the cottage itself, she'd foster the relationship between the two ladies already leaning close to one another, give the marchioness the softness and understanding her son seemed to lack, and ignore the marquess entirely. An excellent plan soon to lead to success.

Seven

R aph should let the yellow be, but devil take it, the color called to him. At least the house was silent enough for him to hear the call. And no one was about to realize he'd actually heard something so ridiculous, listened for it, even. Atlas was in the stables, as usual, and wherever the women were, they were quiet. Thank God. No wailing or moaning or black-laced widow processions of one through the halls. Miss Bellvue and Lady Pratsby had been here less than a fortnight and already they'd made an improvement.

He'd done a good thing. The right thing.

Now he had to get something else done right.

He dipped the bristles of the paintbrush into the pale yellow and smeared it across the empty canvas. Last time he'd started with the darker colors, the pinks and purples of a new day, and those had bled, murky and ugly into the yellow, as if they'd waited there to ruin the lighter color.

Perhaps if he put the yellow on the canvas first, let it dry a bit, then it would not be ruined by—

Glass shattered.

He cursed.

Screaming, angry and sore-throated, ensued.

He threw the paintbrush down and ran.

Following the sounds of breaking glass, following the wails and the—odd—huzzahs, he found the three women in the large, empty ballroom. Like every other room in the house, paintings soared to the ceiling on every inch of the walls. Arched doorways had been carved into the walls, as well, leading to the hallway or to the garden on either side.

In the middle of the room, encircled by the gold inlay of the sunburst on the floor, the three women huddled, a pile of intact saucers and cups nearby with broken cups and saucers scattered around them, a porcelain battlefield.

Miss Bellvue snapped a cup from the pile and handed it to his mother. "Try another."

"Who's it for?" Lady Pratsby asked.

Sniffling, his mother studied the cup, one of the many her houseguests had painted during garden painting parties over the years. "This one is for Miss Scarrington. She's not written me once to offer condolences." Her sniffling turned into a full-out cry, and she threw the cup at the floor, where it smashed into a thousand bits. She snatched a saucer. "And the rector!" *Smash*. She grabbed another. "And the butcher." *Smash*. "And the baker." *Smash*. "None of them have seemed the least bit sad my Edward is go"—a hiccup—"*ooone*." She collapsed in on herself, her shoulders heaving. Then she popped up once more and grabbed as many saucers as she could in one hand, as many cups as possible in the other. She stood slowly, a trembling figure of wrath, and held the pieces high over her head.

"And these," she said, "are for Edward, who had the temerity to die before me. Damn him!" She threw them all at the ground, and her anger shattered around her in tinkling, bouncing bits. Her shoulders heaved, and Miss Bellvue wrapped an arm around her.

Something fragile he'd not let himself feel in years broke with the plates and cups. He shoved the bits away, stuffed them deep down so he did not have to look at them, and stomped farther into the room.

"What the hell is going on here?"

Three women swung around to face him wearing identical glares.

Miss Bellvue stood slowly, her rise smooth and controlled. "Kindly leave, my lord."

His mother reached out an arm toward the remaining pile of dishes and narrowed her eyes at him. "This is for you, who is too cold for a child who lived in *my* womb for nine very, *very* long months." She slammed her arm into the entire pile, sending every single thing scattering, breaking, sliding across the white-and-black marble floor.

Lady Pratsby sniffed at him, bobbing her chin in one defiant nod.

"You're angry with *me*," he said.

His mother stood all at once, her hands fisting in her black skirts. At least she'd left off the veil today. "I am. I am angry at *everyone*."

Lady Pratsby patted her arm. "As you should be, my dear, as you should be."

"I've done nothing," Raph said, placing his fists on his hips.

Miss Bellvue stepped forward, her fists similarly placed, her lips poised around some lecture, no doubt, and porcelain crunched under her slipper. She stopped, looked down, her brows pulling together. Then she looked all about. "We're trapped. I'm not sure my slippers are thick enough to—"

"Bollocks." Raph strode forward, careless of the crunch of drinkware beneath his thick-soled boots. He picked up his mother.

She yelped, and he cradled her like a babe as he moved her out of the circle of danger and placed her carefully on her feet.

He returned and bowed to the viscountess. "May I?"

"By all means." She jumped into his arms, weaving her own around his neck. She fluttered her lashes at him as he carried her to safety.

Then he returned one more time. Didn't bother to bow or ask, he just scooped Miss Bellvue up and tossed her over his shoulder.

She landed there with a grunt. "Lord Waneborough! Let me down!"

Perhaps he should have carried her with the same care as he had the other women, but she was different, and he'd wanted to vex her.

His mother and Lady Pratsby did not seem to mind. In fact their mouths had curved wide with approval. Though why they would approve of his manhandling Miss Bellvue, he'd never know. Their minds were thicker to him than brown paint tipped into a mud puddle.

Miss Bellvue beat against his back. "Put me down!"

"Soon enough," he promised, tightening his arm around her legs. Fine legs, long and lovely and ... what would they look like without the skirts in the way?

He shook his head to shut down that thought, but that brought his chin and nose right up against her ... backside. Nicely rounded, the perfect size for his large hands. Her position over his shoulder stretched the material of her gown taut against it, an arousing sight.

Yes, that was arousal all right, making him hard and yelling at him that he had a free hand to do whatsoever he wished with. Such as cup her arse and—

He plunked her onto the ground next his mother and took a large, very large, step backward.

She glared at him. Worse than glared—she fumed at him.

If she could make it so, the flames from her eyes would shoot out and consume him, turning him to ash in seconds.

He clapped his hands. "All safe now."

They formed a line of solidarity against him.

He crossed his arms over his chest. "Have you had your fun? Or would you like to smash more things?"

Lady Pratsby and Miss Bellvue looked at his mother.

She nodded. "Yes, I'm done. I feel remarkably better. I should have smashed some things months ago. But I did not expect so much ... anger." She peeked up at Raph. "Though some animosity still lingers. I suppose it will fade with time. *You* should hope so at least, son. My ire might cool more quickly if you did not deprive me so."

What the hell did she mean by that? She wanted for nothing. Tobias and Maggie made sure of that.

The other women seemed to know. They smiled, offering comforting expressions that matched their light body leans toward her, promising protection from her villain of a son.

Miss Bellvue turned her regard whip-quick to him. "May I speak with you alone, my lord?"

He bowed, gestured toward one of the arched doorways leading into the garden.

She hesitated to join him, her body, which had so recently been pliant and warm draped over his shoulder, turned rigid like stone.

He rolled his eyes. "Do you wish me to toss you over my shoulder once more?" Because he rather wished that. Easy enough to do. Pleasurable, too, though he shouldn't think it. Or feel it. Bollocks. He needed less painting and more hard labor. If he put his hands and mind to work they wouldn't worry about the feel of Miss Bellvue's backside.

She lifted her skirts, kept his gaze cool as an October breeze, as she swanned forward, skirting the jagged pieces of porcelain, and took off as if a strong gust of wind had lifted her into the air all the way into the garden.

He followed her outside.

She paced back and forth before low hedges grown wild and willful from neglect then stopped pacing and lifted a finger to bite her thumbnail.

"Nervous?" he asked. "Why?"

Her hand flew to her side, finding the shape of a fist. "I'm not. I am merely attempting to find the best words to make my request."

"Just make the request, Miss Bellvue. No special words required."

"True. Your mother wishes to hold a house party."

"No. Sent you to do her dirty work?" He swung back toward the house. "I'll speak with her. You're here to offer company and solace, not to fight her battles with me."

Her hand tightened like a cuff around his wrist, stopping him as surely as an arrow in the chest would.

He turned slowly to face her.

She dropped his hand and pulled her own tight against her belly. "Do not speak with her. I am not fighting her battles. She's entirely given up on the house party. She thinks you do not care enough about her to allow it."

He felt as if a cannon had hit him square in the chest. Every breath, every word, every damn curse knocked right out of him.

She must have seen the shock settling deep and queasy in his body, because she rushed forward. "I do not believe that. You are ... cold. That cannot be denied. But a quick look around this place shows much. If you had not already admitted that the estate was experiencing financial difficulties, I would see it in the roof, the walls, the lack of servants. The wing of the house that's been shut down. The unkept garden. The lack of horses. The—"

"All right, that's enough, Miss Bellvue. You've made your point. And one I was already aware of. We're poor."

She held her chin high. "There is no shame in it, only you cannot hold the house party as your father used to when he lived."

"Had he not held the house party as he used to, perhaps we would not be so badly off."

"Perhaps. But the question is what do we do now?"

"You've lost me, Miss Bellvue."

"We cannot hold the house party, but there must be something else we can do. To please your mother, to create the exuberant and crowded atmosphere she craves."

We. She'd used the word so many times and so easily, as if a *we* existed. "There is nothing," he said. "Thank you for your concern. It confirms I made the right choice bringing you here."

"I—"

"And thank you for the smashed dishes. I think."

Her mouth dropped open. "You're not angry?"

He shrugged. "I've always hated those things. We have cupboards and cupboards filled to brimming with them. The guests were always supposed to take them home, but more often than not, they left them here, and my father considered them priceless works of art, painted as they had been by the hands of some of England's, and Europe's, finest artists. I just thought they took up space. One of my brothers tried to sell them, actually. But William Turner was not amused to find a Mrs. Baker of Fleet Street the owner of his two-whiskey artwork. Threatened legal action, and we had to give him the set instead."

She chuckled, a light-as-songbird sound hidden behind a hand. Then louder. Then she threw her head back and cackled like an old crone. Only there was nothing old or crone-ish about her. The column of her long, slender neck sang to him.

The neck gave way to a creamy expanse of chest, partially exposed by a not-too-low bodice with a flimsy fichu tucked in. At his side, his fingers twitched to touch, to pull the fichu free and other things free as well.

He knotted them together behind his back. "S'not funny, Miss Bellvue. I'm glad the cups were finally put to good use. And that we have some cupboards free for other use."

Her laughter died slowly, and her attention turned toward the arched ballroom doors. "She woke up so angry this morning. We had to do something to let it out."

He nodded. Perfectly understood that. The first time he'd spoken with his father about their failing finances, he'd been angry for months. Perhaps years. Perhaps he still was angry. Something hot and heavy and unpleasant certainly simmered in his blood day and night. He'd ripped his fists into punching bags hung from rafters in the barn, swam till he thought he'd drown. He'd had to move, to let his body work through rage. Many nights he'd stood in the statue hall and thought of breaking every damn one. Shoving each to the floor and watching them shatter with satisfaction. He'd imagined what they'd look like, and he'd smiled. He'd only stopped himself from turning the scene into reality because he'd known their worth. The statues had ruined them. But maybe one day they could save them, too.

Father's damn will had made sure that didn't happen.

"Thank you," he repeated, because he didn't know what else to say, and those were the truest words he could find. "I must go." An urge to touch Miss Bellvue again rode him hard. A misplaced impulse, no doubt. What he truly wished to do was rip something apart as his mother had smashed the cups, but Miss Bellvue stood enticingly before him, and that desire to rip had transferred to her clothes.

No good. Not at all. He backed away slowly then turned all at once, lifting a hand. "Good day, Miss Bellvue."

"Your mother needs company!" she called after him. "Not this solitude that is eating her up."

"That's what I hired you for." He didn't run. But he didn't walk, either. All the way to the barn near the stables where the punching bag hung. Maybe Atlas would wrap his fists and provide a challenge. No. They both had work. Beating one another into an oblivion would have to wait.

Eight

While Franny and Jane were painting still lifes of an exquisitely carved recreation of a man's shaft, Matilda went for a walk. A light afternoon jaunt, she'd told them. But she had a greater purpose, and her steps took her to the main street of the nearby village Fairworth with sweat on her brow.

A great deal of work had been done to take care of the buildings, to keep them clean and tidy despite the general state of disrepair. The feeling of not having quite enough. It proved a more abandoned place than she'd expected, than she remembered. A handful of people walked down the street, and the shops that lined either side were open, but no matter how few they were, *people* were exactly what Franny wanted, what she needed. So many activities could be done in town—attending assemblies, sewing circles, book clubs. And if these things did not yet exist, the marchioness could organize them.

Matilda welcomed the surge of satisfaction rising in her. But memory quickly quashed it.

The baker.

The rector.

The butcher.

All people in town the marchioness had cursed with flung and fractured dishes over a week ago. Why, though? And could her ire be extinguished?

She scanned the signs above the shops on either side of the street. Where to begin? The rector's wife, if he had one, was sure to be a leader in this society. But Matilda would rather seek a more proper introduction there. The baker or butcher, then. Both people she could meet simply by walking into their shops. Her walk had made her peckish, and the wares in the baker's window called to her, so she set her steps that way. The door swung open before she could reach it, and a young boy bustled out, his arms laden with packages.

"Put it right into his lordship's hands!" a voice called out. "And no dawdling!"

"Yes, ma'am," the boy yelled before running off.

Matilda stepped into the shop before the door banged closed.

"Good day," the same boisterous voice said.

"Good day." Matilda bobbed a curtsy.

A woman, the owner of the voice, appeared from the back of the shop. She had not a splash of flour on skin or hair or clothes. "I am Mrs. Popkins, what can I get for you?"

"Whatever's freshest. It smells wonderful in here."

The woman slid behind a case and brought up a flaky pastry. "This do for you?"

"Yes, thank you."

"Who are you?" Mrs. Popkins's gaze riveted on Matilda's face.

"I'm Miss Bellvue. Lady Waneborough's companion."

"You look familiar." Mrs. Popkins's eyes narrowed and her hands found her hips—a thinker's stance.

"I worked at Briarcliff fifteen years ago as well, as Lady Maggie's governess."

The woman's eyes brightened. "Ah, yes. I remember you now. Thought you looked familiar."

"How much do I owe you?"

The woman waved her coin purse away. "I'll bill it to the house."

"I was given to understand"—she did not say by whom because that would give away that it was the marchioness who had offered such information—"that none of the shops in Fairworth allowed the house a line of credit anymore."

The baker shook her head. "Didn't used to. But a few months after the old marquess's death, the young one paid off all our bills one by one. Rumor is he sold a bit of land to do it. And the young gent doesn't run anything up. He pays regular. A trustworthy, responsible fellow."

"Yes." She had no trouble believing it.

"He mentioned a while back that if you came by, we were to give you what you needed."

"How magnanimous." Did his mother know the shops were extending credit once more? Did her anger stem from the fact they had stopped? Or was it shame they'd been unable to pay? Anger at her husband, at herself for not stopping him? Could she have, though? Women were not encouraged to question their husbands, particularly on matters of money.

"If you're looking for the marquess, he's down at the end of the lane. The old cottage at the very end. You'll know it when you see it."

She hadn't been looking for the marquess, but Mrs. Popkins ignited her curiosity. What kept the marquess's attention at the end of the lane?

"Thank you." Matilda bobbed a curtsy and put her hand on the door, the other cupping her pastry. "A quick question before I depart."

"Ask what ya will. I'll answer if I can."

"Does Fairworth boast a book club? Or a sewing circle?"

"'Fraid not. Not much to keep a young mind like yours busy. We work here. Most of our children leave when they can. The marquess, the old one that's turned up his toes, did his best to ruin us all. The young one's doing his best to fix it. But it'll be a while yet, I suspect, before any of us can afford to do more than work."

A shame. A horrid shame that left Matilda carved out. "Surely there are celebrations. Parties."

"The great yearly party up at the house brought a bit of business. Can't say if that'll happen this year with the old marchioness in mourning." Mrs. Popkins shook her head. "That party was the only thing good they did for us. Until the young man, mind you." The woman clicked her tongue against the roof of her mouth. "We haven't even had a harvest celebration in years."

"Oh?"

"A grand thing it was. No reason to celebrate now. The marquess must sell the lands, and the ones he keeps don't seem to do as well as they should."

Too many disasters. How did Waneborough shoulder it all?

Matilda raised her pastry with a smile. "Thank you so much for this. I hope to see you soon."

Mrs. Popkins nodded, and Matilda left the shop. The cottage at the very end of the lane. She set her steps in that direction. It did not take long to find the shabby building with its overgrown garden and sagging roof. It seemed worse off than the other buildings she'd seen.

Despite its saggy gloom, the cottage was a veritable beehive. Women bustled in and out, and men climbed up its walls and on top of the wood-shingle roof. Children played in the small garden to the side and ran about the yard.

Matilda hovered ever closer until a woman with yellow hair and a wide grin caught her eye.

"You're new," the woman said. "Traveling? Staying at the inn?"

Matilda shook her head. "I'm Miss Bellvue, the marchioness's new companion."

"Oh! We've heard about you. Wondered when you'd find your way down here. Louisa will be pleased to see you."

"Why is that?" She could not remember having met a Louisa before.

"You're young. She had a bet going with her husband, Mr. Collins. He said you'd be as old as the marchioness, but Louisa said you'd be young and innocent and bored." The woman narrowed her eyes at Matilda. "You don't seem bored, though she hit the target with young."

"Not so very young anymore."

The woman snorted. "Me neither, according to others. I like to think I've still a spring in my step. I'm Mrs. Sarah Smith. You may call me Sarah, though. Mrs. Smith is my mother-in-law, and she's not someone I'd like to be confused with."

Matilda laughed. "I shall endeavor to keep the two of you separate in my mind. And please do call me Matilda." She'd not had a woman her own age to speak to in years. Having a friend felt novel ... exciting.

"Have you brought the marchioness with you?" Sarah peered over Matilda's shoulder, her previous friendly welcome gone cold.

Ah. More suspicions thrown Lady Waneborough's way. Could anything be done to change that? Franny would have to do the work herself, of course, but would it be in vain if she tried? "No, she's not, though I am sure she would be all curiosity to see the buzz of activity here." She pointed her chin toward the cottage.

Sarah grinned, watching the women bustle in and out. "We're fixing up this old cottage. It's been abandoned, but my cousin Tom just married the butcher's daughter, Molly, and they don't intend to leave Fairworth. Exciting enough, that, but"—she cupped a hand around her mouth and leaned low—"with a six-month babe on the way, they'll need a space all their own. Molly's ma has six younger than Molly, and Tom's ma, my aunt, has four younger than him and two older. Everyone assumes Tom and Molly will be just as ... blessed." She swept her hand toward the cottage. "And this was sitting around unused. When the marquess suggested we fix it up to fit them precisely, we all jumped on it." Her hand moved to cover her eyes, and she looked up. "The men are fixing the things up high, and the ladies are fixing the things inside."

"How perfectly lovely. May I be of any help?"

Sarah took her arm and pulled her inside. "Absolutely."

Five women whipped up from their tasks to look at her with wide, unblinking eyes.

"I've brought reinforcements." Sarah pushed Matilda forward. "Meet Miss Bellvue. She belongs to the marquess."

"I work at the manor house. As the marchioness's companion." She belonged to no one, certainly not the marquess. "Tell me what to do, and I shall do it."

And she did. Every task they set her, from cleaning the fireplace to dusting cobwebs from the corners of the rooms, she achieved. She spoke little and listened much. The women loved one another, knew each other as well as they knew themselves. They were the sort of family Matilda had never really had. And by the time they had the cottage glowing, Matilda glowed, too.

The marchioness needed this, the camaraderie her house party had given her each year, the intimate friendships. She needed human connection and knew it, mourned its loss.

Matilda needed it, too, but she hadn't known it. She did now.

She found Sarah in the small kitchen. "What do you think? Will it do?"

Sarah stepped back from where she'd been washing the last window and stretched her arms up high. "Best be. My body's done."

Matilda pushed her palms into her lower back and arched, leaning her head to the side to work through the tightness in her neck. "Mine as well."

They stepped outside together, and the world was much dimmer than when she'd walked in. The sun slowly fell toward the horizon while Matilda regarded the cottage. Had the men finished the roof?

"I do hope the marchioness has been well without me." Franny was perfectly fine with Jane by her side, but suggesting otherwise could inspire Sarah to sympathy. Hopefully.

Sarah paused before speaking, a silence pregnant with who knew what unsaid words. "The Lady Waneborough ... do you like her? I know I should not speak ill of the marquess's mother but—"

"But you have a mind and a mouth, and they should do as they please. You may freely ask me whatever you wish."

"Just so. I'm afraid few of us in Fairworth feel any kindness for the marchioness. She did nothing to rein in her husband's habits. Indeed, she encouraged them. And the more money the estate lost, the more money *we* lost. Most of my cousins and sisters and brothers have left this town. They went to find jobs elsewhere near big houses that could hire them."

"I understand. It is difficult."

Sarah nodded, brushing dust off her apron. "The marquess is trying to make everything right, though."

That seemed to be Fairworth's rallying cry.

The sun dipped below the line of the cottage's roof, and a figure rose above it, a man's figure. No—the figure of a god from ancient myth. All hard, sinewy muscle. The man—the

93

god, really—lifted his shirt from the band of his pants and wiped the sweat from his brow. But she could not look at his brow when all she saw was the ripple of muscle across his abdomen. Farewell, air! No need for it when the sight of this man, muscled and strong, confident and competent, could sustain her. Obviously competent. That hammer in his hand. That muscle that spoke of labor hard and real and sent a shiver, a tingle of appreciation straight through her body.

She could not see him clearly with the sun behind him. It blinded her, leaving only the outlines of his body visible. He took a few careful strides toward the edge of the roof, looked down, and then every glorious muscle in his body bunched, and he sprang into the air and landed, knees bent, on the ground below. He strode to a fence nearby where his waistcoat and jacket hung, tugged them on, and then strode toward the group of women, dark outline taking on detail—dark hair, broken nose, blue, blue eyes she knew better than she should.

Lord Waneborough was the god. Naturally. He'd been the only man she'd ever met who stole the breath from her body. Every blasted time, too.

The knowledge should have slowed the rapid beat of her pulse because slow pulses should always be paired with men who employed you. A perfectly clear point she'd long known and abided by. But her pulse careened into a crashing roar instead. Because more than a week ago he'd thrown her over his shoulder. Before, she'd had visual appreciation for the man. But since the shoulder incident, she had a visceral one, a preference for taut shoulder muscles like a mountain ledge beneath her soft belly. And now she knew what all that muscle *looked* like, and good God, would she ever be able to forget it?

It would haunt her. A most delicious ghost she should try to deliver herself from.

Instead, she let the moment linger, felt her hand lift, of its own accord, so that her fingertips touched the column of her throat then ventured slowly downward toward the slope of her breast hidden by her spencer. The tingling that had begun there as soon as she'd seen the outline of him above ripened into a deep, yearning ache.

"Good afternoon, ladies. Miss Bellvue." His voice was deep and rich, and it took on a greater richness now that she knew what he looked like beneath his aristocratic trappings. He was a work of art, a marble sculpture come to life, and the artist—labor—had crafted him perfectly.

"Lord Waneborough," she said, "good afternoon."

"What are you doing here?" The words fell hard between them, but a true curiosity in his eyes softened his tone.

"Your mother and Lady Pratsby decided they had no need of me today, so I went for a walk. That brought me here, and I decided to help."

Sarah nudged her with a shoulder. "And a great help she was, my lord. She'll be a mass of aches and pains tomorrow, mark my words."

Matilda smiled. "Gladly earned, too. I will loan you my arms and legs whenever you have need of them as long as I am here."

"We shall quite steal you away from the marchioness, then."

The marquess frowned, clearly unamused by the thrust of the conversation.

"You know how to repair roofs, then?" Matilda asked. She knew the need for distraction when she saw it.

His disapproving brow softened. "I've learned the way of it."

Where had words gone? Nothing existed, frankly, but for his chest barely hidden by thin, sweat-soaked linen. Even now she could not stop staring. They might have to pry her eyeballs from his torso. *Humph.* They could take her sight, but they could never take her imagination. Not that she should imagine. But worse than the unyielding perfection of his physique was what it said about him. Her body fluttered just as much because she was *impressed*. A marquess who could do something practical with his hands, something that sheltered and protected others. She'd known he was capable, competent, but *this* ...

She licked her lips and backed a little away from him, putting Sarah between herself and the marquess.

He merely followed, dancing them into a chase of a waltz only Matilda knew existed. "I'm done here. May I accompany you home, Miss Bellvue?"

"Yes. I would appreciate that. Thank you." No escaping it. They were heading in the same direction, and besides, Matilda had more to learn, questions to ask. She turned to Sarah. "It was lovely to meet you. And the others."

Sarah jumped across the small space between them and dragged Matilda into a hug. "Thank you so very much for your help, Miss Bellvue." She stepped away and curtsied to the marquess. "And yours, too, my lord."

"Of course." A magnaminous nod but softness in his voice.

"Please let me know," Matilda said, "when Molly has her baby. If I am still here, I would like to help in whatever way I can."

The marquess had begun to stare at her as if she'd grown another leg, his head slightly tilted, eyes widened the slightest bit, mouth soft, almost slack, but he extended his hand toward the street, and they began the walk back to Briarcliff.

They walked in silence out of the town and when there was nothing but the yellow-blue of dusk and the deepening greens of the earth all around them, she finally found the words she wished to say. "Do you have memories of the harvest celebrations, or had they already stopped by the time you were born?"

"Why do you ask?"

"More than one person mentioned it today, and I am curious." True enough, that.

"Yes, I remember them." He lifted an arm to scratch his neck, the wool of his jacket sliding tight across the muscles of his shoulders and arms, and something in her belly wound tight, too.

She focused on her feet treading the path beneath the dusty hem of her skirt. "What was it like? Everyone spoke of it fondly."

He huffed, and his arm fell back down to his side. "Everyone looked forward to it, loved it. My parents, my brothers and Maggie, everyone in the village. It felt like we were all working for each other and with each other and celebrating that unity."

"I wish I could have experienced it."

He was silent so long, she looked away from her boots and up at him. And found him looking down at her, the bright blue of his eyes deep wells to lose herself in.

"There's a bonfire." His gaze never once wavered, and her breath caught hot and heavy in her chest. "Lovers dance around it. My mother said it had something to do with an old fertility rite carried over from pagan days."

"It sounds ... enchanting."

He grunted and sliced his gaze to the sky. "I suppose so. Not much reason to celebrate in the last several years. This year, *finally*, it's better. Atlas has suggested selling off the common lands, but ..."

He did not have to finish the sentence. Take away from the people he'd worked so hard to help today? He would never.

He veered off the path and down a hill.

She ran after him. "Where are you going? The house is that way."

He kept walking, didn't look back. "Continue along home. I'm going to take a dip in the lake."

He deserved a dip in the lake after all the work he'd put his body through. The prospect sounded lovely. She imagined him stripping bare, diving deep, coming up glistening with water droplets ...

She shook the image away and stepped back toward the path. "Oh ... have a good time? No. Not a question. Ha ha." Why suddenly such an awkward tongue, a mind that tripped over itself to get to the right words? "Yes. Goodbye!" She waved and ran back toward the path, and she did not know if he chuckled or stopped and waved back because she certainly would not look.

When she reached the path, she marched along it purposefully, but each step seemed to become harder and harder, like she waded through a puddle of molasses. She eventually stopped, looked over her shoulder, and without even thinking —because such actions really were better off without thought —she turned around and retraced her steps.

When the first line of the lake glimmered in sight, a stark blue meeting the green of the rolling hill, she slowed her steps. Her heart beat hard in her ears. God, what she wouldn't do for a tree right about now to hide her prying presence, but none stood tall nearby. So she stood visible on the hill, and she waited.

Where was he? Had he drowned?

And then he appeared, his body rising from the lake as it had risen from the edge of the roof, silhouetted to perfection. Oh, to be a water drop meandering through the grooves of those muscles. Shoulders broad, waist trim, not an ounce of extra on him.

And then he looked at her. Saw her there, tall and straight on the hill, watching him. She did not run because she had made the decision to come here, foolish though it had been, and she was no young girl to be easily embarrassed, to be scandalized and ruined by the sight of a man's naked torso and the curve of the top of his arse.

And Jane had a point. If Matilda's poet never showed up, she would need some memories to keep her warm on cold Cumbrian nights. Her body certainly was ablaze at the moment, and it had nothing to do with the late summer sun sinking into the hills.

Yes. This memory would do quite nicely.

He sank back below the water and took off like a fish. A fast one. While she ached like a starving fisherman on the shore—hungry for him.

She watched another moment more before returning to the house. The man fascinated her in more ways than the physical. Her own experience had taught her that men were careless of things, of people. Her own brother had tossed her aside because her very being, her blood and bone and name, had not lived up to his standards.

Lord Waneborough seemed the opposite. He cared about everything and everyone. Except, perhaps, his mother. At least that was the marchioness's opinion. Matilda could not quite agree.

A harvest celebration.

It would not require the funds of a house party, but it would foster fellow feelings between those who lived in town and those who lived in the house. And he had said the crops had performed better this year. A reason to celebrate. Perhaps she should mention it. And, perhaps, if the marchioness found family in the village, she'd have one less plate to break when rage and sorrow roared in her heart.

Nine

Raph stepped back and squinted at the canvas. No good. Perhaps another step would help. He tried, tilted his head in a different direction and opened his eyes wide this time. Still abysmal. The painting did not at all resemble the sight that had haunted his every sleeping and waking moment for the last eight ... no, nine days.

A simple vision—a woman fully clad in rather dour colors standing on top of a hill, her loosely-tied bonnet barely containing a wealth of dark hair tumbled by hard work, her gaze fully riveted on the lake below and out of sight in the portrait. What she gazed at could not be seen. In a way, the viewer took the place of the thing, the man, she looked upon. Raph in both instances—viewer and, that day, the viewed.

The shiver of cold awareness he'd had upon breaching the surface of the water had alerted him he was being watched, and it had quickly turned into an altogether different kind of awareness when he'd realized who it was.

Miss Bellvue, his mother's stern and soft companion, gazing her fill, brazen and bloody beautiful. Beneath the water, he'd grown hard as a rock. A problem he'd been trying to *remedy* with that dip into the lake, because since the moment he jumped down from that roof and saw her standing before the cottage, dusty and lovely and pink-cheeked with busy happiness, looking for all the world as if she were waiting for *him*, he'd entered into a hell composed entirely of the struggle against his body, which seemed to think she had earned a kiss (or more) for her labor.

His mind knew truth. Miss Bellvue had wandered into town, and used to being useful, had volunteered her time. But his body had seen something different—a woman who shared his tasks, cared for his people, and waited at the end of a long day's labor for him to join her. His body liked that. Loved it. His brain, too, truthfully; but his brain also knew his heart was weaving fantasy from mere coincidence.

Now, his cravat grew too tight, and his pants, too. He'd been too shocked to fight the attraction and his body's reaction over a week ago, but now he'd had practice. His mother's companion was no sort to be lusting after. Although apparently she was exactly the sort he *did* lust after. Had all those years ago, too, when she'd first come to them. No good. He'd hoped painting her would purge him of the unwanted attraction. It had not.

"What's that supposed to be?" Atlas strode into the Purgatorial Painting Parlor and peered over Raph's shoulder.

"Good morning, brother," Raph said. "It's my latest attempt."

Atlas strode farther into the room, stopped close to the painting, leaned forward, and peered at it for several seconds. Then he leaned back and peered at it some more from farther away, then from each side.

"Better," he said. "Though why you would want to paint a log on top of a hill, I'm not entirely sure. Not a particularly picturesque landscape."

"That is because it is *not* a landscape. It's a portrait."

Atlas turned around, a brow raised. "You do know that portraits are of people, yes?"

"Of course I do," Raph snapped.

"Good. Good. Just making sure."

Raph stomped to the painting and yanked it off of the easel. He slung it toward a corner where a half dozen other paintings rested in a graveyard of art. Bad art.

"Not going well, then," Atlas said.

"No." Raph dropped into a chair and hid his eyes with a palm. "Please tell me you have some problem for me to take care of. Something for me to attend to. And that is why you're here."

"No. But I do have a question."

"Please ask. I welcome every distraction."

"Do you know why the ladies have taken at least three jaunts into Fairworth this last week?"

Raph sat up straighter. "By ladies, I assume you mean Mother, Lady Pratsby, and Miss Bellvue."

"Yes. All three of them back and forth as if they have business there."

He shrugged. "Mother needs company. Precisely the purpose for hiring Miss Bellvue. More company resides in Fairworth. It makes sense."

"True, but … Mother has not been on good terms with those in the village for years." Atlas slapped a riding crop against his thigh. "I merely find it curious."

"As long as they're staying quiet, I don't see what it matters. You could ask Mother."

"So could you."

But neither had time.

Still, Raph could not put it behind him as Atlas left. He couldn't focus on a blank canvas when all he saw was the outline of Miss Bellvue's body soft against the summer sky.

When he could not help but wonder what mischief his mother dragged her into.

Damn it all, but especially damn distractions. He had an entire list of things he needed to finish about the estate, and every moment he spent staring at his own poorly painted pictures was wasted. He lurched to his feet and stormed into the hall. Were they home? Or were they in town? He strode upstairs to his mother's quarters and laughter stretched toward him as he approached.

He knocked. "Mother?"

The door flew open, and Miss Bellvue stood before him, blushing prettily, her hair tumbling down her back like she'd just been pleasured well and good.

He almost turned around and ran down the hall, outside, and all the way to the lake.

"Come in, Raphael," his mother called before he could.

He slid past Miss Bellvue as if she were a powder keg set to explode. "I'll not take up your time. I have a question." What had that question been? He had more pressing ones suffocating him now. Like why had flowers taken over the room? They proliferated everywhere. A garland even hung low from the light fixture on the ceiling. "Flowers?" He shook his head. "That's not the question, but I'll deal with this first."

"Isn't it wonderful?" His mother clapped her hands and beamed. We're trying to decide what the perfect combination is for flower crowns. So that all the ladies who wish to may have one during the harvest celebration."

If he'd thought on her answer for a hundred years, he never would have settled on that. "Where did the flowers come from?"

"The garden, of course," Lady Pratsby said. "I hope your gardener won't mind. We all but stripped it bare."

"I *am* the gardener." And he *did* mind. "If you steal all the flowers now, what will be left for the harvest celebration?" Not that there would be one.

"More will bloom," his mother said.

"And since when do we participate in the harvest celebration? It's been over a decade, Mother. We cannot afford to host an event. Surely, you're not considering—"

"Of course, I am! It is our duty to host a gathering, and it is a shame we've not done so in so long. When Miss Bellvue mentioned it the other day—"

"Miss Bellvue?" Raph's attention swung toward her, looking girlish and lovely and more than a little immune to his rage.

She stood tall, chin lifted, shoulders back. No mere flower maiden. A queen of spring decked out for coronation day. "I merely asked a question. And we have been having quite a lovely time with preparations."

"Was no one going to tell me?"

"I didn't wish to bother you," his mother said. "You dislike such frivolous things."

Miss Bellvue seemed to grow several inches as her usually soft jaw took on a militaristic edge. "Franny. You said you would speak with Lord Waneborough. You said it was *your job* to do so. Are you telling me you did *not* do so?"

Lady Pratsby chuckled. "Sounds like she's not telling you *or* the marquess much of anything."

"Franny!" Miss Bellvue said.

Raph stormed toward the door. "Remove all of this. We do not have time or energy to waste on celebrations. We do not have the funds, either, as you should well know, Mother."

"It will not take up any of your precious *time*, Raphael! Or your even more precious money. Your father and I were trying to prevent just this. A preoccupation with something that does not matter."

"Somthing that does not matter?" Raph asked. "Do you mean money?"

She nodded, petals from her crown showering to the floor. "We wanted you to value life, art, compassion. It's why we had the house parties, too. To nurture such things—"

"And what do you think made that house party possible, Mother?" Damn, but he'd had this conversation too many times.

His mother ran across the room to face him chest to chest. Her flower crown had fallen askew. And ... hell ... she did not wear black but soft, silver gray. The sight made him want to sink to his knees, wrap his arms around her legs and weep. She was healing, starting—slowly—to wear the colors his father had only ever wanted her to wear after his death ... anything but black. All the colors of life and living.

He stomped out into the hall. A ridiculous reaction, but better than tears.

His mother followed, grabbed his shoulder, and swung him around. "Listen to me! I know it took money, but the money was always there! And your father said everything would work out as it should, and—"

Raph snorted away the prattle he'd heard too many times and stomped down the hall. "The money is not there now. Hasn't been in ages. I have work to do. No celebration."

"You cold-hearted brute!" she screamed, but lower than usual. As if something deep inside her had broken. Still, a wailing began when the scream died off, keener than since the days after his father's death, as if she mourned something new and just as painful in its loss.

Raph almost turned back around to do a little bit of wailing with her. He kept his steps moving forward.

"Stop!" Miss Bellvue's voice rang clear and sharp as a knife's edge.

He continued forward even when the sound of footsteps behind him increased in pace, grew closer.

Then something hit him in the back of the head.

He stopped, turned.

Miss Bellvue's flower crown lay, petals blasted off, on the ground between them. Now she appeared a goddess of rage, a Hera come to put Zeus to shame.

Did that make *him* Zeus? Bollocks. Not a comparison Raph relished. Inaccurate, too.

She pointed a vengeful finger at him. "You must be a cold-hearted fiend, because no good man would treat his mother so."

He looked over her shoulder, ignoring the blade of guilt she'd lodged in his gut. Lady Pratsby pulled his mother into her parlor, a supporting arm draped around her shoulder.

"You, Miss Bellvue, should not orchestrate a full-scale mutiny."

"I have done no such thing. I mentioned the harvest celebration, asked your mother about it. When she grew excited, she promised me she would speak with you. When she began planning, I assumed she had."

Couldn't argue with that. It wasn't her position to play liaison between himself and his mother, and it *was* her position to make his mother feel better, which planning the celebration seemed to be doing. Miss Bellvue was doing what she should and not doing what she shouldn't. But his rage roared to the heights that hated logic, so he glowered.

"Well, now you know." He took the stairs two steps at a time. "No celebration. I mean *here*. No celebration at Briarcliff. Fairworth may do as it pleases."

She followed behind. "Fairworth and here are one and the same, my lord. They should be."

"That is none of your concern."

"It's not, but your mother is, and she's been better since she started planning, and—"

At the bottom of the stairs, he swung around, and she almost ran right into him. Standing a step above him, they were eye to eye. Nose to nose. Lip to lip.

What had he been about to say?

She seemed to have forgotten her speech as well. Her gaze sizzled into his for a moment and then ... floated. Downward. Snagged on his mouth.

Now *he* looked at *her* mouth.

Bollocks.

His heart sped up, his breathing slowed, and he leaned closer. Her lips—full and pink and looking so soft—parted oh-so slightly. He spun again, pushing against every muscle in his body that screamed for him to stay, and marched off.

Her feet slapped against the marble floor behind him. "Planning this celebration is helping her, and we do not have to spend money. We merely have to invite everyone here."

"Money is not the only thing of value, Miss Bellvue." He stopped, turned back to her one more time even though he knew he shouldn't.

She rocked back on her heels, took several steps backward and away from him.

"Time is of value, too," he said. "And if you've not noticed, I do every damn thing around here but for cooking and undressing you." Bollocks. That had come out wrong. Now he pictured his fingers at her back, undoing her tapes, slipping the sleeves of her plain muslin gown off her shoulders. No. Not images for him. An unfortunate turn of phrase he would not let distract him. He pinched the bridge of his nose. "I'm exhausted, and when my mother decides that studying star patterns is more interesting to her and advantageous to the ages than playing hostess to the village, the duties of the event will fall on my shoulders. And I—"

"Do not have time for that. Yes, I know. I do. And I am horribly sympathetic."

"Ha."

"I am." She did not stomp her foot, but damn if her voice didn't sound like a stomped foot. Kind of adorable, that. Not adorable enough to calm his ire. "You could paint." She turned her head so that her chin almost touched her shoulder.

"Paint." As if he hadn't been every spare minute of his life the last six months. "You've no idea."

She stepped closer, no hesitation evident in the long stride of her legs. "Instead of killing yourself with work. Your mother told me about the will. The stipulations. She said you won't even try."

Worse He'd tried and failed. Over and over again. "It's a waste of time."

"Art? Beauty? The imagination? The act of creation? A waste of time?"

"You sound like my thrice-cursed father."

"*You* are thrice cursed."

Was the insult supposed to be a blow? Barely. Glancing. He'd give her time to rethink her words, who she'd said them to, apologize.

She raised her brows and lifted her chin. "I am not prone to linguistic explosions, as they are often no use, but a man like you does not listen to anything else, I'm afraid. All you have to do, my lord, is *paint something*. Anything. But you won't even try. You're scared. Of a pot of paint and stick with bristles."

Enough! He stormed toward her, grabbed her wrist, and pulled her down the hallway. "Have you visited the Abominable Art Apartment yet? Come, let's go there now."

"Unhand me!" She tugged. He tightened his grip. "Coward," she hissed.

He pulled her through the door. "Welcome to my studio, a

Painting Purgatory. The Chalk Chamber of Horrors." He threw her hand from his grasp and stormed toward the pile of abandoned canvases. "There. *There*, Miss Bellvue, is what you call my fear, my cowardice. Only it is not fear, it is failure. If my mother claimed I have not tried, she lied."

She stood before the pile, hardly breathing, her hair a wild tangle down her back. He stalked toward her. "So take it back. Because while I am many things, even a cold-hearted fiend, I am no coward."

She stumbled backward, and he stalked until her back hit the wall behind the door, and still he stalked until he towered over her, and he could brace his forearms against the wall on either side of her.

"I"—her gaze flicked to the pile of canvases—"I spoke foolishly. Without all the facts. I apologize." Yet her words did not hold meekness. She'd never cower, no matter the threat, and that did something to him, changed him on a bone-deep level, taught him a truth, too. She seemed excellent at revealing those. His new truth? If a lion were to roar through the window behind him and tear at her throat, Raph would tear at the beast, pull it apart with his bare hands, because a woman who faced every threat with such ferocity should never feel threatened, should be protected in whatever brutal way necessary.

But his pride was tattered beneath her claws, and though he wanted to curl around her, kneel perhaps, and offer himself up, he tore at her instead. "If you do not issue a more regretful apology, Miss Bellvue, I'll—"

"What will you do? Dismiss me? Very well—"

He hovered lower over her, stopping her words with a mere whisper of a movement. The air between them flashed into a field charged with lightning. He raised his hand to her jaw.

She flinched, and he saw it then, the gold-green ring

around her brown eyes, glinting with fear. Damn. If only he'd discovered that ring of gold as her eyes had flashed with some other emotion. Happiness, mirth, joy, longing, lust.

But, no. Fear had brought that sunrise color out bright.

He'd become a beast.

But he could be gentle. He could show her how he coveted her. He could ...

He kissed her. A hard meeting of lips filled with every ounce of fury the last half hour, half a year, one and a half decades had wrought in him.

And the soft sigh at the parting of her lips wiped it all away. His own fear and pride, his own anger and bitterness. He slipped his hand behind her neck and held her gently. See. No claws. Not for her.

She melted in his arms, her arms curling up between them, her fingers lightly testing the hardness of his chest. Or the beating of his heart? Test him, mold him, make him better, heal him as she had his mother. Her lips moved on his with sudden boldness, slanting as her hands pressed flat so he could feel the heat of her palms. When he next threw off his clothes, he'd find ten digits branded there. Hers.

Hers?

He ripped away from the kiss, whipping around and striding away from her as he lifted a trembling hand to his mouth where he felt her *still*. Possibly would always feel her. Damn himself to hell and back. He could *not*. For a number of reasons, the most pressing being she was under his care, his employee, and the most annoying being he could not marry her.

And such caresses, seductions really, from a gentleman such as he—though rough around the edges—to a lady such as her—though having worked as long as she had—led only one direction. Right to the altar.

"A ... kiss ..." Her voice shaky yet strong at the same time, a contradiction. He did not turn around. "A kiss is a thing of beauty, too. I can see you understand that well. The art of it. Perhaps, Lord Waneborough ... perhaps you should try to paint a kiss."

He pressed his eyes closed. If he could paint that kiss, keep it, God, he *would*. He tried to brush away the annoying buzz of words eager to describe it—divine, wanton, lovely, tender, ground shaking. He feared he would fall asleep to their whispers.

He turned, finally, to tell her how misplaced her compliments were. If she had any misconceptions they might continue—

Gone. Slipped out while he'd been beating back the newfound rhythm of his body's beating pulse.

Good.

He swiped another empty canvas from a corner and threw it onto the easel. Then he found the blackest paint and swiped it across—the dark of a starless sky. Or the dark of an angry man's heart.

Ten

Matilda sat in the corner of Franny's parlor with her fingertips pressed against her lips. Last night's dinner had not obliterated the sensation of the marquess's lips against her own. A night had not helped it fade. Breaking her fast and a noon tea had not washed her mouth clean of him. The taste of him lingered like a bitter medicine or the ghost of a loved one lost. She, now and again, raised her fingers to her lips to make sure he was not still there.

"What about flowers from town? We could send for some," Franny said. The words rammed into Matilda's gut like a cannonball.

"No." She leaned forward, projecting the word across the room. "You know you cannot do that, Franny."

The marchioness pouted. She'd wrapped her hair in a purple turban because Jane had told her purple suited her, made her look like a flower, and the woman had popped the color, appropriate for mourning, into her outfit every day since.

"I know I cannot, Matilda," the marchioness said, "but it does not stop me from wanting to."

"I am aware that *can't* is very ill at stopping *want*," Matilda said, "but you must learn to live with them both at the same time. And abide by the can't more than the want."

Franny huffed. "Is she always so wise and practical, Jane?"

"Always." Jane crossed the room and opened a window. "Unseasonably hot today." She picked up a copy of *Ackermann's Repository* and fanned herself. "But not only is our girl wise, she is brave. A veritable knight in shining armor."

"You were marvelous yesterday, Matilda. I am as proud of you as if you were my own daughter."

"She could be one day," Jane mumbled.

"Jane!" Matilda flicked a drying flower petal off her chair and speared the older woman with a glare. "Inappropriate."

"Highly unlikely." Franny sighed. "Though I would celebrate such a union."

"Not you, too, Franny!"

"I had hoped for it before, when you were Maggie's governess, but you were both too young." Franny issued a sigh so dreamy it might do Orpheus's work and put them to sleep. "Hopeless with how cold my son's heart is. He'll only take a lady with a fortune, even when our own, delightful Matilda stands beautifully before him."

Matilda rolled her eyes, thought of the kiss. "Nothing can come of it."

Both women studied at her.

"That sounded a tad dreamier in tone," Jane said, "than I am used to her sounding."

"Indeed. When I read the cards for you yesterday, they did suggest you were in for a change of some sort. I assume that meant your cottage, but ... you seem changed *right now*. Do come here, dear one. I've not asked you about your dreams today. They might reveal something of import."

Yes, they would reveal she could not stop thinking of the woman's son, who had swum through her dreams with the same ease he cut through lake waters. No good, that. Besides, Franny's card reading always seemed a bit lethal, a bit too close to something raw in Matilda she'd rather not explore.

She jumped to her feet. "My, it's hot. I think I'll go for a walk. Let us all go together."

"Not me," Jane said, sinking into a chair near her new friend. "My knees don't like the heat."

"I thought they didn't like the cold."

"They don't like any weather."

"Franny?" Matilda asked.

The marchioness waved her toward the door. "Do go. Enjoy yourself."

"I've enjoyed myself enough since being here. It hardly feels like a job at all. More like a holiday."

The marchioness grinned. "Most excellent. I've always prided myself on my hostess abilities."

Jane patted her arm. "See, you are the very best even with so little." She waved Matilda away. "Go, girl. We'll be fine without you."

Still, Matilda hesitated. Who knew what the two women would plot behind her back. She would do her job best to stay nearby if only to keep an eye and ear on them.

"Go!" they yelled together.

"Very well. I am not deaf. I won't be gone long, and please do not anger the marquess any more in the short time I am out."

"*Bah*," his mother said.

Matilda chuckled in the hallway. She agreed. *Bah* to the marquess and his firm lips. *Bah* to his strong hands—calloused and too large for a delicate artist's paintbrush.

When her feet hit the warm ground and the sky opened up before her, she ripped her fichu from her collar and strolled aimlessly, glad she'd forsaken her bonnet. It would only heat her further when she needed no help with that. All she had to do was think of a certain marquess, a sun-filled room, a corner of discarded, unfinished paintings, and the most gentle kiss she'd ever experienced. Or imagined. Or dreamed. He won in all ways.

She'd not lied when she'd called it a thing of beauty, a work of art.

She should have hated it, should have felt threatened by the man giving her an ultimatum—take back her words or …

Or he'd kiss her apparently. And what kind of ultimatum was that? Seemed a better way of getting her to do exactly what he did not want her to do.

She increased her pace. The sun and heat washed giddiness over her limbs, and she wanted to run. She wanted to melt into the ground. She wanted to sleep in the sun. She wanted to kiss again.

Would it be so cold in Cumbria? She hoped not. She wanted a warm home, or at least a home where someone could keep her warm during the cold months.

She stopped walking only when the toe of her boots flirted with the still edge of the lake water. Naturally she'd come here when the marquess-riddled image of the lake had not left her since it had imprinted itself on her brain. No marquess now, though, so she kicked off her shoes, rolled off her stockings, and dipped her toes in. Not enough. Her skin sizzled with heat. She looked around. What were the odds anyone would see her? She'd be quick about it. Twisting her arms behind her back, she loosened the tapes of her gown and shimmied out of it. Then she did the same to her stays and let those drop to the grass too.

Scandalous. She grinned. Her shift flirted with the tops of her shins, and she fisted a hand in the hem, pulled one side to the middle of her thigh, and strode into the water, introducing it to her ankles, calves, and finally her knees. She shivered as a delightful chill quivered up her spine. Perfection.

She gulped in a lungful of air and dove. The lake swallowed her as if she were some watery magical maiden in an Arthurian legend. If only she had a sword to bequeath. Beneath the water, the world went quiet. She exhaled all her breath so that she sank, heavy, to the cooler depths of the lake, and remained there until her lungs burned. Then she shot to the surface with a burst of exhilaration and took off across the lake, awkward and slow, but she soon remembered the way to cut through the water, the movements her father had taught her.

Soon, too, though, she tired, and she rolled onto her back to stare at the sky and smile like a fool as she floated, weightless and unworried.

Except for the worry of the kiss.

The marchioness's disappointment.

And even, if she were being truthful with herself, her Cumbrian cottage.

No, no. She'd think of something else. Her muscles' exertion. The warmth of the day on her skin. The cool water slicing in loving rivulets down a man's muscled back.

She slammed her legs downward and came upright to tread the water. She would not let her mind float toward wayward, wanton thoughts. She pushed her hair from her face and sank below once more before setting off to the shore she'd left behind who knew how long ago now. By the time she reached the bank, her limbs felt heavy and tired, and she was glad for silty sand beneath her feet. She stood, the surface of the water lapping at her waist, wiggled her toes in the lake mud, and—

Ducked back down under the water entirely. Heavens, no.

What in the name of everything good and holy was the marquess doing sitting on the lakeshore, looking out as if ... as if he were waiting for her?

Had below the surface of the water been cool and calm

before? Now it boiled with the inferno of pure panic. She had to stay here, though. Or else he'd see her. In only her chemise, soaked and plastered to her body. No. No, no, no.

Her lungs burned. She couldn't stay here.

No. No, no, no.

She screamed, the sound caught and winnowed into nothing but bubbles by the water and used up the rest of her air. She popped up with gasp, careful to keep her body, if not her nose, below the surface. He likely could not see her, but she wrapped her arms around her chest, her belly, just in case.

He was on his feet, striding toward the water's edge. "Miss Bellvue, are you in need of help?" Worry drew his brows into sharp slants.

"No." She threw up a palm to keep him away. "I'm perfectly fine." The man had thrown her across his shoulder to keep her safe from glass shards and full dress had done nothing to hide his muscle. A wet chemise would do even less. "Do not ... do not come any closer. In fact ... could you leave? Please?"

"If something is amiss, I—"

"Nothing is amiss! I was out for a swim. You startled me, so I ducked below the water." She tried out a laugh. It sounded fake. "But I cannot come out with you there. You understand, yes? Do please leave."

He marched back up the hill and the hard beat of her pulse everywhere in her body calmed a bit. Then he sat down in the same spot as before, and it started back up—harder, more brutal this time.

"Pardon *me*, Lord Waneborough, but I asked you to *leave*." She exhaled so hard, the water rippled before her. "It is rather ungentlemanly of you not to do so."

"I'll close my eyes," he called out. "I wish to speak with you, and now is as good a time as any. In fact, it's the only time. I've wasted minutes of the day waiting for you to come out of there."

Right. He would make a mountain of himself, then, and would not move. Very well. She was not overly modest, and she had made certain decisions when she disrobed and dove into a lake. Anyone could have walked by, after all. She must face the logical consequences.

"Close your eyes, then," she said.

"Closed."

She peered at him, but at the distance that separated them, she couldn't quite make out if he lied or not. She thought he spoke truth, so she wrapped her arms tighter about her body and stood, slowly, gaze trained to the marquess with his knees pulled up, forearms resting atop them.

Why must he be so very virile? And why must she notice?

She stood entirely and waded toward the shore, each step difficult after her exercise. With each inch her body climbed higher above the surface of the water, the colder she grew until her teeth chattered. Had it truly been sweltering moments before? When had the air chilled so?

Finally, she reached her pile of clothes, but she hesitated.

"Miss Bellvue?" he called, his eyes still closed. "Since I cannot tell whether you have drowned through sight, perhaps you might give me a verbal confirmation you are still alive."

"I—" she began to say, but it came out all wrong, high and squeaky. She cleared her throat. "I am well." But not truly. She was soaked, her chemise clinging to her, and if she put her gown on, that would soon be soaked, too. "Do not open your eyes," she commanded.

He grunted.

She peeled the shift from her body, standing in the late summer air in nothing but what she'd been born with for a breath or two before she knelt and grabbed her dry gown and pulled it over her head. No shift. No stays. Heaven help her.

She twisted her arms behind her back to tie the tapes of her gown, but it was more difficult than untying them had been. She huffed, closed her eyes, made up her mind.

"All right, my lord. I am ... presentable. As is possible at this very moment. In fact—"

He opened his eyes, and his gaze found her as if magnetized by her form.

She held her loose gown to her chest and walked barefoot toward him, turning her back to him when he jumped to his feet. The air fell cool on her revealed back, and she slammed her eyes closed to ... Well, no reason. Just because it seemed the thing to do as she said, "Would you please tie me up?"

Heavens. Humiliating. But—

His fingers on her back sucked all thought, all breath from her body, and her eyes shot open. He tugged the tapes deftly together, and she looked over her shoulder, watched him with his head bowed low, the thick, dark fringe of his eyelashes hiding his eyes. She bit her lip. When had she ever done such a thing before? But it seemed the thing to do when something electric and needy rolled to life low in her belly. He tied the last one, and for a hot second, his hands pressed, firm and warm, into her back as he drew a deep breath that seemed to rumble the sky.

Then he stepped away, and as air rushed between them, it rushed into her lungs.

"Here." He slipped from his loose brown jacket and held it out. "You've gooseflesh across your shoulders."

She shrugged first one arm then the other into the jacket, not knowing how to tell him *No thank you, I don't think I can handle being surrounded by your scent anymore than I already am.* He smelled like summer. And the coming fall. At the same time. An impossibility, that. Yet possible in him, it seemed.

So she said, "My hair is wet." And rolled her eyes and hid

her face. Mortification, thy name is Matilda. Who was she, a spinster of four and thirty, to be feeling so ... young ... around such a man?

"Sit," he said, his voice gruff, his own movements jerky as he sank to his rear in the grass and contemplated the sky.

She stood. "I sit, my lord, but only because I wish to." She sat.

He grunted. "I do not remember you being so ... contrary."

"Yes, well, I have learned to be so, and it has often bene-fited me."

A breeze blew between them, and she pulled his jacket tighter around her. *Don't breathe, don't breathe, don't breathe. Don't take him into your lungs more than you already have.*

She cleared her throat. "You wished to speak with me?"

He drew his knees up so he sat in the same position as earlier with his forearms resting on his knees. "I am sorry, Miss Bellvue. Quite, quite sorry. I acted reprehensibly, and I can offer no justification because such brutish acts should never be justified. Although I ... Despite my horrid words, I did not kiss you to scare you. Or out of anger."

She raised a brow.

"I know. Impossible to believe. But somehow, in the middle of all the irrational rage, I realized what a beast I was being. And you were scared. And I hated that I'd made you that way, and I kissed you because I wanted to make it better. An unasked-for kiss is an odd peace offering, I suppose, and the thrust of my ratiocinations impossible to follow." She would not argue that point. "And it does not matter why," he said. "It merely matters, I hope, that you have my deepest, most sincerest, apology."

What could she say? She could not ask whether he regretted the kiss. Though she rather wished she knew the answer. She could not ask if his feelings about it were as complicated as her own. She'd wanted to slap him, but she'd also wanted him to kiss her again.

Again. Would he do so now if requested?

She almost laughed. She could not lean over and simply present her lips for his very thorough inspection.

"I will not ask you to stay after all that," he said. "And everything I have, which is not much, is at your disposal for leaving Briarcliff as soon as you wish."

She shook her head. "I suppose I should apologize, too. I accused you of not trying, and you have been. I called you a coward, and you are not. You are not, perhaps, the best son. But Franny, perhaps, has not been the best mother. Who am I to judge another's circumstance. I made assumptions, and I should not have."

"No assumption should be met with aggression."

"True." She paused and considered her next words carefully, considered the truth of them. "My lord, I do not wish to leave. Not yet."

He fell back to the ground, arms spread to either side, eyes staring wide at the blue-gray sky. "Thank *God*." She chuckled, and he sat up, sneaking her a sheepish look. "There's a bit of my mother in me sometimes. A bit of the dramatic."

"It suits you. Had I not been so shocked, I would have fallen into a fit of giggles when you called that room the Chalk Chamber of Horrors." She laughed now, and it lit something bright inside her.

"I—" His mouth hung open for several pulse beats, then slowly closed. He seemed to be gnawing on words as he regarded the lake.

"Yes?"

"Nothing. I'm partial to the Purgatorial Painting Parlor."

She almost laughed again, but the grumbled nature of his *nothing* stayed her mirth. "Oh, very fine indeed," she said. "But ... it's not nothing. If you need to speak, you may to me. I have enormous ears. It's why I've been such a successful companion. I listen most sympathetically."

He snorted. "Your ears are the perfect size."

"No." She pushed a wet, heavy lock of hair behind an ear and showed him. "See? Elephantine."

He pinched her earlobe between finger and thumb and tugged lightly. "Perfect size. Dainty and delicious." A wolf's grin.

And he didn't let go. The rough pads of his finger and thumb warmed the lobe of her ear, and his knuckles lightly grazed the hidden spot of her neck behind her ear. Who knew it was so sensitive, so attuned to pleasure? She could not rip her gaze from the sight of his forearm—the white linen sleeves of his shirt rolled up past his elbow, the dark dusting of hair across the tanned skin and corded muscle. She shivered.

"You're cold. We should return."

"No. Your jacket is warming me well enough." She wanted to hear his secrets. She had no right to them, of course, and, oh, it likely made her a busybody, but she'd been brought here to heal, and he seemed part of what needed healing.

He narrowed his eyes at her but resettled into the earth too many inches away.

She resettled, too, but this time into the wool of his coat, the heated scent of him wrapped entirely around her. She cleared her throat. "No matter their size, my ears are excellent nonetheless. Would you like to try them?"

His gaze dipped to her neck, her jaw ... her lips? "Yes." His voice rough as bark. "Yes." Smoother this time. "I suppose it won't hurt to try talking to someone other than Atlas. He snorts more than one would wish, and usually, by the end of the chat, either one or both of us are entirely foxed."

"No spirits here now."

He nodded. "Very well. But what do I say?"

"Whatever you wish to say. Whatever will be more ... cleansing to say."

He sucked in a breath so heavy he should have dragged the entire lake into his lungs. "Yesterday, when I was so beastly, I'd been attempting, as I do every day, to fulfill the dictates of my father's will."

"The ones about painting?"

"I've ruined more canvas than I can count in the last six months. You saw the pile. And I'd just had another failure when I discovered the three of you were plotting."

"I object to the term plotting. We were *planning*. Entirely different things."

He sliced her a look that made her cower back into his coat. "In truth, the harvest celebration is not a horrible idea. I am merely not used to any sort of excess, and ... my father used to procure things we did not need. I would discover them later. More art, more artists to support, rugs, furniture. Once he hired circus performers to amuse the guests of the house party. I never knew until it was too late to curtail the damage. When I discovered the plotting yesterday ..." He paused, raised an eyebrow in her direction, waited for her to object once more.

She nodded, acceding for the moment.

"When I discovered the *plotting*, all my anger came roaring back. He's not let me go, not even from the grave."

He had more to say. The set of his jaw held the weight of unsaid words, so she'd give him silence until he had the strength the speak the weight away. She pulled his jacket tighter around her. A chill had rolled through the air while they sat talking, winter announcing its intent. Thank heavens she'd taken her dip today. It might have been her last chance to do so. The jacket would not pull any tighter, but she tried, dove her nose into the lapels and came up not so much with warmth but the scent of him—sun and hay and horse, man, soap, and the slight note of paint, turpentine to wash it away. A fascinating concoction, much like the man himself.

"I offer no justification for my actions, Miss Bellvue. I've not been myself since ... Ha. I should say since my father's death, but"—he dropped his face into his palms, tried to rub the exhaustion it away and failed—"it's been much longer than that."

"Fifteen years?" A whispered question. She remembered the day. So very well. How he'd been wild and silent at the the same time. Grieving and full of rage but worried for her above it all.

"About that, yes. Fifteen years of fighting with my father and mother over every single ha'penny. Fifteen years of deception with my siblings to earn enough coin to keep the house from falling down, to keep the farms running, to support the artists my father made promises to. Fifteen years of watching everyone in Fairworth turn on us. Rightfully so. And Miss Bellvue, I am so damn tired."

"Perhaps you need a ... a day of diversion. Tell me—what do you enjoy doing when you're not keeping an estate afloat?"

He blinked. "I ... I can't remember. What do *you* find diverting?"

"A question meant to distract me, my lord. I'll not fall for it." But she was not sure she had an answer for him. She, too, had been busy and breathless the last fifteen years. "When, my lord, was the last time you did something ... fun? What is the last thing you remember doing that made you smile?"

He cast her a swift glance before returning his gaze to the lake. "A production of *Hamlet* at the Theatre Royal. I can't remember when. Quite some time ago. I sold our box. An extravagance we could ill afford."

"You enjoy theatre? That's art!"

"I suppose. It's different, though. It's art come to life. An escape for a few hours' time."

And he hadn't escaped at all since that unremembered last time. She ached a bit for him. More than a bit, actually.

He shook his head. "To attend the theatre now would be selfish." He dropped his hands between his knees. "A single trip to London could solve everything, though."

The heiresses.

"Your mother is convinced that will not save you but ruin you. Just so you know."

"Oh, I know. She left me the tarot cards she pulled for both candidates for the position of my wife. All cards of death and chaos."

Matilda sucked in breath then chuckled. "Perhaps you should heed them."

He snorted, picked a blade of grass and tossed it away.

"She pulled cards for me," Matilda said.

"And?"

"I don't remember much. I was holding a vase above my head while dressed in a curtain and posing for a portrait Jane was drawing. Your mother is teaching her how to draw. But they spoke of change. And that's true enough for me."

The marquess blinked then threw his head back and laughed like he wanted the stars to hear the sound.

She could not look away from the strong column of his throat, could not close her ears to the rich melody of his laughter. And something that spoke of forever settled in her belly. A warmth she'd never rid herself of despite the chill. Not when she was with him, at least.

When he managed to suppress his laughter, he said, "I do not laugh at change, you understand. It's the picture of you posing in a curtain that turned me inside out. I should have liked to see that. I would have found it diverting, indeed. Are you an painter?"

"No. But I do love it. The colors, the lines and shapes, the emotion." She wrapped her arms around her legs with a sigh

125

and poked her chin into her knees. "Good art can make you feel everything. The way life does."

"See. I do not understand. Drawings copy life. Mimic it. It cannot hold a candle to life. Ever. Whatever emotion we see in the world, as soon as we put it onto some sort of dead canvas, it's diluted."

She rolled to her knees, faced him, and shook her head. "No. No, that's not right at all." She pointed at a fuzzy white cloud floating like a lamb across the sky. "See that." She grabbed a stick from nearby and dug it into the dirt between them. She drew the lumpy outline of the cloud above. "And see that? It is an imitation, yes, and a crude one, but you know it's a ... a happy cloud. Now watch." She reached down and wiped the cloud away then drew something else—another cloud, this one long and sharp and thin. "And this one ... there are no clouds in the sky like this right now, but if there were, you'd know what they mean."

"A storm."

"Yes. Precisely. You know it from the drawing." She sat back on her heels, grinning. "There is beauty in the world and there is beauty in the representation of it. Surely you can see it."

He leaned back, pressing his palms into the earth behind him and opening his broad chest for her study.

No. Not for her study.

"You see," she insisted. "You must admit that—"

"Nature can be represented by lines and squiggles. Yes, I see that. But look there." He pointed to the lake. See the way the surface of the water has turned to glass? How it's smooth until the wind ripples it? See how it becomes another sky when it's so still?"

She held her breath. She did see. "That can be shown in paint, my lord."

He snorted. "Paint can *try*."

She laughed then, sending her mirth stars-ward, too. When she tipped her face back down to earth, he was studying her. He studied, briefly, the cloud she'd etched into the soil, then turned his face to the sky, studying the real thing.

"You see," she said. "The lake and sky you showed me, well, I see it as well as you do. We see the same thing. But if someone paints it, it's not just a sky and lake, it's *their* sky and lake. An interpretation. And that interpretation carries a message, an emotion."

He looked once more at her cloud, then dropped his gaze to her. "And what message are you sending with your dirt scribbles?"

"That I know the general outline of a cloud."

"Hm." He shook his head. "I'm afraid I do not understand." His hand rose between them, and when he rested his forearm on his knee, his knuckles almost brushed her leg. "I cannot, Miss Bellvue. But perhaps you should take it upon yourself to teach me."

Teach him? She couldn't. Could she? Perhaps doing so was her next step, what must be done to heal this home. "I'll try my best, my lord, if …"

"Say it. Your ultimatum."

"You agree to let your mother add in some measure to the harvest celebration." He began to object, chiseled lips parting. She pressed a finger against them. "As long as she does not spend excessively, of course."

"As long as she does not spend at all," he ground out, her finger still in the way.

My, but his lips were soft. She whipped the digit and its attached hand back to her lap. "At all. Do we have an agreement?"

He stood, gaze heavy on the sky-reflecting lake. "We do." Then he strode away, leaving Matilda with a plan, a bit of a chill, a jacket, and his scent wrapped tight around her.

Eleven

P ainting lessons. No, more like art appreciation lessons. What sort of hell had Raph created with his own cursed lips? "Teach me," he'd said because his mother's companion had sounded rather like she had all the answers. He'd actually looked at her line drawing in the dirt, trying to figure it out, trying read the meaning she'd left in it when he *knew* there was none. He'd thought maybe if he could see *her* cloud, what *she* thought clouds meant, how she *felt* about them, he might get closer to ... to ... oh, who the hell knew.

Bah *and* bollocks.

Now here he was, obliged to listen to Miss Bellvue wax poetic about the very thing he cared for least. She'd told him to bring nothing but an open mind on their excursion today, so he stuffed his empty hands in the pockets of his old greatcoat as he marched toward the barn.

Open? His mind had never been more cluttered.

With images of a water sprite lifting from the surface of the lake, floating belly up on the glass, the slope of her breasts evident under the soaked cotton of her chemise.

He should not have sat on the bank and stared. But what else was a man in thrall to do?

Now she haunted him, obsessed him, demanded in his dreams the last three nights since their conversation at the lake that he prostrate himself before her. Which in his dream, Raph had been more than glad to do. Luckily, estate matters had kept him busy. Luckily, the cold breeze that day at the lake had heralded colder weather. She'd be all buttoned up, prim and proper, and if his cock got any ridiculous rogue ideas, his own greatcoat could hide the evidence.

He kicked at a bit of hay as he entered the barn and stopped entirely when he heard her laughter. Atlas's too, rising together like music—deep and high at the same time. Atlas had a good voice, the sort of baritone that could put you to sleep if it didn't keep you up wondering why in hell a man like that—a battle-scared soldier—needed a voice *like that*. Only like an angel if the angel came from hell, but hell, apparently created mesmerizing musicians.

Raph would bet Miss Bellvue had a lovely voice, too. High and with a hint of a laugh always at its edges.

The laughter died, and their voices rose in its place.

"You let me know, Matilda." Atlas's voice. "And I'll offer you my protection."

"I'd be quite glad for it," she responded. "One needs strong, capable arms in such situations."

Raph strode forward, unclenching his jaw. "If *Miss Bellvue* needs strong, capable arms, mine are at her service." And if she needed to be addressed by her Christian name, someone other than Atlas should do it.

Atlas's head whipped up, his gaze shifting from Miss Bellvue to Raph. "Brother. You might become used to lifting no more than a paintbrush and pallet. Then, where will Miss Bellvue be?"

"One painting," Raph said, checking the saddled horses,

"and then never again. What is it I'll be saving Miss Bellvue from?"

"Mother."

"Ah." Made sense, but ... "Why does this require strength of limb?"

"Because men are involved?"

Raph put a hand over the bristling hair at the back of his neck. "Oh? How so?" Surprising he kept his voice so calm.

"Your mother," Miss Bellvue said, "has suggested we invite several young and strapping single gentleman to the harvest celebration. She and Jane have turned matchmaker."

"For whom?" Raph demanded.

Atlas and Miss Bellvue blinked at him.

"For you?" he asked her.

Atlas laughed. "Who else, brother?"

The idea sat like bad cheese in Raph's gut. "There will be no suitors at the havest celebration. No guests other than those from the village. Tell my mother that, and—no. I'll tell her that when we return. Let's go, Miss Bellvue." He approached her, crowded Atlas out of the way where he'd been waiting to lift her onto her horse, and let his own hands hover around her waist, waiting to do just that. "Where are we going?"

"To the village."

He nodded, clenched his tingling hands, then spread them wide and wrapped them about her. Big hands. Small waist. Did something to his brain. Scrambled it. He threw her up into the saddle and released her when she seemed steady, mounted his own horse, and they led their mounts out of the barn.

Atlas waved. "Have fun!"

Raph cursed.

Miss Bellvue waved back then turned to him. "I doubt you will have fun, but I hope I shall."

"Where're the art supplies?" he asked. Business. All business. Stay on task.

"None today."

He turned to her. "Pardon me? You're supposed to teach me to paint, and I know I'm a novice, but I can't paint without paints."

"It became patently evident to me the last we spoke—"

Three days ago by the lake when her skin had seemed almost translucent and her hair had tangled down her back, wetting his coat.

"That you need training on a basic level."

"And you are suddenly an expert?"

She peered at him, a single brow raised beneath a jaunty little cap that looked a bit like it might rest easy on Robin Hood's head. "My, you're testy this morning. You are the one who asked me to help you. I never claimed to be an expert. And your own expertise is so ... how do I say this delicately?"

"Nonexistent?"

"Well, there is the pile of paintings, so you do have experience putting brush to canvas, but Atlas told me you painted a stick and called it a portrait."

"Atlas now, is it?" His voiced sounded gruff, like bark on a tree. Such familiarity so quickly. How had that occurred? "How often have you two conversed?"

"None at all. I've seen him in passing a few times, but this morning was our first true encounter, but he insisted I call him by his given name, so ..." She shrugged.

Didn't make him feel better. But why should he care? He could not be so familiar with her, but if Atlas and she were friendly, it might keep her around longer. Mother improved significantly in the few short weeks she'd been here. He'd keep her as long as he could.

He hunched his shoulders. "You were saying?"

She blinked, blinked again, then—"Ah! Yes. You are so

lacking in certain foundational basics that even my own sparse knowledge can, hopefully, prove of some use to you."

"That's your attempt at delicacy?"

"I'm afraid so."

"You're not wrong. I'll behave."

When the fields gave way to forest, and shadows fell across them, striated with golden light, she said, "Thank you, my lord."

"Oh? For what?" He knew, but didn't particularly wish to speak of it. He'd not truly been thinking when he'd rummaged through the closed nursery to find the old toy and deliver it to her, still dusty.

"For the toy theatre. A well-loved plaything, it seems."

"How do you know it was me?" He kept his gaze cast down and his voice neutral.

"Because you are the only person I've discussed the theatre with since being here, and because it appeared just after that conversation. Thank you. It's charming. I confess I was almost late this morning because of it. I got lost playing with it." Her cheeks heated red, and it was with goddamn delight he watched that flush, knowing he'd put it there. "But why?"

Because she'd asked him if he did anything for fun, and he'd returned the question, and she'd not answered it, and the truth had hit him like a sledgehammer. Those fifteen years he'd been working his soul to airy thinness, she'd been doing the same. If his body ached for rest, his soul for diversion, so too did hers. Likely. He hoped. Or his silly gift was sillier than he thought.

"I thought you might need a diversion," he said. "But I have no way of providing one. No money. You know. But I enjoyed that as a child. I thought it might ... amuse you."

"It did. It does." Soft words.

"You could have been late because of it. I would not have minded."

"Thank you."

"Perhaps we should go back." He looked over his shoulder. "You can play with it as long as you like, and—"

She laughed. "No, no. Let us hurry on."

"But you need a rest. And I'm setting more work before you." He couldn't like it. Hated it, really.

"Lord Waneborough." Her soft brown eyes were shadowed by her bonnet's brim, and her pretty lips curved with some gentle emotion.

"Yes?"

"I am sure I will find our efforts today entirely diverting. Not like work at all. Do not worry for me."

He grunted. "If you tire, you must tell me."

"Hm." She leaned forward and patted her mount's neck. "I am tired. Tired of roaming. I should like a home to call my own. I have had many homes with many families, but I have always moved on from each one. I wish to stay someplace, to belong someplace." She flushed. "I apologize. I don't know why I said that. It's not your burden but mine."

A sentiment that felt wrong. On too many levels to count. To begin with, taking on her sorrows and desires didn't feel like a burden, but a privilege. Should it fall to him. But then also the odd fact that he had a home, but he felt entirely alone.

"Your family is still ... uninterested in your fate?" She startled, tossed him a stiff look. "Apologies. Maggie told me some of what you told her when last you were here."

"You know of my brother, then?"

He nodded.

"I have not heard from him in years," she admitted. "Do you remember the cottage I told you of?"

"The one you plan to leave for once your work here is done?"

She nodded. "I inherited it from a great-aunt who hated my stepbrother with a passion. She'd lived there for years with her best friend. They"—she flicked a glance at Raph—"loved one another deeply, and her friend told me, when I met her once in London after my aunt passed away, that she wanted the cottage to go to a woman who needed it."

"You *need* it?" The idea of her in need at all made him grumbly.

"It will be my home, and home is what I need."

Fairview appeared before them, and they rode the rest of the way in silence. Raph dismounted first and helped her to her feet—hands on waist again, muscles tense again, the tension boiling every muscle and nerve in his body. Again.

He jerked his hands away from her once her perfect little half boots touched the ground. She didn't notice. His hands, the tension, the nerves. She turned right to Fairview, small and sweet before them, placing her hands on her hips.

"Now," she said, "come stand beside me."

"Need pencils at least," he mumbled.

"What do you see?"

"Paper'd be nice, too."

"Lord Waneborough. What do you see?"

He scratched the back of his neck. Bollocks. "I see a village. Mr. Johnson, the butcher, over there." He waved. "Do you want something from the bakery?"

"You'll not distract me, Lord Waneborough."

He growled.

She startled.

So did he. What in hell had he growled for?

"Call me Raph," he said. Ah, that's why he'd growled. "If you're using my brother's given name, you can use mine, too."

"I'm not entirely sure that's appropriate, my lord."

"Here. When we're art-ing. Call me Raph, then." Grasping at straws, or ... "I've been the marquess since before I actually had the title. Perhaps if I strip myself of it I can be more than a tired, frustrated bear."

"You *are* a bear ... Raph."

Damn, but that sounded inexplicably perfect.

"Now," she said, "tell me what else you see."

"Am I to call you Miss Bellvue still?"

Her arms dropped to her sides, and she almost folded in half as she let out a frustrated blow of air that may have turned slightly into a groan as she rose to her full height once more. She forced a large smile and turned to him like an automaton. "You may call me Matilda. Now will you tell me what else you see?"

"Yes, *Matilda*, I will." That sounded damn good, too. He looked out across the street. Lines, she'd said. Art was lines. "The houses and buildings make ... sharp lines against the sky. And the road narrows to a point." Colors, too. That, he knew. "Blue sky. Brown dirt. Brown sh—other stuff, too. White-washed walls. Some pink fabric in Mrs. Decorte's window."

"A good starting place. Now, what emotions do you feel when you look at it all?"

He rolled his eyes, crossed his arms over his chest. "You've been prying into my mother's chest for weeks now, but you can't have mine."

"I've no use for your chest, my lord—"

"Raph."

"I merely wish you to explore what emotions you might want to communicate if you were to paint a picture of this village as we view it this very moment."

"Frustration, Matilda. Is that what you want?"

"It's good enough, yes."

He took a half step that brought them closer together.

She looked up, craning her neck, and the brim of her annoyingly jaunty little hat shadowed her face. "What else?" she demanded.

Solitude, loneliness, being shut out and exiled. No way in bloody hell he'd say all that. "The desire to toss you back up onto that horse and smack its rear to send you reeling back home."

"My home will be in Cumbria, my lord."

He almost kissed her then. No reason for it, but he flinched downward for her lips, honing in on what he remembered tasted like honey. Then he jerked away from her, strode down the street. Wanted emotions, did she? Fine.

She scrambled to catch up, and when she was in step with him, he said, "Failure. And abandonment."

A sudden inhalation across those lips. "What colors?"

"Red."

"Interesting. Why red?"

"It's the color of my father's favorite curtains. I'll show them to you when we return. Useless things. Don't even hang before a window. Cost a fortune. Fine velvet, thick. They hang across one end of the portrait gallery and are used to hide whatever newest prize he'd found until his chosen moment to reveal it. Not even art themselves. Used to hide it. Used to bloody bankrupt us."

She didn't flinch at his language, merely continued to step calmly beside him. "Red, then. A red town with points and lines."

He stopped, looked up, shook his head and looked again. Yes—points and lines and anger. But ... "No. Wrong. Maybe I'd paint my father's portrait red. But this town ... I've discovered I quite like yellow lately."

"It's a pretty color." She'd stopped, too, wrapping her arms behind her back and looking up at him again, that brim shadowing her eyes.

"Looks like piss when I try to use it."

"Why yellow? I assume it's not because of its ... piss quality."

He chuckled, the muscles uncurling along his back. "No.

Because of its sunrise quality. Yellow is new light. And this town is becoming new. Trying to be."

"And you're helping it."

"Trying." He closed his eye and raised his face to the sky.

First, he felt the soft touch of her fingertips. Her gloves, really, but warm with a slight pressure on the back of his hand. Then, her entire hand wrapped around his, holding it, squeezed.

He opened his eyes.

She didn't look at him. She looked at Fairworth. "Trying and doing." She tugged him toward the bakery. "Come, you've earned a prize. But you're not done yet."

He let her drag him forward and found himself smiling. Hell. Hadn't done that in ages. Should have wiped it clean off his face, but he let it linger, draining away only when the bakery door shut behind them.

Two flaky pastries later, and they were strolling back down the street once more, waving to the men and women of the town, stopping to chat. Surprising how many women remembered her from her help with the old cottage. Not surprising perhaps. He'd been impressed with her that day. Since their interactions in London, he'd thought her the sort that liked to take charge, tell others what to do, but she'd let others instruct her, teach her, that day, and apparently they admired her because of it.

He admired her, too. Both bits of her—the part that could join the group and help alongside everyone else and the part that liked to tell him what to do. She challenged him, and that had startled him at first. Few challenged him and almost none with actual reason to do so. But he'd begun to see her challenges were not without cause. She did not do so unless it was justified.

"The bakery," she said.

"Pardon? I was woolgathering."

"The bakery. How would you paint it? Colors, shapes, etcetera."

"Brown. A very soft brown. Lots of circles. Fluffiness."

She laughed, and he wanted to scoop up the sound, bottle it, pocket it, save it for later after she left.

He shoved his hands in his pockets. "I'm aware fluffiness is not a color or shape."

"Oh, no, it is a shape. I see precisely what you mean. Now do the butcher—oh, no, perhaps not. How about ... your mother."

"Hm." His steps slowed. "If you had asked me that a fortnight ago, I would have said black, unceasing black. Whatever shape wailing is."

"And now?"

"Orange, I think."

"Oh, yes, I see that. And wild, curling tendrils."

He nodded. "Coming alive, bursting out of the ground."

"And your brothers? Color? Shape?"

"Easy." He dug his teeth into his pastry, tore, chewed, swallowed. She did the same, and he tried not to watch her ruby-red lips as they worked around the sweetness. "Crows."

"Crows. Interesting." She peeked up at him, licking a flake off her lip. "Do they like shiny things?"

"Lysander, perhaps. But that is not why. They are so very ... dour. That is why. And intelligent. I do not know what I would have done all these years without them. You must understand I do not call them crows in any derogatory way."

She held up her hands, palms flat, shaking her hand. "I am not judging. This is your artistic interpretation, my l—" He glared. "Raph." She narrowed her eyes at him. "I can't 'my lord' you even a little?" He glared. "I shall if I wish or if it's necessary. And don't you glare at me. If I addressed you as

Raph in front of your mother and Jane, we'd both pay for it dearly."

"I don't see how that is when they forced you to be on friendly terms with them from the moment you arrived in my house."

Her head bounced from one shoulder to the other. "Yes, well, you must take my word for it, Raph When Alone and My Lord When Not."

Hell, but he wanted to slip his hand into hers. He inched his fingers toward hers.

"And what of your marriage prospects?" she asked.

He jerked his hand back. "I don't know what you mean."

"The two women you've been sniffing about. Color? Shape?" She looked away from him, taking another bite of the pastry she'd almost entirely demolished.

"Ah. I can't rightly say."

"Why not?" She looked down at her feet.

"Because the colors and lines, as you've so forcefully showed me today, stem from emotion, and I feel none for any of them. Unless you count boredom. What color is that? A bit of dread, perhaps. Is there a shape for dread?"

The pastry fell from her hand, dropping into the dust at their feet.

"Bollocks," he hissed. "Come on, then. Let's get you another."

Her arm snaked out, caught his elbow, stopped him. "No. I was almost done. I am merely startled by your answer. I know you marry for practical reasons, but one hopes that you can find affection even in such an arrangement."

He shrugged, his gaze riveted on her hand curved around his elbow, creating rivers of sensation through wool and linen.

She snatched her hand away, held it to her belly.

He started walking once more, slowly, waiting for her to

join him. When she did, he said, "It is not ... precisely what I wish, but it is what I will do." He'd never admitted that to anyone before. And he couldn't say why he did now except that he saw so many parallels between them, and that connection invited familiarity, trust.

"What do you mean?" she asked.

"I mean that what I want is to improve the estate and the lives of my family. It is not to marry without affection, though that is the means by which I will procure what I truly want."

"Unless you win your inheritance."

He nodded.

"I understand," she said. "What I want is a home, and the Cumbrian cottage is the means, though ..." A hesitation that lasted several slowly measured strides.

He liked that about her, too. She strode like she wasn't wearing skirts, and could keep up with him without him having to mince his steps or plod at a frustratingly slow pace.

She cleared her throat, continued, "Though I do not want Cumbria." She mashed the words together, her face smooshing up, and ended the revelation with a groan, dropping her face into her hands. She popped back up quick enough, shook off her ... whatever emotion it was, and asked, "What do you want, then? From a wife?"

"Ah." His steps hitched. Not a question he'd expected from her. But he did not mind answering it. If Atlas had asked, he would have grunted and strode away. If his mother had inquired, he would have rolled his eyes and stomped about, raving about the reasons he couldn't have what he wanted. If Maggie or Tobias had asked, he would have gotten Tobias drunk or distracted him with some ridiculous question.

But it was Miss Bellvue asking. *Matilda.* And he would answer. He owed her after that disastrous kiss. He owed her for healing his mother. And if anyone would understand, it was she. "I want a partner. A true partner. Like my sister has in her husband. If there's one thing I admire my parents for, it's their marriage. They loved one another completely, even if it was straight into their family's downfall. My mother loved my father so entirely, she could not bear to deny him. My father loved her so thoroughly, he wanted to give her what she loved most outside of him—art." Stupid, perhaps, to admire it when it had led to such ill.

After a silence, she said, "It's not stupid to say what you feel and want out loud. I suppose I sound naïve to you, but I think it's important to do so. How else can you make happen what you want to happen? If you hide it, you can never bring it into the light."

"That *is* naïve."

"It's not. You want to repair the harm done by your father, and you state it, live it, every day. Your intentions are not hidden."

"And that is why I must wed. And what of Cumbria? Did you state that into being?"

She took a long while pulling in a soft breath and letting it go again. "I never dared to. Some people just get lucky."

"Lucky? To get what you want and have it come at a cost?" A home, but in a place she did not relish living. "And why do you dislike Cumbria so much?" He knew why he disliked it. Too bloody far away.

"I fear I will be lonely there. I'm a professional companion. Providing company is my expertise. I've always thought it would be lovely to have no one's whims to cater to other than my own, to live every day by my own desires instead of some other woman's. But … the closer I come to that day, the more I fear I'll enjoy it for a month or two then wake up terribly bored and lonely and end up wandering the hills and washes until I'm one of those sobbing ghost ladies William Wordsworth so enjoys penning poetry about."

That about killed him. "You'll just stay *here* then. At Briarcliff." Excellent idea. Problem solved.

She laughed. "No."

He felt a frown furrow his brows.

"I have a home, and it is not here. I will go wherever it is." She stared into some vision he could not see for a breath, then turned to him with a sunny grin. "Let us return to Briarcliff."

They found the horses and mounted and still his hand on her waist, still the tension and nerves and ... something else, something deeper, cutting bone, branding muscle.

They rode slowly back home, stopping often so she could ask him the colors and shapes of things.

The sun—yellow and circle, of course. *Come along, Matilda, too easy.*

The lightning-blighted tree in the forest—jagged but beautiful, silver and black.

The path between the village and Briarcliff—curvy, broad, empty, a sketch, not a full painting.

Briarcliff itself. He'd refused to answer that one, had rubbed his heart and mumbled something about being tired of the game.

When they dismounted inside the stables, Atlas nowhere to be seen, she said, "I have one final challenge for you, my lord."

He'd let that one slide. "Oh?"

She nodded and plucked the little hat from her head, so he could finally see her eyes clearly. It was like a sunrise or walking out of a pitch-dark closet into a sun-bright room.

"Me," she said. "Color and shape, my lord. I expect an answer on the morrow."

His gut churned and his chest pounded into life. Not a damn stick by a lake, that was for certain. But what?

Bollocks. He excelled at tests, but this one he might very well fail because assigning *Matilda* shape and color in a game driven by emotion seemed dangerous indeed. He did not wish to pry into those pinks and purples and greens. Because unlike the women he had his sights on in London, Matilda had shape and color. But he couldn't afford to put them on canvas and make them visible.

Twelve

The sky wept for an entire damn week and flooded fields that needed new irrigation. And by the time the sun peeked out, bashful like it knew what it had done, Raph never wanted to see another drop of water or speck of mud again in his life.

A portion of one crop ruined possibly. Time would reveal all.

He stepped out of his bathtub and dressed himself. He hadn't had a valet in over a decade. What the hell would he do with one should he acquire the funds to employ one now? No doubt, though, whomever he chose to wed would consider it a requirement of her status. The proper number and type of servants. And they'd be able to afford it, too.

He threw on his greatcoat and boots and stomped into the hall. The boots were ruined—mud-caked and cracked—and he'd have to find a way to procure another pair. Boots were necessities if valets were not.

"Lord Waneborough?" Mrs. Counts, their housekeeper, paced toward him. "Your mother is requesting your presence in the ballroom."

More smashed plates? Something else unexpected?

"Thank you, Mrs. Counts. I'll attend her before I leave."

All the doors of the ballroom were thrown open, and on one side, several sheets that had been stitched together hung from the windows of the room to the balcony on the other side, creating a curtain that hid the wall. A chair and a table sat before it, the table laid with some food that smelled warm and rich and made Raph's stomach growl with hunger.

His steps slowed as he entered. "What in hell ..."

The curtain quivered and split near the middle, and his mother appeared. "Raphael, you're here. Excellent. Have a seat. Have a seat. Now we can begin."

"Begin what? What is going on?" And where was Matilda? Miss Bellvue, he should persevere in calling her, and he would around his mother, as she'd asked. But in the solitude of his brain, her Christian name only seemed right. *Matilda*, soft and strong.

His mother stood tall, wiggled her shoulders, cleared her throat, and clasped her hands before her. "Tonight, my lord, for your entertainment, we present to you the Shakespearean classic *Twelfth Night*." She swept her arms toward the ceiling and turned her body to follow their arc. "Comedy." She swept everything the other direction. "Heartache." She turned to him and held her arms out wide. "Women dressing as men. A complete scandal of course, but at Briarcliff, we spurn such ridiculously prudish notions. Art is art, my son, and"—she cupped her palm around her mouth and leaned toward Raph —"wait until you see Matilda in a pair of breeches."

"Franny!" Matilda's voice rose high and disapproving from behind the curtain.

Raph's mother waggled her eyebrows and straightened. "Prepare to be delighted, for without further ado, or perhaps I should say with much ado"—she snickered—"I present to you *Twelfth Night*, abridged. And with some ... modifications."

"Have you been drinking, Mother?"

"I have had a glass or two of ratafia. No more. Nothing to worry about. Just enough to spur the imagination into its most passionate realms!"

"I do not have time for this."

The curtains parted, and Matilda's head appeared in the middle. Just her head. "My lord, when was the last time you ate?"

"I ... I cannot say." At the thought of food, his stomach rumbled like thunder. "It doesn't matter."

Her gaze flickered to his abdomen then back up to his face. "Just as I thought. You've barely stopped in the last week. Do you see the table of food by that chair?" He didn't glance at it, but he smelled it. He crossed his arms over his chest. "That food is placed there for you. And we have chiseled Shakespeare down to a single half hour."

"I did say abridged, my dear," his mother offered.

Matilda rustled the curtains, demanding his attention. "You must eat. You are no good to anyone if you pass out in the fields. In fact, you'd be a decided distraction. So sit, my lord, and eat, and watch our terribly silly production. Even Lord Atlas is backstage to help."

"When has he had time to—"

"He has not. But we handed him a book with the right lines marked, and he'll read when we tell him. You see, he has decided to embarrass himself for your leisure. So sit, eat, watch, and walk away a half hour from now the richer in many matters."

He sat slowly, seduced as much by the play they intended to perform as he was by the fresh bread and butter. "Very well. You have one half hour."

She grinned and disappeared in a flurry behind the curtain.

His mother clapped her hands and disappeared as well.

Then the curtains parted, and Raph almost jumped from his chair.

Matilda lay face down on the floor, her body heaving as if she were hurt and breathing hard. She couldn't be, though. They'd just spoken. He'd heard no fall. His heart raced anyway.

Then she lifted her head, and her face glowed with delight and not a little mischief, and Raph clenched the ends of the chair arms and relaxed. Fine. She was fine.

He might not be. A home theatrical? Was that how they'd spent their rainy days indoors while he'd wrestled Mother Nature for control of the land? He pulled a hunk of bread off the plate and slathered it in butter without watching his movements.

Matilda pulled herself upright and smoothed her skirts, then dropped the dress right from her body to stand before him in a linen shirt, cravat, and breeches. *His* linen shirt, cravat, and breeches. Much too big for her. She wailed about a storm, a shipwreck, and the loss of her brother to the sea. Then she soliloquized about the need to disguise herself as a man. He'd never understood that part of the play. Fuzzy justifications.

He raised a hand.

She stopped speaking when it became apparent he would not put the hand down.

"Yes?" she inquired.

"The play does not begin with a washed-up body on the seashore. It begins at the duke's house."

"I'm aware, my lord, but your mother did explain the bit about modifications. And we are attempting to convey the gist of the plot in a single half hour."

"I see. I expect more of this rearranging and creative interpretation, then."

"Much more of it, my lord."

147

He settled back into his chair. "Very well. Continue."

She did, stomping behind the parted curtain, which pulled to the side farther, revealing her sitting and playing some tune at a pianoforte.

Atlas paced with a stormy brow behind her.

Raph laughed.

Atlas scowled right at him.

Raph tempered his humor and bowed his head. "Apologies. Continue."

Matilda pinged away with little skill at the pianoforte. And Atlas came to a stop behind her, lifted his chin, and pulled a book from behind his back. Peering into it, he spoke, brow furrowed. "If music be the food of love, play on, / Give me excess of it that, surfeiting, / The appetite may sicken and so die. / That strain again! It had a dying fall. / O, it came o'er my ear like the sweet sound / That breathes upon a bank of violets, / Stealing and giving odour! Enough; no more, / 'Tis not so sweet now as it was before." His brother scowled the entire time he recited the words, but the lines themselves sounded sweet in his deep voice, a voice that spoke poetry well.

His brother's voice soon lulled him into a warm relaxation, and whatever worries he'd had on entering the room disappeared. The play was silly, very much so. Matilda played a woman pretending to be a man, Atlas played the duke, their mother Malvolio, and Lady Pratsby the clown. And whomever was available played Olivia. It was a complete and utter mess. They did not know lines and seemed to make up their dialogue on the spot, and it only roughly resembled Shakespeare's comedy.

But Raph laughed, damn how he laughed until it shook his rain-soaked muddy soul and broke up the brittle bits the last week had crusted around him. When the players took their bows and he stood to give them a standing ovation, he felt better than he had in years; better for having escaped the sour sky and drenched earth and heavy responsibility, if only for a half hour.

"What in heaven's name prompted the lot of you to perform such a thing?" he asked.

"It was all Matilda," his mother said. "She thought it might be fun while it rained, keep us occupied. And it did. She also suggested we invite you to be our audience, to pin you down for a bit in order to fill your belly."

"Crafty woman," he said.

"I'm glad you enjoyed it, my lord," Matilda said, having exchanged her pants for skirts in the final scene. "And I am relieved to see you enjoyed your dinner as well."

God, he had. He'd not thought to slow down enough to eat. What a damn fool he was.

She bustled about the table, stacking plates and cups. "Now you may leave, my lord."

"Do be careful, Raphael," his mother called from the makeshift stage.

"Good to see you for once, young man." Lady Pratsby waved.

Were they trying to get rid of him?

And why did a sudden reluctance to go swamp him, sticking his feet to the floor?

Matilda lifted the tray that had once contained food and moved toward the door with an unconscious sway of her hips that snagged his gaze and flipped his belly over. Again. Then again.

What if he took another half hour? He was useful to no one dead on his feet, after all, and he had several questions about that production he'd just witnessed. He rushed after Matilda, stopping her at the door and taking the tray from her hands.

"Let me," he said.

She blinked, and her mouth parted in a slight moue of shock, but she relinquished her grasp.

"I should be angry with you," he said. "I do not usually enjoy being manipulated in such a fashion. Or any fashion. The only thing that saves you is that I was ravenous. And there was food."

"I'd calculated on that, Raph." She glanced across the room.

And his mother and Lady Pratsby's heads whipped toward their tasks. They whistled different tunes.

"My lord," Matilda amended.

He disliked that more than he disliked having been maneuvered into sitting, resting, eating, and enjoying a ridiculous production of one of his favorite plays.

"How did you know *Twelfth Night* is my favorite?" he asked.

"Is it? I did not know. I merely chose one I enjoy. About loss and longing and the risk of not ever getting what you want."

He breathed deeply, letting her words settle into his skin. "I suppose it is. Yet it makes you laugh all the same."

"I think ... if you can find something to laugh at, no matter how bad things are, you know you will survive. Laughter is life."

"I do not laugh often."

"A pity. I am glad you laughed today. You have a wonderful laugh. Quite echoes on these walls."

He suppressed another laugh. Also suppressed the desire to close the distance between them and give her reason to find more in life than laughter.

"My lord?" She inched closer, dropped the tenor of her voice. "I also wish to thank you. For your gift."

Ah. He'd hoped she'd not mention it. "'Twas nothing. Just an old thing I had lying around, thought you'd find useful." A ragged hem, holes in the pockets, not good enough, but all he could manage.

"It's scandalous. I should not have accepted it. I would not have had your note not explained what you meant by it."

"What's scandalous is you without a way to dress properly after swimming on a hot day. The banyan will cover you better, and you'll be able to dress *yourself* in it. And no one here will care nor speak of your activities. I thought, perhaps, it would help you do something you clearly enjoy more easily." She swam well, and more importantly, she enjoyed it. He wanted to watch her swim again, wanted to watch her troubles sink down to the bottom of the lake, wanted to join her. "Have you, er, used it yet?" A hell of a question. Wasn't sure he wanted the answer or not.

She shook her head, seemed about to say something, sparked by a mischeiveous glint in her eye.

But the door at the end of the ballroom swung open, and he stepped away from her as if pushed by a bolt of electricity. "Yes, Mrs. Counts?"

"My lord," the housekeeper said, "young Tom from the village is here, says his wife is in labor. I told him there's nothing we can do, but he's beside himself, he is. What—"

Matilda stepped forward, unaware of the electric bolt Raph had used to put distance between them. Her hand laid firm on his arm, and she looked up at him with determination in her brown eyes. "We must help. In whatever way we can."

And they would. Not just because she insisted, not because any of their number could do something particularly useful in such a situation, but because it was the very center of Raph's being to look out for his own, and because, peering into Matilda's eyes, he knew the same impulse moved her, too.

Thirteen

$\sim$

R aph at her side, Matilda ran outside. The others
followed close behind, and they skid to a jumbled stop
before the cart where the young Tom sat.

"What's happened?" Raph asked. "Is Molly well?"

Tom nodded. "For now. I went to get the midwife, but
she's out of town. No one expected the babe for another
month. At least. She left with Molly's mother. To the neighboring town to help Molly's sister. She's in labor, too. Right
good timing they have. I ... I didn't know where else to
turn."

"It's good you came here," Matilda said.

Beside her, Raph, tight-jawed and pale, shook his head.
"Aren't there ladies in the village to help?"

She laid a hand on his forearm. "It *is* right he's come here."

Raph hissed, "I'm not a trained midwife."

Matilda turned to face the assembled crowd. "She needs
the knowledgeable presence of an experienced mother to guide
her and to give her comfort. Franny, Jane. You know what to
do, I suppose."

Franny stepped forward with a confident stride. "I've had

six children. I know how it goes. Good thing you came to us right away."

"And I've had three," Jane said. "We *can* help."

Matilda turned to Atlas, ignoring the surge of pride rising through her for the women. "Lord Atlas, we'll need blankets. I think."

"Yes," Franny added. "Lots of them."

"Can you gather them?" Matilda asked.

Atlas took off toward the house like he knew exactly what he was about. The rest turned toward the cart.

Tom made a choking noise. "Not enough room for *everyone*."

Raph's gaze fell once more on Matilda, as if he looked to her for guidance.

"Right," she said. "We'll send Franny and Jane in the dog cart. You can ride to the village on your horse, Lord Waneborough, and Lord Atlas will take the other horse when he appears, bringing extra supplies."

"What will you do?" Raph asked.

"I'll stay here and finished knitting the blanket I've been making for the new arrival. I thought I had more time."

He shook his head, pulled her off to the side. "You must come, too."

Tom helped Jane and Franny into the cart as Atlas barreled down the stairs, his arms piled high with clean linens.

"There's no need for me," she told Raph. "I'll be in the way."

"No. What if the baby's on the way and Mother decides to do a card reading for it? What if Atlas passes out? Or Tom. What if something goes wrong with Molly?"

She wrapped her hand around his forearm and squeezed. "You will know what to do. Don't you always know the best thing to do in any situation?"

"Not *this kind* of situation. I can manage when fields are

flooding or some other such disaster, but *this*? This is entirely beyond me, Miss Bellvue. I ... I would like you to be there, too."

Something about the way he said *like* made it sound more like *need*, and Matilda wavered. In more ways than one.

Atlas bumped into them, eyes wide, arms free of blankets. "Mother has the linens, Matilda. I'll just ... return to the stables now." He turned and ran.

Matilda sighed, pinched the bridge of her nose. "Very well then. I'm coming. Let's get to the stable, and—ack!"

Raph grabbed her arm and pulled her that way, calling out, "We'll meet you at the old cottage. Mother, keep the linens clean!"

Franny huffed, no doubt insulted he'd assume she'd do otherwise.

They traveled the path to Fairwoth with a quick-paced hoofbeat that kicked up mud and sent Matilda's heart jumping into her throat. And when they arrived at the old cottage, he swung her down so quickly she barely had time to register his strong, warm hands on her waist. They lingered. Until a scream split the air and Raph snapped his hands to his side.

Matilda took a steadying breath and patted him on the back. "You do not have to come in."

He looked like he might not, but then straightened his lapels and followed her inside. They found Molly on a small bed upstairs, her straw-colored hair plastered to her temples and her belly rising like a moon beneath the covers before her.

She seemed to melt into the bed when she saw them. "Oh, Miss Bellvue. Has the midwife come?"

Matilda rushed to her side, took her hand. "No. But I am here, and your Tom is on his way with help. I am sorry your mother is not here." She remembered Tom's mother had died.

"She's visiting my sister in Crestwood with Alma."

Matilda glanced her question at Raph.

"Alma Smith is the midwife," he said, looking out the window. "Ah, here they come. I'll go help." He stomped down the stairs and out the door.

Matilda sat on the other side of the bed and took Molly's hand in her own. "Does it hurt dreadfully?"

The pale-faced woman pulled her lips between her teeth, pressed her eyes closed, and answered with a minute nod.

Then people descended upon them—Tom, Raph, Franny, and Jane.

But not Raph and Tom for long. Franny and Jane pushed Matilda to the side, took Molly's hands in their own and began a barrage of questions she raced to keep up with.

Matilda found her way to the back of the small room, standing before the clearly befuddled men. "Follow me."

She traipsed back down the stairs, and they followed like pups at her heel. She led them to the kitchen then turned with a bright smile to Tom. "Could you please make some tea? I don't know where everything is." A bit of a lie, that. She'd helped organize the kitchen herself.

But he nodded and set to work, and the trembling about his limbs stopped.

She pulled Raph to the side. "You must take him to the pub."

Raph's face became a thundercloud. "And why would I do that? Are you trying to get rid of me? I know I'm useless, but—"

She laid a hand on his wrist, and the touch seemed to calm him. His brow unfolded and his lips softened. "Not at all. I need your help. Tom is clearly—"

A wailing cry rent the air—Molly's—and Tom lunged for the doorway, and likely the stairs beyond.

"Catch him!" Matilda hissed.

Without a single question or moment of hesitation, Raph caught him.

"Let me go!" Tom threw an elbow at Raph's chin, but the marquess dodged it and held him tighter.

Matilda stood before him. "It will likely be best if you wait this out, Tom. Go with Lord Waneborough to the pub, and we'll take care of Molly here. She'll be fine, and when you return, you'll have a lovely baby to coo over."

His heavy breathing lightened as his gaze flickered to the ceiling. Hesitation.

Raph squashed it. He let the other man go, but not far, wrapping a single arm around his shoulders and guiding him toward the door. "In the dog cart with you. I'm in a mood to celebrate tonight. Your good fortune. Drinks are on me. For all who want them."

The dear man didn't even cringe when he said it, though he must be crying inside. Matilda would find a way to pay him back.

She followed them outside, and once the marquess had Tom settled, wary, in the back of the cart, he sidled up to Matilda.

"This is your plan, then? To inebriate the man so he can't think about what's happening here?"

She shrugged. "No. Not inebriation. Just enough ale or what have you to take the worry off a bit. I've seen it work before in the families I've worked for. He needs distraction, and you'll provide it for him."

"It's just a babe. They're born every day."

"Yes, and just as often, women die of it."

He made a sound in his throat like he meant to speak but something stopped it. The sound of a stone that should have skipped across the surface of a lake but which had sunk instead.

"Consider how you would feel if your wife were in labor.

Would you not be the tiniest bit worried? Especially if you loved her as Tom seems to love his Molly?"

He swallowed hard, and she could see the lump traveling down his throat. "I'll do as you say. Give the man a distraction."

"I'll retrieve you when the babe's come. If it comes tonight, that is."

His eyes flew open wide. "It might not come tonight?"

She gave another shrug. "You really know nothing about this, do you?" He glared and lumbered up onto the dogcart. "Everything will be fine," she assured him.

"Hear that, Tom?" Raph said, grabbing the reins. "If Miss Bellvue says it, I guarantee it's true." He narrowed his eyes on her. "I have that feeling about you."

"And what feeling is that?"

"That you're so entirely competent you always get what you want."

She grinned then shooed them away and returned inside to miraculous silence. He thought her competent. Shouldn't tickle her as much as it did, shouldn't bloom pride in her belly, but it did.

A low moan from upstairs. She made her way toward it, pushed the door open at the top of the stairs, and hovered in the doorway.

"It's all about timing, my dear, and patience," Franny said, patting Molly's hand.

"It's going to hurt," Jane said, squeezing the other hand.

Molly whimpered.

"But we'll be right here with you," Franny assured her. "And after everything you've told us, I'm positive this is happening exactly as it should. Right on time and perfectly safe. "My Raphael came three weeks later than he should have, happy as a lark, right where he was. But my only daughter, Maggie, bounced into the world three weeks early, if you can believe it. She likely needed the right moon for her kind of living."

The woman's whimper became a low moan.

Franny stood and brought a cup from across the room, put it to Molly's lips. "Here. Drink this. Jane and I will be quiet for a bit now, and you tell us if you need us."

Matilda ducked out of the room before anyone saw her, pride for a bright glow in her chest. Franny lived beyond the pale, as she liked to say, but she had a large, kind heart.

She made her way slowly down the stairs and back to the kitchen to prepare a repast for anyone who should need it. She was no cook, so she'd have to see what she could find. Or perhaps take a trip to the bakery. Molly was well with Jane and Franny and Tom distracted with Lord Waneborough.

Raph.

Her lips curled into a smile. Such a contradiction of a man. Used to power, he gave it to others easily when necessary. Attuned to the beauty of the natural world, he failed to see it in things made by man's hands. Justifiably angry at his parents, he still rather loved them. A man who kissed softly when angry and—

A scream.

Jane's voice, alert and sure. "They're coming faster now."

Another scream.

Matilda bounded up the stairs two at a time, skirts hitched high just in time to hear Molly curse the marchioness, and she entered the room just in time to see the marchioness smile.

Fourteen

The candles in the pub blinked like stars and ... *her* eyes.

Raph shook his head. Three ales had clearly been too many. Matilda had brown eyes with goldish-greenish mossy rings around them. But they sparked like candles. And she *had* specifically asked him to think of her in terms of shape and color. So *technically*—

"My lord. My lord?" Tom elbowed him.

Atlas leaned over and flicked Raph's forehead. "Raph. *My lord*. Wake up."

"I'm awake," Raph grumbled. "Just not particularly coherent."

"Me neither." Atlas yawned.

"Do you think we can go back yet?" Tom asked. He braced his elbows on the table and raked his fingers through his hair.

Raph stabbed a finger into the beaten table top. "Matilda said—"

Atlas made an odd sound, half laugh, half snort. "*Matilda* is it?"

Raph pointed his tankard at his brother. "It's what you call her. Why not me?"

"Who's Matilda?" Tom asked.

"The lady my brother is sweet on," Atlas said at the same time Raph said, "The marchioness's companion."

Tom slapped the tabletop. "Miss Bellvue? Congrat"—he hiccuped—"ulations, my lord! A new marchioness, and a plum one, too. You should know we all like her."

Raph tried not to preen, because he wasn't going to marry Matilda, but he liked that Fairworth liked her, and he liked the feeling of being congratulated for catching her.

But he'd not caught her. So he shook his head, pressed his palms to the table, and stood. "I'll go to the cottage and see how things are progressing." He nodded at Mrs. Watkins, the innkeeper's wife, and she yawned. "We can't sleep here." He shook his head. "No. We can. S'an inn." Three ales definitely too many on a day he'd eaten so little. Nothing except for the meal during the play. Made him smile, that did, made him think of Matilda. Ma-til-da. Lovely name. Lovelier woman. "I'll go see how things are progressing." Hadn't he said that already?

He strode for the exit and reached for the door handle. It flew open, and he lurched back to avoid his nose being knocked from his face. "Watch where—"

Matilda stared up at him, her face a painting of joy.

Their gazes held for a heartbeat with no clear intention other than to look, to memorize perhaps, then she threw herself at him, jumping, wrapping her arms around his neck, whispering in his ear, "It's a beautiful baby girl, and she's perfect and the mother is well, and Tom can come back home!"

He held her, breathed her in, had too much ale lazing through his blood to ignore how right she felt in his arms.

Then she was out of them again, flinging herself away

from him and running toward the table where Atlas and Tom sat. He leaned against the doorframe and watched her.

The men stood so abruptly from the table, their chairs toppled backward, and she flitted about them, righting them, before joining them as they rushed for the door.

Atlas and Tom jumped into the dogcart, waking the horse, and Raph, standing beside it, held out his hand to Matilda.

She shook her head. "No thank you. I rode the horse. I think I'm going to go back to Briarcliff." She yawned through her smile.

"Alone?" he asked. "In the dark?"

She nodded, a sleepy little thing. Of course she wanted to return. She'd been working while he'd been celebrating.

He stepped away from the cart, nodded at Atlas, who held the reins. "I'll escort you."

"You do not have to. You want to see the baby, I'm sure."

"I'll return tomorrow." He strode to her side, looking up and down the street, spotting the horse, and taking its reins. "Come on, then. Up you go."

She shook her head. "I'll walk."

"Very well." He led the horse and they stepped down the street beside one another as the cart rumbled off in the other direction. They walked in silence until Fairworth dwindled in size behind them and only their steps and the light, chilly breeze bothered the grasses.

"She's well?" he asked in the darkness, needing to say something, to hear her voice in response. "The mother?"

Matilda yawned, stumbled a bit. "Oh, yes—oop!" She caught and held her breath.

Because he'd wrapped an arm around her shoulders, pulled her tight to his side.

"You're falling asleep standing up," he said. "You should ride the rest of the way."

He wished the damn horse wasn't saddled. He'd ride with

her, hold her in his arms and—he shook his head. He had to stop this madness, but he wasn't sure even sobering up would save him.

"I'd rather walk. I'm feeling more energetic as we speak."

He snorted, and she leaned more deeply into his embrace. Briarcliff became a pinpoint at the end of the road.

"Oh!" She snapped upright, but he did not let her get too far away from him. "The baby's name. I must tell you."

"What is it?"

"Briar."

Bollocks. "Why?"

"Because the people at Briarcliff came to her rescue. You'll simply adore this next bit. She's been given a middle name, too. Francesca."

He swallowed hard and spoke past the lump in his throat. "Briar Francesca? That's a mouthful."

She nodded. "After your mother. But it was going to be Briar Franny, and oh, Raph, it sounded too close to a thorny backside to me. So I convinced them"—she yawned—"otherwise. Your mother will have friends in town now. After this. And especially after the harvest celebration. And then my work here will be done."

Briarcliff grew larger with each step. His home. But not hers. He swallowed hard and looked for distraction. "You've lived in many places. What is your favorite?" Good enough.

She shivered. "Here. Briarcliff."

He could have received no better answer. No worse one, either. He should not pry further. Still, he had to know. "Why?"

"It was the first place I came to after my brother tossed me out. I had prepared myself for ... horrors, I suppose. One hears stories. About the life of a governess." She wrapped her arms tight about her middle, as if warding off those stories. "About predatory husbands and sons who think they own every woman in their midst. But I came here. I'm not sure your father even knew my name, and your mother treated me like a daughter, and you and your brothers, when you noticed me, were so ... polite." She laughed, a small thing. "The house was beautiful and so full of people and art and activity. It seemed as if every corner held some surprise. It took quite a bit of self-control to keep your sister on a schedule. I felt like I'd found an oasis."

"And then I sent you away."

She gave a heavy exhale. "I was not so lucky everywhere else. Those stories I'd heard had basis in fact, but I survived."

"I am sorry you had to leave. I am sorry you had to live days and months anything less than happy. I am sorry I made you miserable."

She stopped, and her hands sought out his, held him at arm's length. "You did no such thing. I was there that day. I saw you, and you stood strong, making promises to me that you've kept for years, more worried about my fate than your own. And even though you sent me away, I knew that should a position become too untenable, I would merely have to write to you, and you'd find me a new place. Thank you. How did you do that, anyway? How does a young gentleman who spends most of his time in the country have his finger on the pulse of families in need of governesses and companions?"

"Mother knew. Not me. She might not be proper ton, but she has contacts, still, among the set. It's likely why you ended up a companion to so many widows instead of governess to young children."

"Ah. Well, my thanks to the both of you. I prefer working as a companion." She wove their hands together and squeezed them sighed. "Living with Jane has been lovely. I will be sad to leave her."

"I wish you didn't have to."

"I am choosing to." But the tone of her voice sounded darker than the night outside the windows.

Emotions thunked like rocks in Raph's chest—relief for his mother, pride that the relationship between the village and house was healing, dread that the woman walking next to him would leave soon. Almost everything winding its way toward perfection.

"There's a problem," he said, jumping at a remaining wobbly bit of life.

"Oh?"

"I still can't paint."

"Ah." She yawned and rested her head on his shoulder. "Shall we return to our lesson? You have not had much time to consider my final challenge to you."

He knew the answer to that—what color and shape she was to him. But he could never put them into words. So he weakly said, "Thank you."

She laughed. "I have not helped you paint a thing. No need for thanks."

"No, thank you for my mother. I would never have thought to try to repair her relationship with the village. She's never seemed to have any interest."

"She likes people. And the house party brought the people to her. You do not need to thank me. You hired me to help her. I'm merely doing what you brought me here for."

He slipped his hands to her wrists and turned her to face him, letting his thumb and forefinger encircle the delicate bones there. "Nevertheless, you have my gratitude."

If it had not been dark, he might have seen a pink blush steal across her cheeks. She ducked her head and made a dismissive buzzing sound in her throat.

He ducked his head, too, looking for her face, needing to see it awash in pale moonlight, needing her to know he spoke true. She had his deepest gratitude. And more. "Matilda."

She looked up, and her features became fae for the briefest breath. Startling beauty. Shy eyes. Lips like flower petals in the dark.

He kissed her.

And she did not waste any time kissing him back.

Their arms wound round each other, palms and fingernails finding necks and jawlines.

This was his thank you. And this was *stay*. And this was *please*. Things he shouldn't say, wouldn't. But he dove deep to find answers to his entreaties anyway, splitting her lips with his tongue as he splayed his fingers of one hand over the back of her head and used his other hand to span her lower back, press her soft belly against his hardening body. She welcomed his invasion and started tiny explorations of her own, teeth pulling at his bottom lip, lips scattering the tiniest of kisses along his jawline, sending tendrils of starlight skating across his skin.

She was lush and warm everywhere he touched, and everywhere he touched felt like it was meant to be. The small dip of her lower back—the valley his hand fit perfectly into. The slope of her neck into shoulder—a spice field for his nose to explore. The lush curve of her breast beneath her gown—a mystery every bit of him wanted to solve. Her mouth—his. Her petal-soft skin—his. Her lashes, long and dark and fluttering shadows on her cheeks—*his*.

Not his. Never his. Even though every inch of her felt like it.

He kissed her more to forget such dreary practicalities.

She moaned and arched, curving her belly against his erection. Damn, but he was hard; hard and needing only her.

"Touch me," he begged. Hopefully, the two words belonged more to the three ales than to him, but him and they had become the same. "Touch me," he begged again.

Her hands left the angles of his face and shoulders and

crept beneath his coat, flattened against his chest, and drew sharp lines down his abdomen.

"Damn clothes," he hissed.

"I agree." A whisper as her hands fisted in his shirt.

"What ...?"

"You said to touch you, but I have only so far touched wool and linen. Do you not wish me to—"

"Yes." He grabbed his shirt and pulled its hem free from his riding britches. Her hands slipped beneath, found his skin, and bunched his muscles beneath her touch. "Sorceress," he said into a kiss.

"You feel as beautiful as you look." She sighed.

The lake rose up in his memory as it must be doing in her own.

"Did you like looking at me?" he asked.

"Yes." No hesitation when she admitted that.

He clutched the hair at the base of her neck and pulled her head back, baring her skin for his lips, his teeth, a frantic line licked up her throat, then a hard, clashing kiss—as hard as the moonlight was soft, as hard as him.

She seemed to like it. She wiggled closer, arching and grasping at him, curling and uncurling her hands on his abdomen like a cat.

The sound of wheels rolling slowly, the shake of a horse's harness.

Bollocks.

Raph set Matilda from him. Their chests heaved to the same racing rhythm, and her hands flew up to press against her lips for a flurry of moments before balling into fists and pressing into her gut.

"I'm sorry," she said. "I should not have—"

"I'm the one who should not have. Who should apologize." He wouldn't, though. His life was meant for duty, and he'd take that kiss for himself, not apologize for pillaging it.

"The horse." He took the reins. "Go in and get some sleep, Matilda. Miss Bellvue." *Bah*. What to call her now when Matilda could be kissed but shouldn't be, and Miss Bellvue could *not* be kissed, yet he wanted to? "I'll stable the beast."

"Yes. Right. Um." She looked in several directions, her gaze sticking to the approaching cart, Atlas holding the reins, the shapes of two women in the back slumped against one another. "Good night, Raph." A hissing inhalation. "My lord. Good night."

He led the horse to the stables without another word. What could he say when he'd rather be kissing a woman he couldn't have?

If he were to paint Matilda this night, she'd have bars of moonlight and shadow across her, a star-shaped key somewhere, lost, locking her up tight. Locking her away from him.

He had to leave. Return to London and to his duty. Tomorrow. Before he lost the will to do what he'd always known he'd have to. Sell his soul to save his family.

~

Matilda wore the marquess's old banyan crossed tight around her body, too big, and pulled up to her nose to smell the remnants of his scent. She lay in bed after she'd helped the older women settle down for the night. She was exhausted. But she might never sleep again. Had anyone in the history of kisses been kissed just so? Hard and soft, as if he thought her fragile but could not keep his passion at bay.

She'd been kissed before, unfortunately. By two different employers. What was it about wealthy men that made them think every woman in their employ must wish to share their bedsheets? Matilda had promptly left those positions, writing to Raph both times to inquire if he knew anyone in need.

She rolled over and shoved her face into her pillow for a little scream.

Well, a rather large scream.

She'd been turning to Raph for years, acting as if it were the most natural thing in the world to take help from a man who offered it, a man who clearly liked to save damsels in distress, everyone in distress really.

But perhaps it had been more than that. Perhaps she'd been waiting for him to offer something else. No. Surely not. She'd always found him handsome. Who would not? And she'd always appreciated his support. She'd never expected more than that, nor even dreamed of it.

She winced as she turned on her side and rolled into a ball, hugging her knees, drowning in the warm, frayed banyan. She should not lie to herself. She'd thought it a time or two, built her own airy castles in which he rode up and asked for her hand.

Instead, he'd rode up and asked for her to help his mother. Not what she'd envisioned.

But the kiss.

Kisses.

They turned her inside out. Turned her to water and wind and lightning. Turned her into a rather simpering miss who, really, just wanted another kiss.

And more. Because he seemed to want her to enjoy life. The toy theatre, the banyan for swimming—small gifts she should not cherish. And did. They spoke to the woman she'd never had the chance to be, not to the companion she'd become. They said, I know you, what you like, what you want, and I want you to have more of it.

She couldn't have *any* of it—not the life of a woman, not the love of a man, not the kisses. Not a home where all those things resided.

Because he needed money, one thing she decidedly did not have much of. A small annuity. A smaller savings. A cottage.

She looked about the room she'd decorated with her few possessions. She had these things, too—sketches and scarves and a jewelry box. Of no value to anyone but herself.

And she wanted him to have what he'd worked so hard for —his home and family restored. She needed to leave. As soon as could be. After the harvest celebration. This place felt more and more a comfortable haven, and she could not risk it feeling more than that, could not risk it becoming a home. Home could not be *here*, because if it was, she'd be locked out of it forever.

Fifteen

R aph found himself surrounded, enemy armies on all sides. What advice would Atlas give on surviving such a fray? And would advice regarding bullets and bayonets suffice for a battlefield of disengaged misses and their competitive parents?

"Lord Waneborough," Mrs. Delaney said, her bosom brushing precariously close to the cutlery as she leaned over the table toward him, "we had expected to meet with you earlier than this since we learned of your arrival in town."

"Oh?" Mrs. Sawyer said, then took a sip from her wineglass. "*We* saw him three days ago." She set her glass delicately on the table and pulled up tall, her gaze straying from Mrs. Delaney's.

Tobias grinned. Didn't even hide it, damn him.

They'd not sat in any particular or formal order that evening. Only Raph was titled, so he'd bowed to their conventions and sat between the two young women, Maggie on one side and Miss Delaney on the other. Tobias sat across from him, and Tobias's stern father and the two other fathers in attendance clustered around the head of the table, discussing

170

business matters. Mrs. Blake barely seemed to sit at all. She bustled about, directing the footmen as if they were dancers in a Russian ballet. Miss Delaney and Miss Sawyer played with their food. Miss Delaney with her asparagus and Miss Sawyer her wine, tapping the tines of her fork against the stem of the glass.

Plan a party, Maggie had said. We'll ask Tobias's father to host, she'd said. He is the common mutual acquaintance of us all, she'd said. If it's his party, there will be no pressure on you, only the opportunity to mingle and better acquaint yourself with the ladies. *She'd said.* An excellent idea he now cursed to perdition.

Raph glared at Maggie, the stem of his own wineglass feeling fragile in his tightening grip.

She winced and mouthed an apology before taking a hefty swallow of her wine. "I am afraid I must apologize, Mrs. Delaney. I've monopolized Raph's attention since he arrived in London."

More correct to say since he'd fled Briarcliff. Even more accurate to admit he'd fled Matilda and his out-of-control feelings for her.

She *should* try to fix this mess. A dinner party. Indeed.

"Petunia, darling," Mrs. Delaney said. "Do tell Lord Waneborough about Sir Wiggles."

Raph turned to his left where Miss Delaney sat directly beside him. Petunia, apparently. How had he not know that was her name? "Sir ... Wiggles?"

Miss Delaney startled and dropped her fork to her plate along with the asparagus she'd been flopping in the air.

How bored was she? And why did she startle when he addressed her and not when her mother did? Must have learned to tune the other woman's voice out entirely.

"Oh, my lord." She dropped her gaze to her lap. "Sir Wiggles is my cat."

"He has, my lord," her mother said, "one eye. Quite looks like a pirate. He's missing an ear, too, and half his tail."

"Sounds like quite the character," Raph said, more interested in the cat than he had been in anything else that had been said at that table that night. "How did he acquire such an interesting visage?"

"He fights other cats," Miss Delaney said, her hands growing white-knuckled clasped in her lap.

How was it not even a battle-hardened cat she called Sir Wiggles could rouse her to passion? Why did she seem so frightened of him? Was it Tobias who had told him he could not marry a girl with no spirit? Perhaps he had the right of it. Because he could not imagine this girl stomping into Fairworth and joining a cleaning of a cottage. Nor could he imagine her ordering them all about during an emergency.

He could see *someone*, though. Quite easily.

He took a gulp of his wine and washed the image away. "The creature sounds fascinating. I should like to meet him."

She began to shake.

Bollocks. This would never work.

"Does anyone need more wine?" Mrs. Blake asked, her voice as chipper as Miss Delaney's was terrified.

"I'll take a bit more," Raph said, raising his glass.

"My daughter has a pet, my lord!" Mrs. Sawyer almost jumped out of her chair and fell into the table as she volleyed for his attention.

At the other end of the table, her husband looked up, blinked at his wife, then returned to his conversation with Mr. Delaney and Mr. Blake.

Mrs. Blake directed a footman to fill Raph's glass then gestured to Tobias's. "There we go. Everyone happy." She grinned. She truly believed it, bless her.

Tobias thanked his mother and the footman, then took

another sip of wine, eyes glittering above the ruby liquid, over an amused smirk. Raph wanted to hit him.

Maggie watched it all with a wary, polite smile. He would never take her advice again. Perhaps it was the fact she was a new mother. All her good ideas went to the babe.

Raph turned to Miss Sawyer, sitting on his other side. "You, too, have a pet?"

"I do." She took a sip of wine.

He waited for more. Received nothing. Cleared his throat. "A cat as well?"

"A pig."

Hell, he'd not expected that. He almost laughed. But finally, a common element to speak of. "I've a few pigs at Briarcliff."

"Mine is cute." She sipped her wine and spoke without even looking at him.

"Pardon?"

"I assume yours is large. And muddy. Mine is small. And clean."

"I am sure, my lord," Mrs. Sawyer said from across the table, "that your pig, large and muddy though it may be, is also cute."

He nodded. "It's an unusual pet for a lady. Does it have a name?"

Finally, she looked at him, a slow turn of the head that brought a frosty blade of a gaze slicing into his own. "Lucifer."

"Ah. Quite ... creative."

Mrs. Sawyer held her arm over the table, almost knocking over a candlestick with a lit candle atop it. "Our Laticia is very pious, my lord."

Maggie lunged for the candle, sending a fork flinging across the room, but steadied the candle before it could set the entire table aflame. She smiled as she settled back into her chair, but Raph saw it—the fear in her eyes. His sister was out of her depths.

He cleared his throat, ignored Mrs. Sawyer, and directed his next query to the pious daughter with the porcine pet. "Is the pig a tad ... devious in nature?"

Miss Sawyer turned back to her wine. "He's perfect in every way. An angel. And I will not have him put out of doors when I ... relocate."

"She knits sweaters for the pig." Mrs. Delaney spoke out of the corner of her mouth and snorted.

Miss Sawyer's gaze whipped up like a knifepoint to the older woman. "And what of it?"

"Laticia, love," the girl's mother said, "I'm sure Mrs. Sawyer meant nothing disparaging." She glared at the other mother.

Who glared right back.

Bollocks. They were going to come to blows. All over a pig with a bespoke wardrobe. Probably dressed more finely than Raph.

Maggie stood up, her chair screeching across the floor. "Mr. Blake, I am afraid I hear Merry upstairs crying for me. Would you mind terribly if we retired to the parlor? I'll soothe Merry then bring her down for everyone to coo over."

"Oh!" Mrs. Blake said. "We have a lovely pudding still." She tore at the corner of a serviette. "But Merry ..." She threw the cloth on the table with a decisive nod. "The baby must come first. Come along, Maggie."

Mr. Blake grunted. "But I like pudding."

Mrs. Blake had already bustled from the room with a gesture to the footmen that must have meant *Wrap it up, boys!* because they'd begun to pull plates and cups from the table with brutal efficiency.

Mr. Blake sighed, straightened his coat, then left the room, and in a flurry, everyone followed, the two mothers jostling for position in line behind Mr. Blake, and their daughters filing out last.

Raph remained. So did Tobias.

Raph sighed into the palms of his hands. "If you laugh, Tobias, I'll lay you flat."

"You do realize," Tobias said before he finished off the rest of his wine, "that you can't marry either of those women."

He was coming to realize that, yes. But what other choice did he have?

"Have you, ah, tried for your inheritance yet?" Tobias asked.

Raph pushed up from the table, and the slam of his palms jangled every bit of china and cutlery atop it. "Of course I have. None of it good."

"Pity. You should follow Maggie upstairs. She's almost completed her work of art. Merry has slowed her down a bit, but I'm sure your mother will be quite pleased with the outcome."

Twin firework bursts of jealousy and relief exploded in his chest.

"She means to gift the proceeds from the sale of her inheritance to Briarcliff, to bring on more staff."

That would help. Perhaps they could bring back the young people who'd left to find positions in other places, show them that opportunity existed in Fairworth. At the same time, it rankled, that Maggie would so freely and without question hand over her inheritance. She'd earned it. Their father had, after all, wasted her dowry on who knows what.

Keep it, he wanted to say. But he said nothing because he was selfish, and followed Tobias into the hallway.

"Go," Tobias said. "I'll keep the stories of pet pigs flowing like a river at flood so there's plenty to entertain you when you return."

"Can't you just send them away?"

"Yes, but what would I do for entertainment? And then you'd have to court two other chits with title-minded mamas."

Raph grunted and headed up the stairs as Tobias slipped into the eerily quiet parlor. Why was he off to visit Maggie and the babe again? Oh yes—artistic advice.

He found Maggie with the child suckling at her bosom in an upstairs sitting room. She pulled a small blanket to cover the sight and smiled at him. "I hope you do not mind. I did not like the idea of a wet nurse."

He waved a hand at her and walked to the window. Outside, London had been swallowed by fog. He'd been here a week and lived in nothing but fog morning, noon, and night. What was it like at Briarcliff right now? Was Matilda enjoying the weather? He clenched his hands, hoping the slice of his nails into the rough skin of his palms would cut the image of Matilda away.

"What are you doing up here, Raph?" Maggie asked.

"Tobias said you're almost done earning your inheritance."

"Ah. Yes. I'll write Mother when it's complete."

He turned to face her and leaned against the windowsill. "How'd you do it?"

"I thought of Father a bit. The ways he'd loved me, and the ways he'd failed me. And I put in a bit of my current"— she kissed the baby's head—"exhaustion, and I think I made something true."

"True." Matilda had called art shapes and color and feelings, an individual's interpretation of something real. Maggie called it truth. "How do you know what lines and shapes and emotions are true enough for an idea?"

She shrugged. "You know."

Merry must have gotten what she wanted because Maggie sat her upright, rested her on her shoulder, and patted her back until the little bundle burped. Then Maggie held Merry out to Raph. "Would you like to hold her? You'll likely have one within the year, depending on when you wed."

Raph strode to her, took the babe, and grinned at the little darling. "Four months, are you? You've plumped up nicely. Nice and rosy."

The baby gurgled.

He kissed her nose and felt something in him thump and fight and settle down deep in his chest with a growl.

Bollocks.

He wanted a baby.

That's what he was here for, though, was it not? To get a wife who, presumably, he'd get with child? The little bundle in his arms yawned, and he laid her on his shoulder, rubbed circles into her tiny back as he paced the room before her mother.

"Which woman do you approve of, Maggie?" he asked. "I need you to choose because I find I cannot."

Maggie tapped her fingers on the polished arm of the small chair she sat in, a thoughtful motion that gave rhythm and urgency to the slow eyeroll she used to study the room. No, not the room. She'd laid out possibilities in the air before her, and those she studied with her measured pace.

"I think," she said, "you must determine which woman you see yourself living with for the rest of your life—the one who prefers piratical cats or the one who prefers perfect pigs."

He closed his eyes, Merry's tiny flickering heartbeat fluttering against his chest, and considered it. He imagined the wedding day and the wedding night, the breakfast tables and walks to the village. He imagined the trips to London and the way each woman's belly would swell with his child there. He imagined how he'd feel when it was the babe's time to enter the world. As terrified as Tom had been? As nervous as he was delighted and amazed?

He tried to at least. But no crisp details would come. Not

even pigs and cats wandered round the corners of the visions —more London fog than sunlight through a clean window.

He opened his eyes. "Bollocks."

"Bollocks you've come to an answer or bollocks you've not?"

"Matilda said—" He bit the sentence clean in two before he could finish it and started again. "Miss Bellvue said that a man who loved his wife would feel a bit of dread when she gave birth. Don't ask. There was a hullabaloo in the village, and Briarcliff helped."

"Oh, I heard all about it in a letter from Mother. And Miss Bellvue is right, I think. Tobias was ... well, I've never seen him so stony, so serious. Is that what you're trying to imagine, with Miss Sawyer and Miss Delaney?"

He nodded, handed Merry back to her mama. "I should return downstairs."

"Don't make a decision tonight, Raph. Think on it a bit, and if you truly cannot imagine yourself with either of those women, then try again next season. No contracts have been signed. You've not talked courtship with either of their fathers."

"But everyone knows my intentions, unspoken though they may be."

"And they have so much money they'll find a man to replace you soon enough. The women do not lack for suitors, nor those with titles either. They will waste no more time on you if you tell them you've fallen in love elsewhere."

"Fallen in love? Ha. That is not in my future."

"Hm. When do you return to Briarcliff?"

"Once I've made a decision."

"Well"—Maggie stood with a sigh, patting her child's rear gently—"when you arrive, please do give *Matilda* my regards." She sauntered past Raph with a grin.

Raph almost melted into the floor but found his footing

quickly and set his feet toward the downstairs parlor. When he entered the room, the ladies stood, and he waved them back down.

"It has been a lovely evening," he said, "but I am afraid I must leave. I received a missive from my brother in the country just before I left for the evening, and leaving it unread is more distraction for my poor brain than you beauties deserve." He actually did feel anxious to open Atlas's letter. "We're in the middle of trying a new irrigation system on a field, and one of the villagers recently had a child, named her for my mother. I'm hoping he sends news of the babe."

Mrs. Sawyer drew her chin back into her neck. "You are so very hands on, then? Don't you hire someone to do all that?"

He shrugged. "We do not have the funds for that." Something the woman should already know. "Thank you for coming." He bowed and left.

The walk to Tobias's townhouse was short, but Raph almost lost his way. A London fog could disorient him more quickly than a storm in the woods surrounding Briarcliff, but he found his way and found his room and kicked the door shut before ripping his cravat off and settling at the writing desk. He leaned back, tapped its top, and contemplated the painted wall. Tobias *would* paint a room pink. A nice pink, though, dark and dusky with a bit of a rose about it.

A woman he was not supposed to think of—ever—would look lovely in just such a shade.

He dipped an imagined paintbrush into a white paint of fancy and wiped the image clean. But the ghost of a woman's figure in a dusky pink gown still haunted him. He shook his head, tapped the polished oak harder, faster.

Miss Delaney. Sweet Miss Petunia Delaney with the piratical cat or reserved Miss Laticia Sawyer with the perfect pig?

Could he have the animals instead? Just them, wandering

through Briarcliff. They sounded delightful. Interesting at least. And Matilda no doubt would find them amusing and—

No.

Focus. He growled, grabbed the letter from Atlas, ripped it open, and read.

Atlas wrote that Matilda had intercepted several letters from their mother to various personages in town, inviting them to the harvest celebration. Bollocks. But also, bless that beautiful woman. He could feel confident his mother wouldn't be able to revert to extravagance under Matilda's watch. But ... perhaps he should ask Maggie and Tobias to visit for the event. That would please his mother.

What else? He returned his attention to the page.

His mother and Lady Pratsby had begun to torment Matilda with an old superstition. Something about apples and mirrors and discovering your true love. He remembered it well. Matilda, apparently, had started avoiding the fruit, which had begun to appear on every tray of food she was served.

Raph laughed. Hell, he wished he could be there, watching her calm frustration rise. He wished he could be there when she finally gave in and did as the superstition said —bit an apple and looked in a mirror to see your true love. She'd cave eventually, but would likely never tell his mother and Lady Pratsby when she did.

No time for such heavy need to be somewhere else. He ignored it and read once more.

Additionally, Atlas wrote that Matilda had started riding out once a day, in the afternoon, when his mother and Lady Pratsby were napping, and Atlas sometimes joined her. And Atlas had begun joining the women for dinner every evening. Where, it seemed, Matilda regularly regaled him with stories from her previous positions.

"Bollocks." Raph threw the letter down, where it fluttered without the satisfying thump or crash he truly desired. The estate must be falling to pieces even more. What the hell did Atlas think he was doing, acting like he did not have work to do? Because he must certainly be at leisure if he was courting Matilda over candle-shadowed dinner tables and brisk country rides through autumn air. And courting was certainly what it all seemed like.

But if any man was going to court Miss Matilda Bellvue it was—

Bollocks.

It couldn't be him. No amount of wanting could make it so.

Didn't keep jealousy from biting hard, clamping down like a wolf's jaw and tearing through skin and muscle to pierce his beating heart.

Raph tried to swallow it down, extinguish it entirely as he stared at the fire across the room, crackling merrily as if the estate wasn't two steps away from disaster, as if Raph himself weren't a bloody mess. A mighty good metaphor for Atlas—cheerful and courting in the midst of ruin. Damn him to hell.

And what could Raph give her to match Atlas's cheer and freedom? An old banyan and an even older toy. Yes, before he'd left, he'd found the plays that went with the theatre and stacked them neat outside her bedchamber door like a cursed offering to a goddess. He scrubbed at his face. He'd known his mother would keep her on her toes, and he wanted to give her something that might lighten her free hours with a bit of delight.

She was spending her free hours with Atlas instead. Naturally, she'd pick a man over a child's toy.

What a fool he was.

Raph stood and strode to the wardrobe. In less than a minute he had his trunk open and was throwing his clothing inside. He never brought much and hadn't had a valet to scold him in years, so it was short and messy work. And necessary, if he were to return to Briarcliff tomorrow.

And it seemed he must cut his trip to London short, put off his decision another month longer, and return home before the entire estate collapsed without him to keep it upright.

His only calming thought as he fell into bed was that Matilda would keep everything from complete ruin. Shape of an oak and colors of the earth, she was—strong and soft and entirely dependable.

He'd just have to keep his distance from her inviting shade once he returned because while he could trust her, he could not trust himself around her to ruin everything he'd worked so hard to achieve.

Sixteen

M atilda could not enter a room without seeing an apple shining like a sun from some piece of furniture. A week ago, the fruit had appeared with every meal, but since Raph's return home, they had more than multiplied. There had been one on the table by her bed when she woke that morning, then an entire basket of them had been waiting on the breakfast table when she'd arrived, a yawn stretching her body, to break her fast. Another had been sitting atop her book in the marchioness's parlor. And now there was one on the shelf in the library.

How did Jane and Franny know where she would be? Or had they merely placed an apple in every room of the house?

She wished she'd never asked Franny the question about the old superstitions.

She wished, equally as fervently, that someone a century or so ago had not decided that a harvest tradition involved apples, mirrors, and the discovery of true love.

A charming tradition—if a lady ate an apple before a mirror at the end of October, she'd see in its surface the reflection of her sweetheart.

Charming if two tenacious ladies had not decided Matilda herself should discover her true love by just such a means.

Franny and Jane had been odd since the night of little Briar's birth, the night they'd interrupted the Something That Should Never Have Happened.

They'd said nothing, so it was reasonable to hope they'd seen nothing. Yet ... they were up to something. Four letters had held Raph's franking signature on the outside and invitations to young, eligible gentlemen to attend the harvest celebration on the inside. How had they managed the signature with the marquess in London? More pressingly, had there been more than four epistles? Had the four been merely the ones she'd caught? He had returned last night, but if Franny had truly determined to sneak invitations past him, past them, she would continue her attempts nonetheless.

The mere thought made Matilda tired. She needed sustenance. She strode to the bookshelf and whipped the apple up, breathed on a portion of its bright skin, and shined it across her sleeve.

She opened her mouth to bite into it but stopped. A mirror glinted across the room. Why not? Then she could tell them she saw the image of no one looking back at her or, better yet, the image of a willowy poet named Baxter who liked to wander the Cumbrian landscape for inspiration. She knew exactly how she'd tell them, too, with fireworks in her eyes and her hands fluttering together over her heart.

She chuckled and wove her way to the mirror. As usual, her hair was a tad unruly. Jane had been drawing her swooning on a settee this morning, and her coiffure had never quite recovered. Dark, curly wisps escaped to frame her face, and her skin was pink from the cold in places. She should have worn a more sensible gown, but Jane, ever vigilant in her new pursuit of sketching, had insisted Matilda provide decent décolletage.

She pulled her shawl tighter around her shoulders and

frowned at the apple. Then she closed her eyes and tried not to imagine a thing. Except perhaps Baxter the imaginary poet. She bit into the fruit and an explosion of taste rippled across her tongue, sweet and tart and nothing worth frowning over, and as her smile once more smoothed the corners of her lips upward, her mind imagined what it shouldn't.

The Something That Should Never Have Happened.

The kiss beneath the moon. Starlight rushing through her blood and Raph's hands, large and warm, ... everywhere. His lips tasting her as if she were the season's bounty, as if she were an apple both tart and sweet, and her clinging to him like he was the last warm day of summer.

She swallowed the apple and opened her eyes.

"Are you unwell, Miss Bellvue?" Raph stood behind her, and he blinked at her from the mirror's reflection, a strand of hair falling over his brow and concern turning his sky-blue eyes to stormy gray.

She yelped and spun around, dropping the apple.

He knelt and picked it up, handed it out to her. "I apologize if I scared you. I see you found my gift."

"Your gift?"

"Atlas wrote. Said you'd developed a fondness for the fruit."

She shook her head and reached for the apple. "Thank you. It's more your mother's fondness than mine." She snatched it to her as if he might bite it out of her grasp. Or bite her.

She wouldn't mind.

Oh no. No, no, no. Naughty thoughts could go far, far away. Yet every moment near him spawned a new one. Such as what would it be like to have him press her up against the bookcase. And would he touch her roughly after ten days away? Or would he touch her softly, and show her that muscle could be gentle.

Oh no. No, no, no. She swept to the side and around him, remembering her manners at the door. She stopped, looked over her shoulder. "I hope you had a fruitful trip, my lord."

Fruitful. Yes! He was likely engaged to be wed now, and that would fix everything. Because she would never, *never* touch a man engaged to another woman. She relaxed, turned all the way around. He was nothing to fear now. Her own lusts would soon dissolve, and she could ignore that feeling in the gut that felt like a spear had found its way entirely through her middle and be around him without danger.

"Am I to congratulate you?" she asked.

He ruffled a hand through his hair, his gaze intent on her. "You should have kept walking, Miss Bellvue."

What was he doing? Walking closer. No, *stalking* closer, looking rather predatory, his hair a bit wild, his muscles rippling beneath linen and wool. Why must he be so magnificent? She tried to move, but she'd turned to stone. No going anywhere.

He stopped right before her, leaned close. Not touching, though, thank heavens. If he touched her, she'd turn to stardust and dissipate in the air. But it would be a happy dissipation. Oh to be touched by him. She could still feel it when she closed her eyes. When she opened, them, too. Honestly, she felt it still with every breath she dragged into her pitifully Raph-focused body.

He breathed deep, shuddered, his eyes never closing, never straying from *her*.

She must be turning stardust limb by limb. Her legs likely weren't there any longer. She couldn't quite feel them, and she reached for the doorframe to steady herself, to hold up her weight when she rather reach for him. Doorframes offered poor substitutes for her true desires, but she locked them down, held them tight, and tossed the key. He belonged to another woman now.

186

Though he was not acting like it.

"You"—her voice sounded like a toad's croak so she cleared it—"you're betrothed now?"

"No."

She melted. Thank heavens for doorframes, entirely not-Raph-like though they may be. "But your entire purpose—"

"Is to sacrifice what I want to build the family back up."

He sounded tired. So very tired. She wanted to run her fingers down his cheek and knead the stiff muscles of his neck. She kept her hands very much to herself. Besides, if she let go of the wall, she'd fall flat on her face. Still melted, after all.

"Do you truly have to do so?" she asked, knowing the cursed answer.

"Maggie is close to earning her inheritance."

Not an answer.

"And Theo, surely will do so soon. Perhaps Lysander." Finally, he broke his gaze from hers to drop his head into his palms, and he stood so close, his rogue lock of hair almost grazed her head. Then his head popped back up, his eyes blazing. "My mother told me Atlas was here. Where is he?"

She shook her head. "I've not seen him all day."

He snorted, whipped around, and paced away from her. "I've heard differently."

Oh, there were her legs—feeling flooding through them, finding purpose. She strode after him. "You have a tone, my lord, that I do not welcome."

He laughed, a curt affair that curdled her previous desire.

She pulled that spear from her gut and trained it his way. "Please do speak your meaning."

He spun, legs wide, hands finding his hips. "You and Atlas are spending an irresponsible amount of time together." Her mouth fell open, but no words fell out. "You must know, Miss Bellvue, he cannot marry you. Like me, he'll be obliged to wed wisely."

"And marrying me is not wise?"

"Not for him. Not for me." The last word rolled his lips into a sour frown he directed at the ceiling.

And it cooled her quickly burning ire like a winter wind. This was no good. Not his words, not her feelings. She should leave. Smart thing would be to leave.

"I am sorry," he said. "I do not mean to always yell at you."

"I yelled right back. Will you send me away."

"God no. I should. But I won't. I'm considering waiting. To take a wife. I could not make a decision, and Maggie thinks I need not rush one." He scratched the back of his neck and looked so unsure, so small for such a big man. Yet, his brows slashed across his face, and his lips held a tilt of defiance. Whatever hopelessness he looked on, he did so with courage.

"Wise. I would not want you to make a choice that made you miserable."

He lifted his gaze slowly until it locked with her own. Oh. Misery had already settled deep inside him. She ventured another step closer, her feet obeying the commands of her heart when her mind—logical, practical thing that it was—had given no such orders. She stopped until she could touch him, and she did, placing her fingertips, devoid of gloves, against the skin of his wrist, right where the pulse beats. His pulse beat quickly, then even more so as she rubbed the pad of her thumb back and forth across it.

"You need to leave, Matilda. This room. Right now." His voice rough, though he bowed over her, spoke the words softly against her temple.

"I know it is absurd, but I want to know you're well, that you'll not sink into misery."

"I—"

"No. You should not have to be miserable." Her hand became a manacle on his wrist. "Do not marry if it does not please you."

"You must leave, *now*, Matilda."

She did not.

His hand turned twisted out of her grip only to grasp her hand, twine their fingers together. "If you do not leave, Matilda, I will ensure a lack of misery. For us both. At least for the next hour or so."

Her heart beat hard against her ribs.

"I have spent ten days riding hard, trying to forget what you taste like under moonlight, trying to become better acquainted with women I don't care for and who do not care for me, agonizing over what I don't want and what I do. Do you know why I've returned home unsuccessful?"

She shook her head, and he leaned so near her, the slight movement brought his lips up against her forehead. Her heart missed a beat, and he hissed, his body tightening, his weaving so strongly with hers, he might never let go.

"No." Of course she did not know.

"I left because I was jealous. Of Atlas. Of his time spent with you. So I gathered an entire crop of damn apples for you because I wanted to be near you when you finally did it—gave into superstition. And Mother tells me you're *with Atlas* in here, and *my apples*, and I ran, Matilda. I ran to find you and to plant Atlas a facer if necessary. Not bloody thinking, was I?"

No reason to answer that, and he didn't seem to want an answer anyway. He nudged his nose into her hair at her temple and simply breathed for several moments.

"There is no reason," she said, "for you to be jealous of Lord Atlas. I do not view him in any sort of amorous way." My, what a speech when words flitted away from her like nervous birds from a branch before a storm. But these words had seemed imperative to say. "Neither does he view me that way."

Raph exhaled and released her hand.

But not her.

His arms wound round her, and he dropped his face into the curve of her shoulder and neck, nodding, as if reassuring himself of the veracity of her words. He lifted his head just a bit so his lips brushed against her ear. "Leave this room, Matilda. Because I want you more than is practical. I want you against the bookshelf and on the rug. I want you in the chair and in the window seat. I want to strip you bare and kiss every damn inch of you, and make you scream my name, and if you don't leave, I will. I swear I'll give up every damn thing for one more taste of you. Leave, because I am a man who has lived in ruin most of his life, and I will gladly go there again for you. I will lay waste to everything I've earned for the feel of your lips against mine." He kissed her temple, punctuation for his final words. "Leave. Now."

Leave him? When she was where she'd dreamed of being every night since his absence? Leave him when she didn't have to look into a mirror or eat an apple to know who she wanted, who her soul called out to? She'd have to leave him. Eventually.

Today, this very moment, if she sought to bring the pleasure of her dreams and her own wandering fingers to life in the welcome embrace of his arms, he'd let her. He would not stop what she wished to do. Leave?

She went up on tiptoe and kissed him, softly, eyes closed, every other bit of her body on and open and begging him to deepen it. "No," she whispered into the kiss. "I'll not leave. Not today."

His arms became chains around her and his tongue parted her lips and swept into her mouth as he hugged her so tight, her feet nearly left the ground.

Then they did leave the ground. He picked her up like a child, and she held on tight, arms around his neck, lips clinging to his, and their bodies sank together. Onto what? Who cared. He kissed her still, one of his strong arms supporting her back, the other finding her ankle and exploring upward, over calf and knee, branding her inner thigh with a splayed hand, hot and seeking ever higher.

"You should have said no, Matilda."

"I'll say no later. Just kiss me now, and"—she fit her hand over his, her skirts between their skin, and she dragged that hand higher until his fingers touched her just where they had in her dreams, until his head rolled back on his neck with a moan that pitched her own pleasure higher—"we can say no later."

They'd have to. Later, they would both be strong. But they'd been strong so long they were brittle, warped and weathered by time and responsibility and burdens. And loneliness. And here in this dream moment, breathless and beautiful, they could let all that go. Kiss each other into a rebirth, and hope that when the tight, twisting pleasure surging through her—the very sensation lifting her higher than the beaten roof, as high as the clouds and spiraling off into the stars—finally broke, as she knew it must, it would remake her strong enough to resist him. But no resisting now. Later.

His hand explored her, stroked her, pleased her, and she pulled his head up from where it rested on the back of their chair, his jaw hard and eyes closed. She kissed that jaw until it softened, kissed his eyes until they opened, and then she held his gaze, refused to give it up until he slanted his lips across hers and drank from her deeply, his tongue stroking into her mouth as his fingers stroked inside of her.

"I'll give you something all your own." His voice gruff and low so only she could hear. "And I'll take for myself as well. Your moan in my ear—mine forever. We can pretend it never happened after this, that it was a dream, but by God, I'll make it a dream you return to every night." His fingers worked between her legs, parting and stroking, his thumb frantic but meticulous at that little pulsing bud.

"I dreamed of this," she panted. Waking and sleeping.

His thumb found the buzzing center of pleasure at her core and circled it.

Barely able to speak, she fisted her hands in his hair and arched against his palm. "I'll always dream of this."

His thumb ever circling, he slipped one finger inside her, then another, and she clung to him, needing her breasts against his chest, needing *him*. And he must have needed her, too, because he crashed her to him so tight, the arm at her back a steel bar, pinning her. But not a prison. A heaven as her body fell apart, as he gave her a reason to need him more. As if she needed another. And this one crashed waves of pleasure against her, through her. She wrapped her arms tight around his neck as she shook, kissing every bit of skin she could reach.

And as her muscles became heavy as the ocean, he cradled her in his arms and said, "I've dreamed of it, too."

His words should have increased her pleasure, rocked her high into happiness, but they turned a summer-blue sky to winter gray, and she pressed her forehead to his chest, closed her eyes, and held back tears.

Seventeen

Raph stared at the blank canvas in his painting room and tried to forget their tryst—too short and hot, too perfect—and all the places he'd told Matilda he wanted her. A partial list only, but they needed forgetting, too, because now that he'd felt her body shatter beneath his hand, now that he'd kissed her as she'd moaned her pleasure, those mere imaginings had come to vivid life.

He'd left out of his list the ways that mattered most, though, the more dangerous forms of wanting. He wanted her beside him during the days and nearby during the evenings. He wanted to pick her brain and lean on her, to help him shatter a few plates when he was angry and teach him the color of emotions when he was too confused to understand anything but the basics.

A greater danger than any poverty he'd ever faced—the poverty of life once Matilda left.

Yet he still itched to run after her, to make sure she wasn't near Atlas, to find her and walk with her, to ask about her cottage. Had she ever visited it? Did she have plans to change it? Would she be lonely there? How close was the nearest neighbor? What would she do if she were injured or ill?

Horrid plan, really, to seclude oneself like that. She shouldn't do it. She was too intelligent to do it.

But she wanted a home, and damn everything, he wanted her to have one.

He splashed a brush into brown paint and drew a square on the canvas. Then more squares, smaller this time, and soon he had a child's approximation of a house. Briarcliff but cottage sized.

Once she left, he'd never have reason to contact her again. All these years, he'd had reason—to check up on the young woman his family had failed, to help her when he could in any means possible. But she wouldn't need his help any longer. He slashed through the house with a blobby wet brush.

An exclamation—half scream, half wail—floated down the hall.

Bollocks. Not again. Thought they were past the wailing.

Raph didn't run this time. Mother had friends around her now. When he came to her sitting room, he flung open the door, bracing himself for the sight of Matilda comforting his mother.

"Are you well?" he asked, his gaze swinging everywhere, finding no one. "Are you hurt?" His mother beamed up at him from her writing desk where she sat. Alone. "Where are Lady Pratsby and Miss Bellvue?"

"Matilda is taking a walk, I'm told, and Jane is napping." She stood in a flurry of flounces and bounced toward him, waving a piece of unfolded paper in his face. "I am so glad you're here, Raphael. Look. Just read. Maggie has *done it*. She has won her father's inheritance." She shoved something else beneath his nose—a bit of fine silk, heavily embroidered.

Raph took the cloth between finger and thumb. It was a

lovely soft yellow, and the embroidery made a repeating pattern of daffodils. His sister's design? Her work of art?

He raised a brow. "Flowers?"

"Yes." His mother stared dreamily at the square, her orange turban listing to one side. "Your sister has designed a silk with your father's favorite flower."

"I did not know father's favorite flowers were daffodils." But he had known his favorite animal to be the bear. They'd pretend to be bears when he was little, fishing with paws and climbing into bear dens to sleep for the winter.

"Oh, it might not be, but he always told Maggie it was. It was special for them. He found her one day after she ran off. She was hiding in a field of them, and he told her"—she swallowed hard and pressed a fluttering hand to her belly—"that of course he'd find his two favorites keeping one another company."

Raph's heart restricted, shrunk to the size of a cherry pit. He'd had special moments with his father once, too, but not since the day he'd discovered the ruin of their finances. He'd been embarrassed and flustered but happy to let Raph take control. Beneath his shamefaced red cheeks and slouched shoulders, he'd looked on Raph with a spark of pride. Raph would never forget his words: "I have not been the best marquess, but I have tried to be a loving father. I am proud of you. You will be, are, better than me."

The words had enraged Raph then. How could he claim to be a loving father when he'd ruined them all for his own amusement, when he'd been so careless?

Yet ... that pride. Damn, how he'd wanted it. Still did.

He slammed a door closed on that thought. "You're going to give Maggie her inheritance now?"

His mother nodded. "And she may do with it as she pleases." She sniffed. "Even if that is selling it and giving the money to you."

That had been the plan. They'd all agreed. One by one, they'd earn their inheritance, sell it off, and pour the funds into the estate.

"I must write to Zander." Only he would know the value of Maggie's inheritance once the painting she'd won was revealed.

"Oh!" She bounced to her feet. "Will he be coming, do you think? For a visit? Perhaps he'll arrive in time for the harvest celebration. Wouldn't that be perfection! Since you won't allow me any guests. And perhaps he and Matilda will take to one another and then—"

Raph left. Not the polite thing to do, but he'd rather walk straight into hell on his own two feet than listen to his mother pair off Matilda with his brothers.

Atlas ran down the hallway, breathless, face white with panic. "I heard Mother. Is she—"

"Fine. Maggie has earned her inheritance, and it sent her into histrionics." He strode past Atlas.

Atlas kept up with him easily, long legs settling into a calm stride behind him. "That's excellent."

"We'll use the money to hire new servants, employ the villagers, bring their families home."

"Yes." They jolted down the stairs together, and when they stopped at the bottom, Atlas spoke soft words with a blank face tilted toward the vaulted ceiling. "Sometimes I feel Father isn't buried far enough down. Other times I ... miss him." He snorted. "Doesn't deserve it. But ... do you remember that time he took us out in the rowboat and we pretended to be pirates? He never broke the game all day long. Tucked us into bed with an eye patch on. And when I enlisted, he cried." Atlas licked his lips, paused, then continued. "Said he was proud of me but also scared to lose me."

Raph remembered it all and wished he didn't. Would be

so much easier to hate the man if could forget all his kindnesses.

"No." Raph left his brother, cutting right when Atlas went outside, letting in a wind that wrapped a promise of winter around him. He found the study and prepared a pen and soon had a letter folded and franked to send to Lysander. Zander would know the price and the person who would pay it. Maybe then, money in hand, they could begin to heal.

Eighteen

⟡

The sun rose early the day of the harvest celebration and remained bright and happy from sunup to sundown. But despite the weather's cheerful glow, by the end of the day, Matilda felt ready to jump right from her skin. She needed to run or swim across the lake and back. Or have another session beneath Raph's clever fingers.

She'd not seen him, though. Not since their encounter in the library. Likely, he'd been busy bringing in the harvest. But also likely, he was avoiding her. As she should him. But avoidance did not tame the imagination, and hers seemed particularly determined to fixate on Raph. Amongst the others harvesting the crops, shirtless and sweaty.

She should not let her mind wander such directions. Now was the time for *no* if the day in the library had not been. She focused instead on the preparations. And as the sun set low on the horizon, a chill slipped into the air. A fog accompanied it, rolling the day into an early autumn evening. She watched from her bedchamber window as men from the village, Tom included, arrived at Briarcliff hauling wood. Raph and his mother had decided that though they could not host a large party offering food and cider or wine, they could host the bonfire. Flower crowns had been made, and Jane and Franny had organized games for the children. There would be dancing beneath the stars. A celebration, indeed.

Matilda pushed open her trunk and pulled out her mother's shawl. She packed it away every summer and pulled it out again every autumn. She wrapped it around her shoulders and checked her image in the mirror. A red gown the color of a newly fallen leaf and the cream-colored shawl paired well together. Her curls bounced about, unruly things, and more so than usual because she'd woven the crown Franny had made for her into the plait she'd wound round the top of her head. A very rural coiffure. She looked well, though. It suited her. On the outside, she appeared merry, ready for an evening of diversion. On the inside, she felt wiggly and wanting.

She'd never do it. Never banish her need, never be able to ignore the call of her soul to his. Nor did she wish to. She wanted Raph's kiss, his touch, his wild words, and she'd denied herself so much for so long.

Why deny herself this? Him?

She would soon leave. She would likely not marry, and hadn't Jane been telling her that she would need warm memories to help her survive the cold Cumbrian nights? She had one. Why not make others?

Why not?

He clearly felt some attraction for her. And he gave so much to everyone else that it made him quite grouchy quite often. But there was a softness once one scratched below that grouchy surface, a willingness to give everything. That willingness turned Matilda's affection into something *more*. She had often spent her years giving to those who needed it. Well, he needed some comfort now, didn't he? He was grieving many things wasn't he? And there was more than one way to comfort a human. They both would benefit from giving in.

Why not?

The risk of a babe.

The corners of her lips turned up. Her heart thought a babe no risk at all, though her brain knew better. Because she would have to tell him, and he would insist on marrying her, and that marriage would ruin him, ruin all his hard work. He needed a wealthy wife, and she could not do that. But still there were obviously other ways to gain pleasure without taking such a risk. She knew that from her books. And she knew that from the kisses they'd shared.

Why not?

Her door flew open, and Jane flew in. She grabbed Matilda by the hand and pulled her out.

"No running," Matilda lectured. "Your knees, Jane, your *knees*."

"*Bah*. I feel young as a spring lamb today. Come along. We'll not miss any of the festivities."

Matilda laughed and let the older woman drag her away down the stairs and out of the house, but as soon as they were outside, she lost her to the crowd. People had already arrived, and Franny greeted them with a wide grin on her face but a shyness in her eyes. Matilda could not help but smile and feel a bit of pride that she would not be leaving Franny as wrecked by grief and loss as she'd found her.

A raucous bout of laughter seemed to split the sky, and following the sound, she found him. Raph looked newly showered, his hair damp and curling at the ends, his shirt crisp and clean. As if he could feel her gaze on him, his head turned a bit, and he saw her. Something flashed bright in his eyes then he turned his back to her.

That ... hurt. Like a knife in the hand. But the pain lasted just a breath, leaving her with her next exhale, the following inhale pulled in irritation to fill her to brimming. Kiss her then cut her, would he?

Oh, she knew every reason under the autumn sky for him to have done that. He'd told her very convincing ones. And the ones he had not spoken out loud were even more convincing. He needed money. She had none.

But after his kisses, she needed something a bit more ... feral. A wildness had grown inside her, and his look, his touch only could tame it. Or grow to more rampant proportions.

Why not?

She stalked toward him, tapped him on the shoulder.

He stiffened, as if he knew who she was without seeing her, but he turned around, bowed. "Miss Bellvue. You are looking"—his eyes flared bright—"lovely this evening." He scowled. "I know that shawl. You've worn it before. When you were here the first time. You've nothing newer?"

"It was my mother's."

"Ah. Would you like a new one?"

She shook her head. "May I speak with you, my lord? About something other than shawls?"

His eyes widened just a bit, and he crossed his arms over his chest. "That request had the edge of a command in it." She lifted a brow, challenging him further. "There's much to do here."

"And many hands to do the work, my lord. I ask only a minute or so of your time." She turned and walked away from the crowd, rounding the house to find semiprivacy in the gardens. She did not look back to see if he followed, but she felt the heavy heat of his gaze on her neck. He followed, of that she was sure.

When the rumble of the gathering revelers receded to a hum, she whipped around to face him. She clenched her hands in her skirts and swallowed her fear. "Why not, my lord? I have not been able to rid myself of that question. It has haunted me so that I have finally, possibly against my better judgment, decided to put the question to you. Why not?"

"Why not ... what?"

"Why not give in to the attraction between us? Just for a night. A single moment in time during which you live like a man who can take something, someone, for himself instead of for others. And during which I enjoy human companionship the like of which I'll likely never experience again."

In the gathering evening light, his cheeks flushed, and the boy in him returned with that heat—open and flustered and the tiniest bit soft.

"Are you propositioning me?" he asked.

"I suppose I am. Perhaps I have read things between us wrong, but I do not think I have. You have told me yourself that—"

"I want you, Matilda."

Now heat washed over *her*. To hear him say it so brazenly, as if it were as much a fact as the color of the sky above lit a fire of desire in her that would not soon be doused.

He strode closer, reached for her, and the warmth of his knuckles brushed her cheek if his actual skin did not before he dropped his hand to his side. "But it is the worst idea to give in. 'Why not?' Because I am a gentleman, and I do not ruin innocent ladies."

"I will not be ruined. I will be the better for it."

"You could become with child."

"We could take precautions, could we not? What we've already done will not put me in a delicate position."

He shook his head. "If I let you into my bed I will never let you out again."

"Then we shall retire to *my* bed, my lord."

He laughed. "God, you're a temptation." He did touch her then, his hand cupping her neck and his fingers spearing into the hair at her nape. He lowered, as if to kiss her, their lips almost touching, his tongue darting out to wet his lip.

"Why not take one night where you do not deny yourself?

I offer it of my own will and for my own selfish reasons. It will not impugn your honor as a gentleman."

He inhaled, exhaled deeply. "I made a fuss." There was a grumble in his voice. "But you were right. This is good. The celebration, everyone at Briarcliff and Fairview coming together. It feels right. Healing. Thank you." An evasion of her question.

"Thank your mother, my lord."

He grunted. "I will." His shoulders, bowed like a tree curved by heavy snow, haunted her. She wanted to see them straight and strong.

Why not?

"Will you answer me?"

"Not yet."

"Will you at least dance with me later? About the fire?"

His breath seemed to catch in his throat, and when he spoke, his words came out rough. "I do not think that a wise idea. It may … appear a declaration."

Ah. She understood. While he could give her a night, several perhaps, he could not give her forever, a declaration of a life spent together.

She reached up and plucked a flower from her hair. She approached him slowly and circled him as if they danced. When she stood before him, she slipped the flower into the small pocket of his waistcoat. She patted the hard plane of muscle over his chest and tilted her face up to him. "There," she said in a bold flirtation. "I cannot claim you. At least let me have this." Let her claim him in secret.

He nodded, a tight bob of the head, the only movement possible in a body wound tight as his was. He strode around her and walked away, growing the distance between them with each step that brought him closer to the gathered crowd. What would his answer be?

Matilda found the nearest bench, weather beaten and half

broken, to support her heavy weight, her tingling limbs. She sat there long enough for the sky to darken from cobalt to navy, stars peeking out of the heavens in places. Part of her longed to join the others, to joke and laugh. But she sat where she was, on the edge of joy, watching as she always did, as everyone else lived. She was being silly. She should not let disappointment wrap her tight. He'd not said no yet. But it held her in its gloomy clutches anyway, and as the men stacked log upon log for the bonfire, as the children ran races and earned prizes from Franny's hand, Matilda watched and did not cry.

There was that one tear, but she wiped it quickly away. Likely not even the thorns on the dying vine beside her saw it.

"Matilda?" A voice, deep and gruff but lyrical from behind her.

She turned around and offered a wobbly smile. "Lord Atlas. I thought I saw you with the others, stacking logs."

"I was, but Mother sent me to look for you. She saw you disappear with Raph. Then Raph returned but you did not. We were worried."

"Oh, do not worry over me. I am made of stout stuff."

"Yes, anyone could see that. But even stout hearts need others to worry for them now and then."

She did not argue that because it felt true, and it felt good to know that when she'd disappeared, others had looked for her. Would they miss her, as she would miss them, when she went home?

Home? She'd never even visited the small cottage. Would it ever feel like home? With the new curtains and books, her knickknacks, and her mother's shawl. When all was set out and arranged to her liking, would it then feel like home—comfortable and warm and lively? Or would it feel empty and lonely and cold?

She pressed her eyes closed to ward off a tear she'd have to hide from Atlas as well as from her neighboring thorns and vines.

He held a hand out to her. "They are about to light the bonfire. Would you like to dance?"

She hesitated to take his hand. He was a handsome man. The scar slashing down his face did nothing to mar his deep, bright eyes and firm, chiseled mouth. But his face was not the one she saw when she closed her eyes, his hand not the one she imagined smoothing down the curves of her body when she lay in bed alone.

Yet she counted him among her friends, and she would not mope when tonight meant such success, such hope for the future. She took his hand and let him pull her to her feet. "Yes, I would like that very much."

He grinned and pulled her across the lawn into the growing dark just as the bonfire took blaze. Together, they laughed and ran toward it, a calling flame she would warm herself by. Tomorrow, she would begin arranging her departure. But tonight ... tonight she would burn bright and dance until the ground beneath her feet melted away, and she floated into the hazy stars above.

She danced and spun and laughed, and all the while felt Raph's gaze on her, felt his hard regard sizzling across her skin. She imagined it was his touch instead. And as long as she danced, he stood on the edge of the light, watching.

Nineteen

M atilda smiled at everyone except for Raph. She whirled from hand to hand, each man jigging her about, but always returning to Atlas, who grinned down at her like a lovestruck fool. If he was in love, no wonder. Every man here should be. She was joy incarnate, a wild fairy caught and teaching them the ways of fire.

He wanted to dance with her, to touch her, to be burned. She'd asked him to dance with her in every way conceivable. A night out of time just for them two. And he'd refused to answer her. Even though he knew his answer.

He threw back a cup of cider and almost gagged at the sweetness. An excellent brew, but too sweet for his mood. He wanted bitter. He wanted burning.

He wanted her.

Instead, she danced in the arms of his jovial brother. Jovial? Atlas? He should be glad to see something on his brother's brow other than violent memories and worry for the future. Instead, he wanted to run his brother through with a sharp implement. Matilda whirled about the fire, flitting from man to man, as all the women were, really, but always back to

Atlas, as if he were that home she wanted so badly. Atlas whirled her away from Raph, finding the other side of the fire.

Raph's jaw turned to stone, and his teeth ached. He wanted to be her home. If only for one night.

He didn't step through the fire, but he felt as hot as if he had as he circled it, chased her, took her hand as she threw her head back in a laugh cut silent as soon as skin met skin.

"Raph," she said, her voice hoarse with some thick emotion.

"Dance with me." He leaned low until his lips brushed her ear. "And only me."

She caught her breath and held it but did not try to wiggle free of his hold. She melted into him, and like pouring wine into a crystal cup, she fit perfectly in his arms. He waltzed her around the fire until the world became a blur, the only solid, clear bit of it her face, her hands on his body, her eyes full of merriment and curiosity and something stronger just for him. A fiddle player slowed the melody and swept starlight round the dancers, but Raph continued waltzing, ducked his head close.

"We should not be so close," she said.

"You should not be dancing with Atlas like you were."

"Harmless. I—"

"Do not dance with him again," Raph growled.

"My." Her voice barely a whisper, and a husky one at that. "How very possessive of you."

He tightened his grip on her hand and shifted his other hand lower on her back. "Yes." All she needed to know. Tonight he possessed her, but also ... "I am yours, Matilda. If you are mine. Tonight."

A laugh bubbled up, sounding a touch nervous, so he waltzed her away from the flame's light and into the darkness to kiss her doubt into determination, and when the night swallowed them whole, he took her hand and ran for the gardens.

"Where are we going?" she hissed, standing in the dark just inside the door. "Where are we?"

"My bedroom. Yours. Doesn't matter." He grabbed her to him and pinned her against the wall of the house. Vines curled up it at her back on either side, slipping into her hair as he tangled their fingers together on the wall by her head and kissed her hard. He kissed down her neck, licked between her breasts, and rocked his hips against her with a groan. "Might not make it that far. Damn." He wouldn't take her outside for anyone to discover. She was his tonight. He flung open the door he knew well, nestled into the brick a few inches from her back, and pulled her through. Good enough.

He slipped to the fireplace, found the tinder box, and set the grate ablaze. She blinked in the new light.

"Ah." She rubbed her hands up and down her arms, her shawl trailing off one shoulder. "Are we calling it the Purgatory Parlor today? Or the Chamber of Horrors?"

"Tonight? Tonight, let's call it the Parlor of Pleasure." He decimated the distance between them in three long strides, cupped her face in his hands, and kissed her long and slow as he walked her backward across the room until her legs hit a couch and she fell onto it with a gasp.

"I can't wait for a bedroom, Matilda."

She clutched at his shoulders, tugged at his cravat. "Don't."

He hit his knees before her and wrapped his hands around her hips, pulled her to the edge of the couch.

"Stay," he ordered.

And she did, wrapping her hands around the edge of the cushions.

He grinned at her as he reached for the hem of her gown. "Good girl."

She arched an eyebrow. "I'm not a girl. And I'm only good when I decide to be."

"I know. It's marvelous." He lifted her hem high, revealing the wool stockings he'd explored so thoroughly earlier.

"What are you—" She swallowed hard. "What are you doing?"

"Exploring the curves of your legs." He ran his hand up her calves. "And testing the warmth of your stockings." He untied one garter and then the other and slid those stockings down her legs.

She shivered. "And?"

"And I'm going to kiss you." He spread her legs wider, wide enough for his shoulders to fit between them. He placed a kiss on the inside of one thigh, right above the knee.

She gripped the cushions tighter. "I've ... I've seen illustrations. I've ... I've read ..."

"Have you? Well now you shall *know*. And *do*." He lifted his head to catch her gaze, and caught her chin as well, holding her steady so she could not look away. "If I have only one night, I'll fit all of them into it. Do you understand?"

"Yes." Then something like mischief blazed through the fog of lust in her eyes, and she jerked her head free, turned it, caught the tip of his thumb between her teeth and sucked it into her mouth.

His cock tightened, and his heart began to beat a frantic pace to the rhythm of tonight. One night. *Our night.*

She grazed her teeth slowly down the digit, then released it. He surged up to kiss her mouth once more before ducking to kiss her in every other way and wrapping his hands around her hips once more. Wool hiding curves should not be so seductive, but he was done for, wound tight and needy. He placed a line of heated promises down the inside of one thigh until his breath warmed the core of her. She shivered with pleasure or perhaps with the foreignness of the sensation in so intimate a place, but he shivered with the anticipation of touching her and tasting her.

She smelled sweet and sultry, and he nipped at her inner thigh as one hand wandered lower, teasing the soft flesh of her belly, sweetly rounded to perfection, then trailing downward, finding the slit between her legs and probing with cautious fingers. If she jerked away from his touch or asked him to stop, he would, but hell, he hoped she didn't.

She flinched a bit, hissed, and he paused, but then she moaned and melted, and he let his fingers explore further, finding her nub. She'd told him once a kiss could be art. He'd show her just how much that was true, give her something of beauty to take home with her.

A pang sliced through him, so he put notions of home aside. Tonight, their night. Nothing else existed outside it, so he kissed her, and when her hands shot away from the cushions to pull at his hair in a fiery, tangled tug, he grinned against her core and did it again. The taste of her curled his nails into her thighs. He didn't want to hurt her, so he flexed them, flattened his palms against soft skin.

She raked her nails against his forearms. Wool and linen protected him, but he felt their points driving him on, sinking his own blunt nails once more into flesh so that she called out a single affirmation.

"Yes."

He kissed the desire that had leapt high as she'd danced around the bonfire against her thighs and higher—against her sweet, damp core. His need raged hotter than the flames outside, curling smoking tendrils of desire across every inch of skin and blood and bone. His wide shoulders between her thighs pressed her legs open, and he took full advantage of the space, teasing with his fingers and licking, sipping, sucking with mouth and tongue.

Her breaths came heavy as her hands reached for him

wherever they could touch. "Pictures. Books." Each words a difficulty. "Cannot ... *convey*. Don't stop."

As if he possessed the ability to do so.

He smoothed a hand up the top of her thigh, under her skirts, around her hip, slipping between her body and the couch to cup her rear and squeeze. She arched her back, and he dug his fingertips into her flesh, pressed the thumb of his other hand into that little nub between her legs that made her writhe. She liked it. And tonight, his only responsibility was to give her what she liked. So he kissed her and teased her until her body wept, her mouth issued a cry—his name—and the heat he'd been boiling in her sparked into fireworks.

He teased her more slowly then, until her rigid, arched body melted into the cushions, and then he left the heaven between her legs to gather her boneless body in his arms and onto his lap as he held her tight against his body. His cock strained against his fall, his own need still a blade within him. But he'd hold her for a while, until at least, she floated back to him from that foggy place she'd drifted to. He'd sent her to.

"I never knew," she said, the words like those of a man who'd drunk two glasses of wine too many. "How marvelous" —she stretched the word out, earning a kiss on the top of her head—"it could feel. Not until the library. Until now." She nuzzled her nose into his chest. "Once will not be enough I'm afraid." A note of sorrow, there, a foreshadowing of the future.

Not tonight.

He lifted her chin with his knuckles until their gazes met in the shadowy light. "Once? Hardly. Dear heart, I'll bring you to the apex of pleasure as many times as I can before the dawn comes."

She pushed upright, hands flat on his chest, her body nudging against the hard, ready length of him, making him grit his teeth. "Again? Can we really? I've read in books ... but books and life, especially *these books*, are often not particularly related to one another."

"And there's more to be done than what we just did. If we're creative. While I cannot create art, I'm particularly imaginative in other areas of life."

She peered up at him with a scowl. "We both know I'm a virgin, but I have no doubt about your ... status. Do you have a mistress?"

"Do you think I have the funds to keep a mistress, Matilda? It has been close to fifteen years since I've touched a woman as I have you."

"That long?"

He nipped her earlobe. "That long. I cannot sleep with anyone in Fairworth. And I do not have the money for London brothels. Neither do I have the time for London widows."

She drew a finger down the line of his jaw. "Poor Raph."

He chuckled. "I've learned to take myself well in hand."

Her scowl returned. "Do you mean ...?"

He took her hand and placed it atop his cock—a pain, a pleasure, to have her there. "Like this, Matilda. But me."

Her fingers stilled, then tightened, then she stroked her fingernails lightly down the bulge at his fall. "Ah. This feels good then?"

He nodded, swallowed hard.

"You've had no pleasure yet," she said.

"Holding you is the most perfect pleasure I can think of."

A shy grin slipped across her face, replaced with the very tip of her pink tongue, licking her lips. "I thought you said you were imaginative, Raph." She placed her lips next to his ear and whispered, "You mentioned bookshelves and chairs and window seats. But what about beds?"

They could be more imaginative than that, too, but to hell

with creativity. He needed to be inside her, to know she was his.

He slung her over his shoulder as she stood and carried her out of the room. If there was time enough between them, he'd do everything their imaginations could devise. But with only one night, creativity could hang. He wanted only her, only the closeness of two bodies, the closeness of two souls.

She laughed and wrapped her arms around his waist as he carted her up the stairs. "Don't drop me!"

Drop her? He swatted her bottom then took the stairs two at at time. "Never."

If it were up to him, he'd never let her go.

Twenty

Raph had just swatted her bottom as if she were a recalcitrant child. And she'd enjoyed it. She'd enjoyed everything he'd done, every time he touched her. And there was to be more. For him, too. She ached to make him feel as light and lovely as he'd made her feel, to be the maker of his pleasure.

He pushed open a door and she entered a room upside down until he set her on her feet. She spun and clung to him for balance, and the room stopped spinning and the shadows gave way to detail.

"My room," she said.

"Was closest," he grunted.

She threw the window curtains wide to see the bonfire rising high into the sky. Laughter echoed up to them.

"I think your mother is dancing with Tom. And look, Jane is holding the baby."

He joined her at the window and stole his hand into hers. He threaded their fingers together, raised them, and kissed her knuckles.

"Your family is happy tonight, Raph," she said. And she

imagined it was their family, a blooming flower of a thought that she turned from quickly. She left his side and bustled about the room, stoking a fire and lighting candles before turning to him once more.

"Well? I'm afraid you're going to have to lead this particular endeavor because though your experience is perhaps dusty, mine is nonexistent."

He didn't look at her, though. He gazed about the room, mouth slightly open, arms slack at his side. "I'm fairly certain the room did not begin this way."

She looked about, too, at the curtains, the books lined across her trunk, the small clock she'd put on the mantel, the blankets she'd piled on the bed, the scarves she'd hung from the bedpost, and the watercolors she'd mounted on the walls. The collected items of her life since leaving home, the way she brought home with her wherever she went.

"I will, of course, take it all down when I leave," she said, her fingers fidgeting with her wrinkled skirts. "I like to have familiar things about me when I'm in a new place."

"Tell me about them."

"Now?" Didn't he want to spend more time doing and less time talking?

He stalked toward her, his blue eyes dark and deep and starless. No. He wanted what he said he did. More, too, but somehow the talking was the difficult bit. The man rarely got what he wanted, though, so she would give him what she could.

"Come, then," she said. "We'll go in chronological order. Everything is a story, you see, a bit of my life in physical form." She led him to the vanity and picked up a small carved box there. "This, you see, is from my girlhood. Besides clothes, it is one of the few things I brought with me to Briarcliff all those years ago." She opened it, and it sprang into musical life briefly before the tinkling tune died out. "I could wind it, but the mechanism is precarious. Sometimes I'm blessed with a note or two."

"A music box."

"A gift from my mother for my tenth birthday. She died not long after, along with the child she was giving birth to."

His hand stole around her neck, and his thumb rubbed comfort into her skin.

She reached into the box and pulled forth a silver chain with a teardrop pearl at its end.

"I've seen you wear that. When you were here the first time."

"You remember a necklace from fifteen years ago?"

He shrugged. "It was around your neck."

No clear way to respond to that, so she held the necklace up. "It's from my father for my sixteenth birthday. He died two years later."

She replaced the necklace, closed the box, and moved on to the next object, a series of watercolors with thick black outlines of every object. "These were done by your sister when I first came here. I think she preferred to sketch than to watercolor, and she gave these to me before I left." They were of Briarcliff and the surrounding lands. "She wanted me to remember this place."

"I remember her making them for you. I thought it silly until you left. Then I was glad to have *something* to give you, since I could not pay your wages."

Her heart thumped out a rhythm only he seemed able to encourage. "You gave me more than you think." A whispered admission. She wished he'd believe the truth of it.

She went around the room, touching each object, explaining it, to calm her heart and explain herself to him. "The blankets are from a family I was governess for. The clock from the first woman I was companion to. The books are presents from Jane. And the curtains are new. I bought them for my cottage. Do you like them?"

He pinched the edge of the fabric between his finger and thumb. "They're sturdy."

"Their color is better shown off in the sunlight." She wrapped her arms around her waist. She loved her things, her little reminders of where she'd been. They always made her feel at home, no matter where she roamed. But under his gaze they felt insubstantial, a game of pretend to a man who'd always had a home.

"It may seem silly to you, but—"

"It does not seem silly. Nothing about you is silly to me. I want to know every corner of you." He cupped his hand around her jaw and brushed his thumb across her lips, silencing her. Then he spun her, trailed his fingers along her back, down then up again, until he reached the tab of her gown, and he pulled it loose. Then the next and the next until the gown gapped and sagged, and her shoulders peeked out. With one large hand, he swept the shoulder of her gown down her arm and placed a kiss along the slope of her neck. "You will soon have everything you desire."

But what she desired was changing. When she closed her eyes, she no longer saw a secluded cottage, picturesque and silent but for the chirp of birds. She saw him. Him only. In the dark and in the light, smiling and glowering, ordering everyone about and worrying with a furrowed brow. Kissing her and touching her and making her want to stay.

Her gown fell to the floor, and she stepped out of it, turned to face him in nothing but stays and shift, her stockings having been abandoned downstairs. She pulled the end of his cravat, hastily and sloppily tied, and she unwrapped him until the dark, sinewy ropes of his neck fell open to her gaze. Then she dropped the linen to the floor and made short work of his waistcoat, tugged at his shirt and pulled it over his head, letting it fall into the pile of discarded clothing.

Bit by bit, she undressed him, peeling back layers hidden to everyone else, but she already knew what she'd find. A body that appealed to her fingertips, and a body that appealed to her heart, honed as it was by care and love, by determination and ambition. He'd cared for her earlier, kissed her where no one else had or likely ever would again.

Now she wanted to return the favor.

She'd never undone a man's garments before, but it had not so far proved too difficult. She flicked open a button of his fall, and it must have lifted him from some daze because he tangled his hands in her hair and crushed his mouth to hers. She worked at his buttons without thought or breath until he pushed away, tugged at her remaining clothing, his own, all their arms windmilling in every direction to strip themselves bare as soon as possible. His boots and stockings, gone; her stays, equally so. Her shift a torn bit of cloth on the floor over his boots. She shivered, naked, as she finally, *finally*, loosed his britches entirely. She pushed them down his hips, then stepped away to view him as he stepped out. He reached for her, and she danced away, fleeing to the window where she flung the curtains closed.

He caught her up in warm strong arms, pressing their bodies together. Nothing between them, every sensation new. "Will you tell me what to do and how to do it?" he growled in her ear.

"I was rather thinking you might order me about."

"Would you like that?"

"Yes." Heat pooled low in her belly, confirming her answer.

"When I lift you up, wrap your legs around me."

She didn't have time to ask questions because he lifted her body and she did as he'd demanded, finding the naked core of her pressed hot against the tight muscle of his abdomen. He held her as if she weighed nothing and nipped at her bottom lip. He carried her to the bed and laid her gently down. She unwound for him, feeling lonely until he rested the long, hard length of his body next to hers.

He ran fingertips lightly over her shoulder, down her arm, her hip, as far down her leg as his own arm length allowed, then back up the center of her, circling her belly button and cupping her breast. He dipped his head and kissed her nipple, and when he met her gaze once more, he wore a small smile.

"You are as beautiful as I knew you would be."

She flattened her hand against his chest. "You're a beautiful man. The strong muscle of you makes me want to touch, but what it says about you is even more beautiful. You built such a body giving your hours and desires to everyone around you, caring for them and shaping a future for them. That is beautiful, and that ... that is ..." What she loved about him. Not words she could say when only one night stretched thin between them. "I think you need to take something for yourself. I want you to take me. For yourself."

He buried his face in the crook of her neck, inhaled deeply, spoke into the warmth of her so she felt his words as much as heard them.

"I will."

Raph kissed her slowly, tenderly, as she explored the mountains and valleys of his muscle. His tongue slipped between her lips and made a slow exploration of its own. She met him and they tangled and got lost in one another for several breaths simply kissing and sighing and touching in a way so sweet Matilda's heart ached.

But the sweetness edged into something altogether different. And his hand, which had been kneading her breast, playing with her nipple, crept over her rib cage into the dip of her waist, smoothed over the flare of her hips, and then between her legs to that place he'd played with before. She knew what would come next, the feelings, at least, of ecstasy and release. As if in anticipation, her body began to tingle, and her hands left the hard beauty of his body to clutch at the sheets on either side of her.

She threw her head back and lengthened her neck, hoping his lips would find the pulse there that she ached for him to kiss, and when he did not, she placed her hand at the cup of his skull and dragged his head down where she wanted it. He kissed and nipped there while he slipped a finger inside of her. She gasped, and he kept kissing and added another finger. She tightened around him, every feeling shooting through her, new yet familiar.

How long had she wanted this? Since she'd eaten an apple and seen him in the mirror behind her? Since his gentle, angry kiss? Since the day she saw him naked at the lake? Since the moment he stepped into Jane's sitting room and asked for her help? Longer. God help her, longer. How was a sheltered girl, alone in the world and scared supposed to meet a man like him, still rather a boy himself, angry and alone, and not fall a little bit in love?

So very long, then. And their bodies together now a blessed culmination of desire and want. Every sensation new, but she'd been waiting for it for so long, every sensation felt exactly right.

She dragged him closer, and he chuckled into her pulse, and her pulse took on the dance of his mirth. She laughed when she should be moaning in ecstasy. But the laugh felt right, too. It felt good, as if they had both needed it. And when his mouth dropped away from her pulse and her neck to suckle at her breast, then she did gasp. And when his thumb flicked over that bud between her legs where all sensation gathered, she remembered. She had wanted to explore the hidden center of him, too.

She broke the trance of his ministrations and found herself pinned. Pleasantly so, yes, but no way to slip curious hands between heated bodies. So she pressed her palms against his chest, a movement which threatened to undo her entirely. She'd always realized she'd enjoyed the sight of muscled thighs —particularly Raph's muscled thighs—in tight buckskins ... but a chest? She'd not given much thought to it. Except that day at the lake. Except for now. Why not stay pinned and explore the wide expanse of muscle so near her lips, kiss the burning skin, press her ear close to hear his heartbeat.

No. She had a mission and would not be distracted. She flattened her palms and shoved. But he did not move. A mountain, he was. So she pushed again, and he lifted his head from her breast and gave her a quizzical stare.

"Yes?" he asked.

"Roll over."

"Giving orders again, Matilda."

"Yes. Roll over."

"Yes, dear heart. Happy to follow your wishes." His lips curled into a delicious grin. "But I've a command for you as well." He lowered his nose and mouth to her neck, her ear, and inhaled deeply, then whispered, "Don't stop touching me."

"Gladly."

He rolled onto his back, and she missed the feel of him immediately, so she rolled over with him, and for several wonderfully warm seconds lay atop him, toe to toe and lip to lip. She kissed him, unable to discern any other option, sweeping her tongue into his mouth, slipping it out and biting his bottom lip.

But then she remembered.

She used the plains of his chest, all of rock and bone, to push herself upright. Remembering how she had wrapped her legs around his waist earlier, she straddled his thighs now.

"Marvelous thighs," she sighed. "As thick with muscle as the rest of you and ... more marvelous and curious than all of that which I ardently admire ..."

His hands wrapped around her thighs, his fingers digging into her skin before he flattened his palms and dragged them up and down her legs from hip to knee. "Does any other lady speak as boldly as you do?" He shook his head, his eyes full of fog and fire. "Forget I asked. I don't care about any other lady. Just you."

Words to unwind her entirely. Words to make her and ruin her, and if she were going to survive, she'd have to pack them up, explore them later from the small parlor of her cottage. When she was alone.

She dragged her gaze away from his dear, handsome face and the length of his sculpted torso to where his shaft jutted up between them. She did not ask permission. Perhaps she should have. Perhaps it was common courtesy, polite. But she did not think he would mind, and without a word, she touched the tip of her thumb to his shaft's tip, and then she leaned over, remembering how he had put his mouth on her. She kissed where her thumb had touched, dragging her fingers down the long length of him. Silky and soft, yet so like a blade beneath the skin. He hissed and arched, and then his hands found her wrists like manacles. He flipped her once more, pinning her again, this time covering the entire length of her body with his. No part of her remained unbranded by his touch.

She'd kept her wits about her while he'd flipped her and kept her hand curved around his shaft.

"Damn, Matilda," he said. "Damn. It has been fifteen years, and I want to sink into you *now*. Hard and fast. But I want this to be good for you, and I want you to be ready for it so there is no pain or as little as possible."

He slipped one hand between her head and the pillow and

fisted his fingers in her curls, tugging her head back and lengthening her neck before kissing a line of fire down her throat and between her breasts. The force of his hold on her hair piqued her desire higher than she'd ever felt it before. To know she could give herself fully and completely to this man, feel his teeth on the vulnerable arch of her throat and know he would not hurt her, that he would take care of her—that thought alone almost made her shatter. She trusted him in all ways and knew he would never let her down. He would never betray her.

So she stroked his hair over his ear and released his shaft to run her other hand up and down his back. "Raph," she said into the salty scent of his skin, "I trust you, and I want to give you what you need, what you want."

His hand caressed her waist from ribs to hip bone over and over again, carving out bits of her and replacing the practical flesh and bone with something bright consisting of stars and sparks as well as the aching need for him to be inside her. She clutched at his shoulders, sinking fingernails into skin.

His hand stopped its metronomic movement at her waist and shifted to her core. "Wet," he whispered into her ear. "Good."

She smoothed her hand lower, found the gentle rise of his backside and squeezed, urging him closer, wanting him as close as possible.

She knew the mechanics. She knew he would never be close enough until he was inside, as his fingers had been earlier. Heat wiggled through her, and she arched her hips against him. "Please, Raph. Must I make another request?"

"A command you mean."

"Yes. A command. Now, Raph." But she heard the begging in her own voice. The *now* could have very well been a *please*. The last time she begged was when her brother had kicked her out of the house. She thought to never do it again, but with this man, the one she trusted? "Please."

He did not betray her. He placed his shaft at her opening and lightly circled the nub pulsing between her legs. "I will go as slow as I can now, but I cannot promise slow later." He had begun to fill her as he spoke, and the sensation pushed all words away. She bit her lip and nodded, and he kissed her and kept kissing her, distracting her from the fullness, but not distracting her. What could possibly distract her from him coming to her completely, taking what she offered him. She almost stiffened when he reached the hilt, almost pushed him away when she felt the too-tightness clenching her muscles like iron bands.

Then, in the sweetest softest voice, his lips near her ear, he whispered, "Relax, dear heart. I will stop and wait until you are ready."

And those words made her ready, melted her into a state of relaxation that should have been impossible with the yearning desire building fire inside her body. She arched her hips to pull him completely into her.

"Hell," he hissed. "No. Heaven." He retreated, and she pulled him back to her, biting her fingernails into the skin of his back.

"Do not leave. I like you here."

"So do I, dear heart, but I must move. You will see. I'm going nowhere."

"Tell me."

"What you're feeling now becomes better when I move. It will spark hotter, gather fury, and ignite everything."

"Like before?" she asked, breathless.

"Better."

"Better?" She laughed. How could that be? But she trusted him, and she found they were already moving together in a slow retreat and return. "What do you need from me?"

Another demand. She could not stop being who she was, and his grin grew lazy and hot and possessive every time she made a demand, commanded him to do something. "Tell me what you need from me." Because she wanted to give to him everything.

"You. Just you. And this." He stroked a steady rhythm in and out of her, his weight braced above her on his forearms, the work causing the muscles in his arms to flex and tighten into rocks.

"What do you like best?" She kissed his bicep.

"You." No hesitation.

She licked the same muscle. Why not? Her mantra of the evening, and it was working splendidly. Perhaps she should accept it as her mantra for life. Why not?

She laughed and managed to say, "Where should I touch you?"

"Everywhere you like."

"No help." She nipped his collarbone.

"If I am no help, dear heart, it is because your every damn touch is perfection. No matter what you do, I'll want more of it."

So she kissed his neck, trailed her fingers down the length of his spine, cupped his muscled backside, counted his ribs, all while he rocked in and out of her, and her body rocked to his rhythm.

He swooped in to kiss her mouth each time he stroked into her, a retreat, yes, but a return home, too. To her. She bit the slope of his neck, and he thrust hard. She cried out at the explosive pleasure, and he moved faster and faster, and so did she, meeting each thrust, and his finger stroked her, too, and then she broke. Pulsing waves of pleasure rippled through her on every level. She broke and clung to him while she whispered she knew not what into his ears, and then he broke, too, shattering, screaming her name. They collapsed together in a sweaty, sated heap.

He rolled away from her.

"Wait!" She flung out an arm, capable of nothing more strenuous, but why in heaven's name was he *leaving*?

He leaned over her and kissed her cheek. "I'm not going anywhere." His voice firm and sure. He tugged the blankets free from her body and pulled them up around her, tucked her in warm and safe and joined her, wrapped her up tight and kissed that little point of her jaw below her ear.

And that shattered her more than the pleasure of their bodies joining had. Because wrapped in his arms, she finally felt like she'd found a home, not in a room, or in a collection of objects, or in a house, but in a person. In him.

Twenty-One

Usually, Raph frowned when forced to put crayon or oil paint to paper, but today, his lips seemed capable of nothing less than a smile. A very large one even though his brain was occupied with very important cogitations.

Namely, he wanted more than one night, and when he'd woken with her by his side, it had seemed oddly possible. Despite the very many and very good reasons it was not possible.

"Good morning, brother."

Raph swung around, dropping the crayon. "Zander! When did you arrive?"

Lysander propped his shoulder on the doorframe and crossed his ankles. "Last night, after you abandoned the party."

"With Matilda." Atlas appeared behind Lysander. "Hmm. I wonder what they were about."

"I was rather hoping to become reacquainted with Miss Bellvue last night," Zander said. "It's been an age. Are we calling her Matilda now?"

"You're not," Raph said, dropping into a nearby chair.

His brothers joined him, sitting side by side on the couch where Raph had brought Matilda to climax the night before. It had been the beginning of something, not the end. A thought that had been growing in shape and size since that moment. Perhaps the best way to do right for his family was not to sacrifice his happiness entirely, but to show them they could have both—the responsibility of rebuilding the family and the happiness of growing it larger.

Bollocks. A mad idea, to be sure. But a tempting madness.

"I'll thank you not to speak so easily of Matilda," Raph said. "You'll afford her your respect, Zander. I assume you've come for Maggie's inheritance?"

Zander shifted, rubbed his palms on his thighs, and nodded. "I'm interested to know what it is and annoyed Father insisted on keeping them secret. How are we to know their value and plan accordingly?"

"Planning was never his strong suit," Atlas said. "Even Mother planned their house parties."

Zander flung his arm out toward Atlas. "He's still sweet on Miss Bellvue, then?"

Atlas grunted, laughed. "I can't talk to her without him flying into a jealous fit."

"What nonsense," Raph grumbled, though he wouldn't deny it. It was a ridiculous truth that blackened his pride. "And what do you mean 'still sweet'?"

"Oh, come now, brother," Zander said. "Do not pretend ignorance. The first time she was here, you couldn't take your eyes off her when she was in a room, and you jumped at fixing any problem she encountered."

"It's true," Atlas said, "And after all these years, looking after her, Zander, I'm afraid he's not simply *sweet* on our Matilda."

Zander clutched his heart. "Never say it, Atlas, never say it. Not our stern, stoic brother."

Atlas cupped a hand around his mouth and pretend whispered, "He's in love with her."

Raph snapped to his feet and returned to his easel. "I can't be in love now, can I?"

"Of course you can," Zander said. "Out of the lot of us, you're the most-likely candidate for such an emotion."

"I don't see how."

"Look." Zander leaned forward, propping his elbows on his thighs. "Atlas doesn't really do relationships. Of any sort."

Atlas grunted but didn't disagree.

"And I'm not interested in any of that nonsense. Theo is too cynical and Drew too busy for falling in love. But you feel deeply. You always have. You love this place and all of us more than any of us deserve, and you tear yourself apart for us every day. Don't think we don't notice. It makes perfect sense you would fall in love."

Atlas nodded. "And with a woman like Matilda." He glanced at Zander. "She's just like Raph. Looking after others. All she wanted when Raph swept her back home was to hie off to a Cumbrian cottage and live her own life, yet here she is, making Mother a new woman and stealing our brother's heart."

Raph curled his fingers into his palms, letting an uncomfortable anger work its way out of him. On the other side of that emotion was something cleaner, newer, brighter.

He uncurled his fingers and sat again. "Suppose I want to ... distract Matilda permanently? I couldn't, could I? Not with our debts and the collapsing wing of the house and crops and fields in desperate need of improvement. We're barely sustainable, and—"

"And the harvest went better than expected this year," Atlas said. "Especially considering the flooding."

"And Father's debts," Zander said, "are close to being paid off. And what need have we of that rotting wing?"

"It's our home," Raph reminded him. "My children's home. And the dower cottage is in need of repairs, too."

Zander waved it all away as Atlas nodded, something almost a smile breaking his face into hope. "All that can come with time. You marry an heiress and you fix it all up now, but then you face years of misery."

"You marry Matilda," Atlas said, "and it takes longer to make it all right, but you have a partner by your side to help, someone who forces you to slow down and eat when the fields are flooded, someone who cares for your family and neighbors as well as you do. Who would be happy if you brought one of the heiresses here? Not them, from what you've told me of them. Certainly not you, and likely no one else."

Zander nodded, his head bobbing up and down like a chicken pecking at feed. "We'd have a nice, newly repaired house, improved fields and farming methods, etcetera, etcetera ... and no one would be able to enjoy it."

It was a potent argument, and one that had been simmering inside Raph. Now it rapidly bubbled into a boil. He wanted a partner like Atlas described, but that partner wanted one night. Because she needed to get to Cumbria.

"Raph?" Matilda's voice entered the room from the hallway before her body did. "Is my shawl still in there?" She appeared in the doorframe, stopping abruptly, blinking. "Oh. Is that ... Lord Lysander." She dipped a curtsy. "How lovely to see you once more."

Zander stood and strode toward her, offered a bow and took her hand to raise it to his lips, casting a challenging look to Raph as he did so. "I am charmed, Miss Bellvue. I was delighted when I heard you had returned to us. I hope your visit will be a long one." He cast a look over his shoulder at the couch. "Is that your shawl? Discarded on the floor as if in a moment of high passion?"

Her brow raised, and her lips pursed. "I remember now. You always were terribly naughty, weren't you."

"Thirteen-year-old boys often are. I merely never grew out of it. I was just leaving to speak with Mother. I'm sure we'll see each other for dinner tonight." He winked and sauntered from the room.

"I'm off, too." Atlas found his feet and grinned at Matilda. "Have a good time last night?"

A rush of red blushed across her cheeks. "It was an ... enchanted evening. Thank you for the dancing."

He strode backward out the door. "Hope to do it next year."

Then they were alone, and his brothers' grins were infectious. Must be because his lips had wrapped themselves up and his eyes could not look away from Matilda, who grinned too, still in the doorway. Too far away.

He picked up her shawl and wrapped it around her shoulders, holding tight to the ends and pulling her closer.

"Thank you," she said.

He shut the door and kissed her. Sweet and slow. A lifetime. Would she want that? Or did she still want her cottage?

She pulled away. "You seem distracted."

"Yes. I was trying crayons again." He looked over his shoulder.

She broke his hold on her and bent to the side to peer more closely at the drawing. "It does not look so bad in the light of day."

"No. Not ... quite so bad. But still rather abysmal." A blur of brights and darks with little shape at all. "It's a blob."

"No. I think it's rather mystical. Pagan. You should show your mother, Raph. She'll approve very much, and you might win your inheritance, and then—" She closed her mouth slowly, killing the sentence with intention.

Good. He didn't like the direction it threatened. He didn't want to throw himself on the sacrificial alter of marriage. He turned her so she faced him. "Thank you for last night."

"Thank *you* for last night."

"Your plans ... When do you leave?"

"Soon. Your mother is so much better, and she has friends in the village now. She only ever needed companionship, people to help her see the light in life after she'd thought it had drained away for good. I am no longer needed here."

Wrong. So very wrong. "What if I asked you to stay?"

She opened her mouth, and fear like he'd never felt before washed over him, turning him colder than a block of ice.

"Don't answer yet. Think on it." He reached around her, picked up a red crayon, and took her hand. "Look."

She unfolded her hand for him, no hesitation, and peered down at the soft, hollow cup of her palm where he pressed the tip of the pastel. He pressed the chalky substance into her skin, curving it round the contours of her inner hand. He drew a line upward, circling her pulse, and then curled a pink tendril of chalk up her arm, stopping here and there to trace patterns.

She giggled, a girlish sound he'd never heard from her before. "It tickles."

But he kept drawing, and when he lifted the crayon, he kissed the skin of her upper arm, right above the final sketch he'd etched onto her. Then he returned his attention to her palm, opening it up for her to view his work. There, in the center of her hand, he'd drawn a heart and vines snaked up and out of it, all the way up her arm where more hearts branched out like leaves and blooms in spring.

He pressed his thumb into the center of the heart. "This is mine, and it is yours. You will always have a home right here, and you may take it with you wherever you go or rest it wherever you choose."

"Raph—"

"You asked me once to think about the shape and color of you, Matilda, and I finally have it figured out. You are the leaping curves of a bonfire and the steady lines of an oak. You are the blue of a late summer lake and red. Red for frustration and for passion and for the blood that beats through veins. If I put all of that on a cursed canvas, it would be utter nonsense. But wrapped up in you, with the curve of your hip and the green ring around your brown fairy eyes, it's entirely right. And wonderful. And … bollocks, I sound an utter fool, but—"

She silenced him with a kiss. There'd been so much kissing since she'd returned to him, and he wanted so much more of it, so he wrapped his arms around her and pulled her in tight, and she wrapped him round with her fire and her steadfastness.

Heiresses? Gone. Forgotten.

Debts and farmlands—tucked away to deal with later.

His own heart curling from her palm up her arm and entirely hers? All that mattered.

Kisses turned to caresses and tugs at cravats and hems and bodices and shirts, and when he picked her up, she wrapped her legs around him. He sat her on the long table, sending papers and crayons and oil paint bladders flying, and her legs pulled him tighter to her.

"Here, Raph," she pleaded. "Now."

She was not leaving *today*, and he had time to give her reason to stay, to change her plans, and find a home with him instead.

He kissed her breast and slipped a hand between her legs, into her, finding her wet and ready. She undid his fall in a few breaths, as if one night of practice was all she needed to become expert. She pushed his breeches down and took his cock in hand with more confidence than last night. She squeezed gently.

"Up and down," he demanded.

"Like this?"

He kissed her neck in answer. "Perfect."

"I strive to do everything well. Now, Raph. I want you inside me now."

Had he ever bristled under her commands? He delighted in giving what she wanted. He slid into her, and they clung to one another tightly until he started to move more quickly. Then she braced her palms on the table behind her, and he grasped her hips with one hand, letting the other slip between her legs, teasing her, building her pleasure.

He thrust again and again until she cried out and bit her beautiful bottom lip, and he felt her convulse around him, watched the pleasure shiver across her face, eyes closed, and the sight of her flushed cheeks and swollen lips sent him over the edge himself. He spilled his seed into her, a dangerous game they played. How many times now had he done so without a word about the consequences? She'd not mentioned it either, but surely she worried.

She collapsed backward onto the table, panting and laughing. "There's something beneath me."

He gathered her back up and put her on her feet where she swayed. He held her steady. "Bollocks. You've landed on a paint bladder. The stuff is all over you."

She peered over her shoulder. "It's a lovely shade of yellow, at least."

Finally, the perfect shade of sunshine. The hope of dawn. Naturally, it would be smeared across this woman's rosy skin. He grabbed a linen square and cleaned it off, lining her spine with kisses. "Nothing to do about where it's on your gown. You'll have to change."

She knelt and retrieved her fallen shawl once more, draping it around her shoulders. "That should hide it until—"

A scream rent the air.

"Bollocks," he said. He ran from the room with hesitation, taking her hand and pulling her with him. Together they ran for his mother's sitting room.

Together. Hopefully they stayed that way.

Twenty-Two

M atilda didn't need the tug of Raph's hand to send her careening down the corridor. Her heart threatened to beat out of her ribs as much because of Raph as because of the scream, the volume of which sent her feet flying. Together, they found her sitting room open. Franny stood in the middle of the room, her hands fists, her eyes blazing with fury, and her salt-and-pepper hair frizzing out from beneath her habitual turban.

"How dare you!" She thrust a finger in Lysander's direction.

He stood pale before her, a paper held lightly in his fingers. For a moment, it seemed like he might hit his knees or fall flat on his face. Some strong emotion swayed him like a wind sways a willow.

Raph stepped forward. "Zander, are you well?"

The younger man held out a hand to keep his brother at bay. "Quite." He sucked in a breath and seemed to find his strength as he took a few steps toward his mother and held out the paper. "Apologies, Mother. You weren't supposed to know I had looked."

"What is that?" Raph demanded, grabbing at the paper.

His mother swiped it away before he could reach it, folded it, and slipped it into her pocket. "You may not look at it." She glared at Lysander. "No one was supposed to look at it, whether I was aware of it or not."

Raph turned to his brother. "What is it?"

"The list of paintings we are to receive as our individual inheritances."

Raph scowled. "I thought it a stipulation of the will that we were not to know."

"It is," their mother snapped.

Matilda approached her carefully and wrapped an arm around her shoulders. "I am sure that Lord Lysander is quite sincere in his apology. Does this"—she flicked a glance at Raph —"impede your children's ability to inherit their paintings? Is it written in the will that—"

"No," Franny snapped. "But it was Edward's wish. He liked a little surprise, a little intrigue." Her eyes welled with tears.

Matilda felt only relief. Relief because everything felt so precarious. Relief because Raph had asked her to stay, and she could not suppress the desire to do so, but the reality of that desire seemed so tenuous, so based on the exact right series of events that would place this family beyond the realm of worry and offer Raph a sliver of hope to not marry money.

She held her hand open lightly, afraid to smudge the drawing in her palm, and she pulled her shawl tighter. Anyone could notice the vine snaking up her arm, blooming into silly hearts that made her smile. It would be terribly unhygienic to leave it, to let it fade away gradually instead of rubbing it from her skin this evening during her bath. Yet, she did not wish to scrub herself clean of the evidence of Raph's ... what? Love? He'd not said that word, and he was a plainspoken man. Surely he would have if he felt it.

Yet, he'd asked her to stay.

"You should leave." Franny trained her gaze on Lysander. "I'll see you at dinner and not a moment sooner. Perhaps I'll have calmed my spirits by then."

"Very well. I'll join Atlas outside. We have much to discuss."

"Don't you dare tell him the contents of that list!"

He bowed low and stopped before leaving, a hand on his brother's shoulder. "We need to talk."

Raph nodded.

Their mother scowled. "Do not ask him to reveal what he knows."

Raph dropped into a chair with a sigh. "I do not see that it matters."

"It was your father's wish." Franny dropped, too. To the floor, becoming a puddle of purple skirts and tears.

Matilda knelt beside her. "He will not ask. I will make sure of it."

Raph grunted, and even that bearish sound made her heart smile. She applied her question from last night to his question from this morning. Why not stay? With him? With the man who'd worked to keep this house standing, to keep the family whole, to keep the lands intact? She'd searched so long for a home, a place she did not bow to anyone's whims, a place she could not be booted from when the desire arose. Was that not Briarcliff? Was that not Raph's arms?

Why not stay?

She loved him.

But she brought nothing but herself and a cold, lonely cottage. And the man needed more. Though he'd made do with much less, hadn't he? And he'd never done a thing to jeopardize it. He wouldn't do so now.

Franny lifted a trembling smile to Matilda. "Will you? Will you exercise your influence to keep my Raphael in line? I—"

She blinked, tilted her head, her gaze snagged on Matilda's arm and her brows furrowing. "What is that?"

Blast. The shawl had slipped when she'd knelt, and Matilda tried to pull it back in place, but it would not cover the whole of Raph's art, and she could not keep Franny's feisty fingers from prying and pulling until the shawl loosed and dangled off one shoulder, revealing all.

Franny gasped and took Matilda's arm at the elbow, cupping it gently with one hand as she traced the air above the poppy-red sketch on Matilda's skin. She traced it from her upper arm and into her elbow, down the length of her forearm and to her palm, which Matilda kept closed.

But no hiding it now, and Franny pried Matilda's fingers open, her hands jolting away from Matilda as if they'd been burned and flying to cover her mouth. She swung her gaze over both Matilda's hands then looked over her shoulder at Raph, zeroing in on his hands, his red-smudged fingers.

Franny gasped again. Then hiccupped. Then wailed a wail that turned into a sobbing cry.

Raph cringed. "Mother, it will wash off. I've not hurt her."

"See. It's coming off," Matilda said, poking at one tendril of the vine and wiping just a little bit away.

"No! Don't you hurt it!" She jumped to her feet, tears streaming down her mottled face, and then flung herself at Raph.

He stood, carrying her with him and setting her on her feet. "I don't understand what is happening." He looked to Matilda for help.

She shrugged.

Franny cupped his face and beamed up at him. "It's the most beautiful thing I've ever seen. That"—she stabbed a finger in Matilda's direction—"is what I've been waiting for you to create."

"A doodle? A sketch?"

"No! A piece of art that conveys your soul, Raphael. That speaks of your heart."

He cleared his throat and shifted from foot to foot, and Matilda would have chuckled at his discomfort had she not felt so entirely lost herself.

"It's a heart, Mother," he said. "Not even a biologically correct one."

"Bollocks."

"Mother!"

"I can curse just as well as you! Now, do you want your inheritance or not?" She stormed toward Matilda, grabbed her wrist and dragged her across the room to stand before Raph.

"Pardon me!" Matilda tugged to free her wrist, but to no avail. "I refuse to be pushed around." She would object no more than that, though, because what had Franny said about his inheritance? If Raph won his, would it matter so much that Matilda had so little?

Franny shook Matilda's hand in Raph's face. "This is your work, is it not?"

"Yes."

"And it means something to you, does it not?"

Raph's gaze lingered on the heart in Matilda's palm, then he raised it slowly. He stared at her with such heat, she could not breathe.

"Yes," he said, "it does."

Franny released Matilda's wrist and pressed both her hands into her breast. "Oh, heavens. The old gods of the harvest have blessed us."

"Mother." Raph's voice took on a low rumble as he rolled his eyes.

Matilda rubbed her wrist where Franny had wrapped her fingers so tightly about it, the paint smudged now there.

Raph stood and came to her. "She didn't hurt you, did she?"

"No. But I do expect her to respect boundaries in the future."

He ducked his head. "Is there a future? It's what I've been trying to find out from you, and all these *things* keep getting in the way."

"Things such as your family? And wills? And pesky little debts?"

"Precisely." He inched closer, swept a lock of hair out of her eye.

She wanted to stay, and the possibility of doing so bloomed true and vibrant before her.

Franny sighed. "Young love. It is the best blessing we could ask for. I will contact Mr. Grant and tell him you've completed the task set before you."

Matilda took his hands in both of hers, squeezed them. "What are you thinking?"

He dipped low, whispered in her ear as he trailed a finger down his drawing. "That I'd like to wash this off you myself."

"Improper timing, my lord." But she grinned. She desired the very same thing. If it must come off, best he help.

His mother pushed them both for the door. "Go be happy together. I'm going to find Jane to tell her the news. I knew the cards could not be wrong! Nor my dreams." She shoved them into the hallway then went to shut the door.

Raph stopped her with one palm flat against it.

"Oof," she said. "What is it now, Raphael?"

"Do you think you could just ... give us all our paintings, Mother?"

"Oh, no. I can't do that."

"It would be immensely helpful," Matilda added.

Annoyance fluttered across Franny's face. "No, my dear. Every one must earn them, just as Raphael and Maggie have. I trust they all will. I birthed a bevy of unartistic brutes, but they all have soul, and that is what matters. Besides"—she swung her gaze toward Raph—"I do not see what is so wrong, Raphael. We have plenty to fill our bellies, the roof over our heads ... Well, most of it is secure ... and we have each other. Which is what matters most. I can talk to you and hug you and drive you wild, and you may do the same to me, and believe me, son, when you can no longer do that, you notice. Your father was handed a fortune he was not equipped to handle. I know that. He knew that. He wanted his sons to learn what truly mattered and how to work for what mattered, as he never quite did. I think you've seen what matters now." She sniffed then slammed the door shut.

They flinched.

"Well," Matilda said, "that was an eventful, what? Quarter hour? Ten minutes?"

"Mother does not believe in uneventful quarter hours. I wish she'd find a better way to express her displeasure than screaming." He rubbed his ear.

A warmth spread through Matilda, and she could not tease anymore. She turned to him, once more taking his hands in hers. "You've done it, Raph." Pride. Ah, yes, that was what the warmth was. And possibility.

He lifted a shaky hand and shoved his fingers through his hair before letting it fall with a slap to his side. "I have. Not that I did anything. I merely ..." He stroked his knuckles down her arm. "I simply could not let you go. Will I have to? Or must I move to Cumbria with you? I'd do it, you know."

She shook her head, pruning back that warmth rising in her like a sun. "I want to. But I am fully aware of how much I have to offer."

"Every good thing."

"Myself only."

"Exactly." He cupped her face.

She leaned into that hand. She leaned into that welcome. "I bring no money to help in your endeavors. You've worked so hard, and—"

"What is all the work for?" His hand swept from her face to her neck and crashed her closer to his body. Their chests met, and she clung to his shoulders to remain steady. "What is it for, Matilda, if not for—"

"Raph." A heavy clearing of the throat from down the hall.

Raph growled, never looking away from her. "Leave, Lysander."

"I do so hate to interrupt this tender moment, but we need to talk, Raph. Now."

"Go." She pressed a hand to his chest and gave him a gentle push.

He didn't budge.

"I'll be here. I'm going nowhere right now. We can continue this conversation when your brother does not need you."

"Not leaving right now? Or ever?"

"We'll discuss it later." But her heart knew the answer.

"An order?"

She raised a brow. "Yes."

He scoffed, but he trailed his finger around the outline of her face, dipped for a quick kiss, heedless of his watching brother, and lifted too soon to stride away from her.

How could she tell him no? How could she leave when he'd become her home? And surely he would not ask her if he thought her staying would impede his work, his plans for his family's future.

If he did not mind, if he felt this thing between them would not topple everything else, she would trust him. Her life had toppled before. Again and again, she'd given up control of every situation in order to survive. But *here* she could breathe. He would not let life unmoor her or circumstance toss her about. He would not toss her about either, unless it was quite a welcome toss in a warm bed.

And no matter how much money an heiress brought to a union with him, she'd prove unlikely to provide what Matilda could—knowledge of how to argue with a stormy man, how to soothe him, how to love him.

Twenty-Three

Raph slammed the door behind him as he entered Zander's room. Couldn't his family be less intrusive? How did they always know the perfect time to interrupt? Some days, the entire last fifteen years felt like an interruption. No more, though. His furrowed brow smoothed out. He'd speak to Zander and return to Matilda and do everything in his power to convince her to stay.

"What is it, Zander? I'm rather busy at the moment."

"You're always busy, and I can't keep it from you any longer." Zander paced from one side of his bedchamber to the other, his arms punctuating each word with wild, wide gesticulations. "I had hoped to have found a solution before now. I had hoped there would prove no problem, but after seeing Mother's list—" He stopped and stared at Raph, his eyes dark and heavy with sorrow.

"Bollocks, Zander. I don't want to know."

"I sold the paintings. Six of them. Throughout the years. Covertly."

"You've sold no paintings. What is this nonsense?"

Zander cupped Raph's shoulders and moved him toward a chair, pressed him to sit, and when Raph did, Zander stepped back several paces, darted around a large armchair, and peeked at Raph from the top of it.

"Stay there until I'm done," he said.

"Zander. Explain. Now."

"The woman who bought the paintings knew a very skilled artist. And she agreed to pay for the copies in addition to the price I asked for the originals. The copies are perfect, Raph. Immaculate."

Raph stood slowly, his nails biting into the frayed material of the armchair. "Are you saying that there are works in Father's collection that are fake?"

Zander closed his eyes and nodded. "Worse than that."

Worse? Hell. What could be ... oh. "The paintings listed as our inheritances?"

Zander nodded again, opened his eyes. "Every one of them. Fakes. It almost makes me think the old man knew. Every other painting in his collection was willed to the Royal Society. But ours?"

Raph's legs gave out, and he dropped back into the chair. "Bloody hell. What do we do?"

"We can't sell them anymore. It would be a criminal act."

"What you've done is already a crime, Zander," Raph snapped. "Why in hell would you do that?"

"I did what I could, just as you did, just as the others have, to keep the pantry stocked and clothes on our backs. Those large sums I gave you the last four years in a row? Did you think those came from my work? The newly rich pay well for me to line their walls with priceless art, but not that well. Even they have their limits. Unlike our father. I was only doing what I could to right his wrongs. And the copies are perfect, Raph. Not even Father noticed. They might as well *be* authentic Rubens and—"

"Would you come out from behind that cursed chair, Lysander? Sit and help me *think*. I'm not going to punch you." Though he rather wanted to. Instead, he pinched the bridge of his nose.

Zander darted out and sat in the chair. "I've been thinking about it nonstop since Father died. No matter what, I had to get them back. They were either going to be willed to some society, as most of them were, or we would sell them, and in either case, handing over copies as authentic works of art ... Father deserved it. No one else, though. And if we were caught? Hell, Raph. I *know* better."

"It does not seem like you do," Raph hissed.

"Getting them back has always been part of the plan. As soon as we'd recovered enough of our funds, paid off enough debts, were lucky with some sort of investment, then I would reach out to the woman once more and buy back the paintings. She *knew* I intended to buy them back. But she's disappeared, and her home is empty. And I can't find a soul who knows where she's gone."

"Your plan was to sell paintings, buy them back, then sell them again?"

"When you put it that way it sounds—"

"Ridiculous, Zander. Utter nonsense. What now?"

"I have a promising lead. The painter. The forger. I've discovered his address."

"And that will help how?" He squeezed his eyes so tightly together, stars blooms on the back of his eyelids.

"Perhaps the painter will know where the buyer is."

Raph dropped his elbows to his thighs and rubbed his face with his palms. Darkness did not clear his head. A sort of keening sound had started, low and long, and it would not stop, try as he might to silence it, and it broke through every semi-coherent thought, breaking it into brittle pieces.

He tried, though. "Maggie's inheritance, which we have

counted on?" He lifted his head, opened his eyes to stare at his brother.

Lysander shook his head.

"And the one Mother just released to me?"

"To you? She did? What for?" He waved his hands before his face. "It doesn't matter. The Rubens Father set for you to inherit—fake as well. But I'll get it back, Raph. I swear I will."

That was it, then. Just like the day his father's land manager had left, swept out the doors with dire predictions of ruin and warnings. A turning point, an end.

He stood, shaky. "I must speak with Matilda."

"Yes. Atlas says she's a good sort. I remember her being dependable enough. And from what I saw in the hallway, I assume I'm soon to offer you both congratulations."

"No." The steps that took Raph toward the door were slow and heavy.

Faster, more frantic steps raced after him, and Zander's hand grabbed his shoulder, spun him around. "What Atlas and I said this morning remains true. We do not need an heiress. We do not need you to sacrifice yourself for—"

"I already have, Lysander. Why should I stop?"

"I saw the way you looked at her. Mere moments ago. You can't, Raph."

"But I might have to." He ripped his shoulder out of his brother's hold and yanked the door open.

Atlas blinked at him. "Something bad is happening."

"True enough," Zander said. "This fool is about to rip his heart out of his chest and stomp on it."

Raph strode for the stairs and jolted down them. "Tell Atlas what you've done, Zander."

"What did you do?" Atlas demanded.

His brothers followed him down the stairs.

"Hell. I'll tell you later. Not in so public a place."

Raph whirled around halfway down the stairs to look up at them, crossing his arms over his chest.

Zander tried to continue down, past Atlas, but Atlas stopped him, palm to shoulder, as tall as Zander even a step below him. "Tell me now." A growl.

Zander winced. "I may have, just a tiny bit, had several paintings copied in order to sell the originals."

"And," Raph added, "in a horrid coincidence that simply cannot be a coincidence, all six paintings Zander had forged are the ones we stand to inherit." Hurt more than it should, the knowledge his father had willed them *fakes*.

Atlas faced Raph, eyes wide. "You think he knew?"

"He must have," Zander said. "He would not have willed forgeries to the Royal Society, so he willed them to us instead."

If it was true ... how cruel. He seemed to be taunting them from beyond the grave, but his father had never taunted. He had been irresponsible and bad with money, but not cruel. It made no sense, and a large part of him wanted to fight the accusation. He could not have known. Or perhaps there was a reason they were unaware of.

"I don't know," he said, the forgiveness that had cracked him open earlier pushed those cracks wider. "It does not sound like him. *Why* would he do it?"

"The why of it doesn't matter," Zander said, "the outcome remains the same. We are left with nothing."

Raph continued down the stairs, the heaviness in his limbs returning as he rounded the stairs at the bottom to— "Matilda."

She stood in the sun-striped hallway, her hands clenched in her skirts. "I'm so sorry. I heard everything. I was ... I was ... well, I rather forget what I was doing. Not eavesdropping, though, Not intentionally. I swear. I—"

He wanted to take her in his arms and dance her out the

door into the sun. He wanted to slip into the lake with her and wash away the last half hour of his life.

Could he now?

"Bollocks."

She tiptoed closer, and Zander and Atlas backed away so slowly, so silently, they might have been ghosts.

"Can I help? I'll do anything you need of me." She wrapped her hands around his arm and pulled him toward a sitting room. Tried to.

He didn't budge.

She squeezed his arm. "Come and sit down. You've had a shock. We'll get you some tea." She sucked in air and tilted her head. "Something stronger, perhaps. Then we'll discuss what's to be done."

There was only one thing to do. Damn Zander.

But he let her drag him into the sitting room as he had at that other turning point in his life. She shut the door softly behind them so that not even a click broke the fragile silence wrapped around them. When she went to pull the bell for tea, he stopped her, led her to a seat and made sure she perched on it before he walked to the window. The garden was tangled and dying, despite his best efforts. Vines around him, too, tangling him up in duty and purpose. No time for want when there was only obligation.

"Raph?"

He glanced over his shoulder at her. She'd turned and leaned against the back of the couch to stare at him.

"Raph, I can help. I don't know how yet, but—"

"This problem is no grieving widow."

She straightened her spine, set her chin strong. "I'm highly aware of the nature of the problem. Your brother is a nodcock. A possibly criminal one. And the funds you had counted on all these months are no longer at your disposal. Even in theory."

Yes, she understood perfectly.

He turned back to the window. "Naturally, I'll pay for your trip to Cumbria."

She stood. The rustle of her skirts and the creak of the old coach his only signal she'd done so. And there—the swift patter of her feet across the threadbare rugs. Then she stood beside him, thrusting that delightfully pointed chin at him.

"Are you truly going to ask me to stay one moment then send me away the next?"

"You'd not even provided me an answer. So you should not be wary of these ... unfolding events. It unfolds in the direction you intended anyway." A lie. She'd been going to agree to stay. He'd known it deep in bone, deep in blood, and deep in his soul, damned to hell as it now was.

"You know what I was going to say, Raph. You know what my answer was going to be."

He flinched. Her words felt like the night stars blinking out all at once.

"I stood in that hallway, so worried. About everything that could happen, that already had happened, and I wanted to make the right choice because, above all, I did not want to ruin everything you'd worked so hard for. I cannot help but but love you. Though it is not wise to do so."

He tried to stop the words, meaningless as they were, but they slipped out anyway. "Then why choose to stay?"

"Because I trusted you! If you were asking me to stay, to marry you, you would not do so lightly. You would not risk everything, hurt everyone, in order to have me. You are not selfish. I chose to stay because I trusted you would never hurt me, never send me away and rescind your support, never take back your heart and throw me into the world alone. I chose to stay because I cannot stop loving you despite the practical reasons I never should, the practical reasons I should not have let myself love you to begin with. I thought perhaps you needed love more than you needed an heiress. I thought you saw that too. I see I am wrong, though." She took a bold, strong step backward away from him, looked him up and down from boots to head, and snorted.

Snorted! She didn't wail or cry or beg and plead. Merely snorted and walked away from him. God, he loved her. He spun around to watch her, and she spun, too. In the doorway, her hands were balls of fury in her skirts, and he was doing what she'd thought he never would—sending her away, betraying her trust, breaking her bond with the home he'd wanted her to have, the home she'd seemed to want for herself.

Hell, he was a beast, wasn't he. Cold and single-minded, with no bloody choice to be otherwise.

"What you have found out today," she said, "is a blow. It makes everything more difficult. I understand that. You must be who you are, and you would not be if you put your own feelings above your purpose, if you put your family's well-being behind your own desires. I understand that."

He stepped toward her. No clear reason for doing so, only that his body insisted.

She flung a hand up, palm out, to stop him. "No. I am leaving. Today. I'll stay in the village until I've figured out my travel plans, and Jane will help me manage those, as she was always meant to do. I hope you find a convenient marriage swiftly, my lord." She turned and took two steps away from him, steps that flayed him, broke his bones, grew a wail long and deep inside his gut.

When she stopped and turned around, the color returning to her face in a rush of pinks and reds and sparking brown-green eyes, his body wove itself back together once more. He saw the truth now. She came to him, he won. She left him, he lost.

She strode right up to him, poked him in the chest, and

when she spoke it was with the resounding fury of a woman scorned. "No! I do not hope you find a convenient marriage, my lord. I do not know the specifics of what I wish for you, but know this, should you and she ever wander my way in Cumbria, I'll slam the door in your face, I'll scratch out her eyes, and curse you both because I'm sure to take your mother's cards with me, learn them, and grow into a witch of absurd power. Absurd power, do you hear me? And I've been ... well, I feel spurned, and even though I see the practicalities of it, I do not like it. There must a be a way other than this."

"Do you think I like it? You'll not have to curse me, Matilda. I already am."

She sniffed, an angry snort that propelled her across the room again. She slammed the door behind her. Didn't even look back. The angry woman he loved and couldn't have—so goddamn beautiful in her fury.

～

Matilda had left several households and families behind her. She'd packed her trunk on many occasions and watched footmen load it onto a cart or carriage or coach before alighting and driving off into an entirely new existence. It's what one did when one's existence was not one's own.

This time proved no different even though it was different in every way that mattered. She'd cared for her charges before, yes, but she'd fallen in love now. She looked around the bedchamber she'd called her own for several speechless moments. Where to start?

A soft knock fell upon her door before it cracked open and Jane entered on quick, silent feet. "We heard a ruckus, Franny and I. Is everything well?"

No. Not particularly.

"I'm leaving, Jane. You may stay as long as you wish. I will abide in the village until my plans for travel to Cumbria are complete. Or you may come with me if you like. I do not wish my change of plans to discomfit you."

Jane perched on the edge of the bed, worry etched into the usually laughing lines of her face. "Sit, Matilda, and speak with me."

Matilda could not. She'd managed not to cry so far, and she would continue to manage thusly until ... until ... well, for as long as possible, at least. Hopefully until she was alone.

With dry eyes, she placed each of her garments carefully in her trunk, removed her paintings from the wall, tugged her scarf of every color from their homes on the bed posts, retrieved her knickknacks—jewelry and music box—and nestled them in for a bumpy ride, hopeful they'd survive one more trip before settling down into their permanent places once and for all.

The toy theatre she left on a table. The banyan she packed. Knew she shouldn't, but she'd not give it back, would wrap herself in it nightly while she cried until she found the anger to burn the damn thing in the garden behind her cottage.

With the room blank and empty, scrubbed clean of *her*, she closed the trunk, locked it, and sat atop it.

"Do you have a preference?" She spoke to Jane without meeting her gaze.

"What has happened, girl? Tell me."

"I'd prefer not to rehash it. I fear I'm overreacting a bit, but I cannot bring myself to care." She'd trusted him, and she should not have. He'd done what everyone else had always done—offered her a home, a family, then stripped it away. With the exception of her brother, she'd known such a thing would happen with the other positions. Yes, she'd entered this position with the same assumptions and expectations, but he'd taught her to want more. He'd made her think she might actually have a home that wasn't a lonely, hollow shell.

More fool her. She should not have been convinced so easily when experience had taught her otherwise.

She heaved in a breath, found it shaky, yet tried to speak anyway. Jane deserved it. "Lord Waneborough and I have had a falling out, and it would be awkward for me to stay a moment longer. I ... cannot."

Jane made a catching sound in her throat, and that dissolved Matilda like she was a tiny sugar cube in a deluge of scalding tea. She dropped her face into her palms and wept, shoulders shaking until a soft, warm arm wrapped around them, pulled her close, then she wept into Jane's shoulder, quieter sobs.

"Shh," Jane clucked. "Shh, now, girl. It's hardest to have a falling *out* when you've fallen *in* first. Love, that is, and anyone with a working pair of eyes can see that's what's happened. Then Franny told me about your arm art, and I can see for myself, all those red tangles like veins snaking up you ... The boy is mad for you ... and just mad. Men in love don't quite know what to do with themselves. They lose their wits for a while."

Matilda brushed her tears off her cheeks and straightened. She peered into her lap for several long moments before speaking. "Whether or not we've fallen *in* hardly matters when we've fallen so far *out* he plans to take another woman's hand in marriage." She sucked in a breath, tried to be practical. "He must, though. I see that. I'm being a widgeon."

"What he must or must not do is for him to decide, and I'll not speak on that."

"Moderation? From you, Jane? I commend you, though I am not sure when you've learned such a skill."

Jane sniffed. "I can have it when it's necessary. Most of the time it isn't. Most of the time, I can poke as I like into others' business and no harm comes of it. That's what the stories about apples and mirrors were all about. Trying to get you to see for yourself what you wanted."

Hardly shocking, that.

"This is big-heart stuff, though," Jane said. "Deep-cut stuff, and the only folks that can fix that are those who have the big hearts and the deep cuts." She sighed, patting Matilda's back, rubbing circles into it as if Matilda were a child. "I'll leave with you. We came together, and we'll leave together. Besides, my daughter has been writing daily from London asking when I plan to return. Think she's lonely. Only natural. But I'll take my leave of Franny today and join you in the village tomorrow."

"A good plan."

Jane rose and made for the door. "I'll send someone your way to help with your trunk."

"Thank you." Matilda held Jane's gaze, hoped the other woman understood. She was thanking her for so much more than finding someone to help with a trunk. She was thanking her for friendship, for a motherly embrace.

"*Bah.*" Jane batted the thanks away but smiled, too, before exiting the room and shutting the door behind her.

A short time later, another knock sounded on the door.

"Come in," Matilda said, trying for a chipper tone and failing.

The door swung open, and Lord Atlas stepped through. She should have known he would be the one sent to help her. She'd not been thinking clearly. There were no footmen at Briarcliff. He asked no questions. Merely lifted her trunk onto one massive shoulder and strode from the room with a soft sadness in his eyes.

Lord Lysander waited in the hall. If he'd had a hat, he

would have been wringing it before him. Without such an accoutrement, he paced, hands clasped behind his back, looking up when they exited her chamber. He strode to them, palms opened wide as if he offered something to them.

"I'll fix it." The pain drowning his words dripped from his face and body as well.

Matilda cocked her head, considered giving him a lecture, but she turned for the stairs instead. "You have been a right nodcock, Lord Lysander, and you *should* try to fix your actions."

The brothers followed her down the stairs, Lord Atlas at the slow, lumbering pace required of a man balancing a heavy object on his shoulder, and Lord Lysander with the manic bounciness of a rabbit.

He was at her side in moments, descending sideways so he could look at her as he spoke. "I know. I know I've done wrong, but I'll fix it, then you'll be able to return."

She reached the bottom of the stairs and continued out through the door. "While you can and should atone for your own mistakes, you cannot atone for the actions of others." A cart and horse already waited for her in the drive. "Thank you, Atlas."

He grunted as he released the trunk into the cart, and she climbed up onto the seat as Atlas joined her and took the reins.

Lord Lysander approached her side, looking up at her. "How can you be so calm? Do you want to leave? Atlas said ... seemed convinced ..." His gaze flashed to his brother. "Said he'd caught the two of you—"

"Zander," Atlas said, a warning growled into his voice, "don't be crass."

"If you leave, Miss Bellvue," Lysander said, "I'll have ruined not just our inheritances, but Raph's future as well. I'll be no better than my father."

She tried to soften her face because she would not soften her words. "That is for you to grapple with, Lord Lysander."

Lord Atlas grunted and whipped the horse into movement, and they trundled along the drive and away from Briarcliff, from Raph, and from a home she very much wished she could have made her own.

Twenty-Four

D arkness could creep into a person even in broad daylight, lapping at the soul like the waters of a lake against the shore, ever encroaching, teasing, taunting.

Raph sat, listless, paralyzed, in those dark waters. Numb, immobile. Usually, he moved from dawn to dusk, dropping into bed on a wave of pure exhaustion. But he could not bring himself to move from his chair in the cursed Purgatorial Painting Parlor. Which was now thrice cursed because it held memories of Matilda. And no longer seemed cursed at all. How could it when he could sit here and drink in her scent. While it lasted, of course. She was gone, and soon those tiny reminders of her would be, too.

Didn't help he stared into that horrible painting he'd done after their night together—darkness and flame, a blur of dark and light. Like him with her? Or without her? He couldn't quite grasp its meaning. Everything fragmented like those saucer shards in the ballroom.

A song reached out to him from the darkness, through the tea and soap scent of her, slow and dreamy, the singer's gruff voice brushing up against the high ping of the pianoforte. It pulled him to his feet and out of the room, down the hall. Then it stopped, and he stopped, too.

Lysander's voice broke into the silence. "No, no, Atlas. Too sentimental. I'm telling you, it has to be a bit rakish. The bawdy ones will sell better."

"Bollocks," Raph muttered. He rushed down the hall, burst into the music room. "What are you two doing?"

Atlas sat at the pianoforte, frowning, and Zander stopped pacing and looked up at Raph.

"We're busy," Lysander said. "So unless you can help, go mope about somewhere else."

"What are you busy doing?" Raph demanded. "I no longer trust your form of business."

Atlas plonked heavily at the keys. "We're writing songs."

"To sell," Zander added. "All above board, of course. And I've a plan to get the paintings back. I always have had a plan, but you exploded before I could explain it."

Raph pinched the bridge of his nose, his body so heavy, so tired, he almost gave way to weakness and leaned against the doorframe. But he found some way to stay upright, to stay strong. He'd done it for fifteen years, and he'd do it for fifty more.

"There is so much to respond to," he said, "I'm not sure where to start." The songs. That was the least rage inducing. "I am aware you sold songs before, but I did not think they were well received."

"They weren't." Atlas pushed back from the instrument. "They were bloody sad. Written after battle, full of death. You wouldn't want to sing those, would you? The Crown wanted songs glorifying battle, full of patriotism and—" His voice ground to a hard halt, and he took a steadying breath. "They were not interested in truth."

"These," Zander added, surging forward to pat the

pianoforte, "will be of the popular variety, bursting with innu-endo and rakishness. I'm helping to ensure the maximum amount of charm, and Atlas is providing the actual musical talent. There's a fellow on Oxford Street. Runs a firm that buys lyrics for various means."

Raph allowed himself to enter the room more fully, found a chair, and dropped into it.

"It's not the same as having an heiress's dowry," Atlas said.

"And it's not as lucrative as selling a Rubens," Zander said, "but it's something."

It was something, and hadn't they pieced together just enough out of thousands of somethings over the years? His gaze caught out the window where the lawn extended outward then dipped out of view. At the bottom, hidden from the house, the lake. He'd never be able to see that damn body of water the same way again. It would always enflame him instead of cool him down.

"What," Raph asked, "is your idea for retrieving our paintings?"

"As I told you, I've been searching for the woman who bought the originals. No luck as of yet, but if I can find her, I can—"

"No." Raph finally allowed himself to meet his brother's gaze. "Don't do a cursed thing, Zander. She obviously has no desire to sell the paintings back. And how are we going to procure them, anyway? With what funds?"

"I'm going to swap them. With the copies."

Atlas and Raph jumped to their feet. "No!" Two voices, one word, one tone as well—unequivocal disagreement.

"Yes." Zander rarely used such a hard voice, but it was all gravel and marble now. "We have achieved two paintings from our cumulative inheritances. I have the most excellent copies of those paintings. I find the woman with the originals and swap them out."

Raph shook his head. "Too dangerous. She sounds like a discerning art collector. I assume she can't be tricked."

"Who was more discerning than our father? And he was tricked. Quite easily. I tell you, this painter, whoever he is, is a genius. No one can tell the difference. Ages the paintings and everything."

"I agree with Raph," Atlas said, "in this one thing at least. Sounds like a horrid plan. Let's stick to the songs." He turned to Raph. "And let us keep working to improve the fields. Think of how well the harvest went this year, even after the flooding. Think of how the village is coming together with the house. Let us stay the course, and let you bring Matilda home."

Raph stomped toward the door with a growl.

"Raaaaaaaaphaeeeeeeel!" His mother's voice howled his name.

The brothers exchanged looks, and Raph flung the door open to rush toward her sitting room. The wailing grew louder.

"Raaaaaaaphaeeeeel!" She swung into view, sliding around a corner and flying down the hallway toward them. Raph caught her as she fell into his arms, panting, punching at his chest with ineffective fists.

"Why has Matilda left?" she demanded. "What have you done to her?"

"Nothing, Mother." Everything, actually. Offered her a home, then snatched it away. Betrayal, really, was what he'd done to her.

"Bring her back. You *love* her."

"I do. But I can't. She wants a home, and I cannot give her one here. I can barely maintain a home for *you* here. Surely you see that. It's the only reason I must marry an heiress. To keep this house, to keep your home, the home of my children."

She stomped her foot, ripping her shoulders out of Raph's grasp. "What *nonsense*. Go get her."

He ached to do so. "I cannot."

"I'll release all your art. Your inheritances. I will. Just bring her back and be happy, Raphael."

"They're fake, Mother." Raphael had not meant to tell her, but perhaps she deserved to know.

Her entire body turned to stone, so motionless not even wind would sway her.

Zander stepped forward, wrapped an arm around her shoulders, and guided her to a seat. "It's my fault, Mother. I found a woman who would buy them and produce copies for me to install here."

She finally blinked to life to gaze at Zander. "And your father never *noticed*?"

Zander shrugged. "No? Maybe? He never said."

"My, what a talented painter. I must meet—"

"Focus, Mother." Raph knelt before her, took her hands in his. "This means even if we earn our inheritances, we cannot sell them to fix the house or improve the estate or hire more staff. You see now. My path is set, immovable."

"No," she said, shaking off his embrace to stand once more. "I don't care. If Matilda leaves, you will feel as dead as I have felt since your father died. I know you will, and that would kill me in a way his death never could have. I know you think I do not care, but I do. Please go get her."

He turned to leave.

"Raph, stop. I know we were wrong and foolish and careless. I know the terms of his will ask too much. Your father knew, he *knew,* he'd ruined his legacy, and he wanted to find immortality in some way. Art does that. It makes you immortal in the way the artist remembered you. He wanted to be remembered in six different ways, how his children remembered him through their art. For better or worse. But none of that matters if you are miserable, Raphael. Better your father is remembered with bitterness than you live in it. *Go get her.* Give her our home, give her your heart to make her home in."

"I cannot."

She fell against him, wetting his waistcoat with great racking sobs, and he wrapped his arms around her, held her tight.

"I am sorry. So terribly sorry." Repeated over and over again, an apology that soothed him a bit, in the strangest way, that lightened him, that calmed some snarly beast inside.

He rubbed a hand down her head and circles into her back, not sure if he could say words of forgiveness, but wanting to give comfort somehow, in any small way. He guided her back to a seat, and she went willingly, hiccupping as her tears slowed.

Atlas handed her a handkerchief, and she took it, dabbing at her swollen eyes.

"I did not realize," she said, speaking in a dreamy way, her gaze fixed somewhere outside the room, "what was lost, what we—your father and I—were damaging. I thought, as did he, that we were exchanging earthly things of man and money for art, matters of the mind, philosophical thought. But we threw much more than that away, didn't we? Our responsibility and duty to others. Man cannot, I suppose, though it is difficult for me to admit, live on art alone. We cannot eat art, at least, and while we may love it, it does not love us back."

She lifted her gaze to Raph's, the haze dropping from her eyes to be replaced by a crystal crispness. "I will not ask for the house party again. I will give up my lady's maid and sell some of the pieces from my personal art collection. Just please bring Matilda back. For you. Because you deserve to have all of us look after you for a change. I should have been looking after you all this while. Your father should have, too. I know this."

She offered no excuses this time for her actions, for his

father, and that soothed him so well something like forgiveness broke through his cracks.

"She's right, Raph." Atlas placed a hand on his shoulder, squeezed. "Let us do the work for you. Bring Matilda home."

They kept using that word—Matilda's favorite, the one thing she wanted more than anything. The thing he'd offered her, other than his own bloody heart, for so brief a moment before taking it back again. How could she trust him after this? Even if he went after her, how could she trust him again?

He couldn't go after her ... could he? God knew he wanted to. Wanted nothing else than to run down the drive until he found her, sling her over his shoulder, and bring her home.

Always back to that word.

But he couldn't because he'd always done this alone, done everything alone.

Bollocks.

He hadn't done it alone, had he? Lysander selling the original paintings. Maggie and Tobias taking care of Mother's needs. Atlas working every duty on the estate he could manage. Drew's tutoring positions and Theo's political caricatures.

Even Matilda, during her few short months here, had given her fair share of help to lighten Raph's load. Hadn't she helped bring Mother and the village together? Hadn't she cared for him when he'd been run down and entertained his mother when he'd not been able to? She'd not brought money with her, but she'd brought herself, and that, more than all the lessening of debt throughout the years had cloaked Raph in gladness, given him hope.

"Bollocks."

His mother gasped, a sound that bounced light into her eyes.

Zander threw his hands in the air. "Finally, he sees it!"

Atlas crossed his arms over his chest and grinned.

"How the hell do I get her back?" Raph asked. "I was a complete arse to her."

"Show her what's in your heart, Raphael," his mother said.

"Toss her over your shoulder and make her come home," Atlas added.

Zander shrugged. "Hell if I know. Wouldn't trust my advice anyway. But if anyone can fix a problem, brother, it's you."

So many problems to fix, always so many problems. This one the most pressing, though, and he would not take a decade and a half to make it better. He'd only just realized he could forgive his parents ... would Matilda be able to forgive him?

Twenty-Five

L ittle Francesca's contented gurgling had become a bit of a wail, and though Matilda did not wish to wake the sleeping mama, she would have to for the poor babe to get some food. Francesca scrunched up her little lips in a way Matilda had come to understand meant, quite clearly, *feed me now*.

"Come along, dear," Matilda said, "give your mother another few minutes." Francesca cracked her lips open and wailed in a sound much like that Matilda had sometimes heard from her namesake. "Very well, then. I must remember, babies cannot be ordered about." Something she'd learned in the last week.

She'd remained in Fairworth much longer than she'd intended, helping Molly with Francesca, learning how to bake bread from Mrs. Popkins, and using her savings to stay at the inn. Jane had left for London days ago. Yet Matilda remained, as if she could not be moved.

She knocked on the door to the only bedchamber in the little cottage. "Molly. Francesca has need of you."

"Come in."

Matilda did so, handed the baby off to its mother, and watched it latch onto her breast in a frantic fumble then fall into a contented rhythm. The mother looked at the child with so much love, touched her so tenderly. An ache grew in Matilda's chest that had little to do with the ache that had been there a week already with no sign of lessening.

A little to do with it, though. Because the man she wanted to make a baby with was the same cursed one who'd sent her away. Yet she could not leave. A curse indeed.

She stepped backward toward the door. "I'll be going now, unles you need anything else, Molly."

"Oh, do stay until Tommy arrives with the cart to take you back."

Matilda laughed. "It's only a short walk. I'll be glad for the exercise."

Molly reached her free hand out toward her. "No! You must stay until Tommy returns."

Matilda raised a brow. "Must I? And why is that?" She'd been governess to enough children to know when she was being distracted from hijinks happening elsewhere.

"Tea!" Molly exclaimed a bit too loudly. "Would you make me some tea?"

"You do realize you're only increasing my desire to see what mischief is about."

Molly bit her lip and draped Francesca over her shoulder. "I know. I'm horrid at this. But I was instructed to keep you here until Tommy came home, and I'd hate to disappoint the marquess."

"Lord Waneborough?" What was he about? No word from him for a week, then he's sneaking about, hiding something from her?

She missed him. She shouldn't, but she did. And she slept with his banyan on, no desire to burn it, either.

"I'm not saying another word." Molly sighed. "But I can't

keep you here against your will, and I suppose it's just about time for Tommy to arrive anyway. I say go and give 'em all hell, Matilda."

"I'm not sure I want to walk blindly into a situation in which I'm required to cast anyone into perdition, but I must admit to curiosity."

Molly grinned. Francesca burped. Matilda took her leave.

The walk back to the inn was short, and she dragged her feet, slowing her usually brisk walk as she approached the inn. She peered into every face she passed, looking for him, knowing she wouldn't have to look. She'd just know. Feel him like the rapid increase of her pulse when he touched her, like the constricting of her chest when they laughed together.

But she made it almost all the way to the Blessed Pig without seeing him or feeling him. What she did feel was a tiny tug of disappointment in her chest. She shouldn't trick herself into thinking she could stay here. She couldn't sell her cottage and buy one here. There wasn't another here. And she knew nothing about building them, the costs, the materials.

If she could sell her cottage, she'd like to gift what she earned to the Bromley family, to Raph, for watching over her all these years, for making her feel loved and wanted not just for what she could give to others, but for herself, and—"Ack!"

She stumbled, tripped over something. She looked down, knelt, found an apple. An apple? And several steps farther ahead, another one. Then another, an entire line of apples leading to the inn door.

"Odd." She stood, followed the trail, and pushed into the inn.

And the world went quiet. Conversations stopped, the sounds of eating froze midair, and even the fire seemed to crackle at a whisper. Everyone looked at her, too, wide-eyed and grinning. More baffling than that, the far wall seemed different. Paintings covered it from left to right, top to bottom.

Then the sound of a chair screeching across the floor shattered it all. She swung toward the noise. Found Raph standing, holding an apple. Looking her straight in the eye, he took a hearty bite, slammed it onto the table, then strode toward her. She clutched her heart because it had gone wild, thumping frantically, trying to jump out of her ribs and past his own, grasping for its home, so close, so walled off from her. She'd expected he would be here because of Molly. Yet seeing him still rather came as a shock.

He didn't let her get far. That strong arm of his snaked around her shoulder as he came to her side and pulled her deeper into the tavern filled with scuffed tables, teetering chairs, faces she knew well now, and paintings. Bad ones, to be sure.

"Raph, what have you done?" she whispered.

He bent at the neck, his lips hovering near her ear. "Not enough. Not for you. But I'll keep trying." He hugged her tight to his side and swept her toward the wall of paintings. He raised a hand toward them. "I present to you, Miss Matilda Bellvue, my very first art exhibition."

"Hopefully his last," someone nearby said. "And look how many apples he's bruised."

"Good thing, the fellow handles a scythe better than he does a paintbrush." She knew that voice—Tom.

"From what I've heard," the first fellow said, "he needs skill with a paintbrush more than he needs skill with the scythe."

Tom leaned low like he would whisper, but did not. "From the situation the marquess seems to be in now with Miss Bellvue, neither scythe nor paintbrush will help him. He needs prowess with quite a different *tool*." He snickered, elbowed his conversational partner.

Raph glared at them then returned his attention to Matilda. "Let's start here." He drew her toward the first three paintings on the left side of the wall. "We'll deal with the middle row only. The rest are variations of a theme. And this one"—he patted the far left middle painting—"is called *Portrait of a Fool*."

"More like the painter is a fool," someone snickered.

Raph snapped around. "That's the entire point, Patrick."

"It's only, my lord, that there's no clear light source," the man named Patrick said.

"And," another one added, "it don't rightly look like a human. And the perspective's all off."

"It's not the quality that matters. It's the message." Raph cleared his throat. "Now, if I can continue?"

Both men nodded.

"Thank you." Raph turned back to Matilda. "The fool is me. Scared. Just as you called me the first day we kissed. You saw me well then. Better than I saw myself."

She tilted her head to view the painting from a different angle. Murky colors, unidentifiable objects. "A portrait?"

"Not you too, Matilda. It's murky because I can't see things clearly. The fool can't."

"Apologies. That's quite thoughtful. Ingeniuous even. Continue."

He drew her to the next painting down the line. "I call this *Family*."

"A field of ... boulders?"

"Yes," he mumbled. "They're strong. They support me even when I'm unaware of it. I've been terribly unaware of it."

"Ah."

"This is horrifyingly difficult to do, Matilda. In front of everyone like this. I'd rather have Mother read cards for me than do this."

"Ah. That difficult, then?"

"But I'll do this for you. Follow me." He dragged her to the next paintings, these with brighter colors—yellows, rusts, indigoes. "It's ah ..." He lowered his voice, ducked low so only she could hear. "Sunrise and such, you know. Because that's you. You're the shape and color of the blood in my veins, the heart in my chest, but you're also this—a new beginning." His voice sounded gruff, and when she peered up at him, his face was red, his eyes full of doubt. But also of determination.

"I don't know what to say, Raph."

"Don't say anything yet. Come along." He dragged her toward the door.

"Oy! My lord!" Mr. Watkins, the innkeeper, called after them. "Make sure to come back for the paintings. Don't want 'em scaring the customers off."

Raph waved a hand before the door closed behind them. He picked her up and threw her atop a horse. She gasped as the ground fell away from her feet, and he mounted behind her, pulled her tight to his chest and urged the horse into a gallop.

She held tight, too, and when she looked up at him, the hard edge of his jaw said he was not in the mood for conversation. Yet she had a world of questions and wanted answers. She could not bring herself to ask them, though. Not like this, held tight by him, his scent surrounding her, his arm a band protecting her from the precariousness of her perch. Clearly he'd done all this for a reason, and she would listen.

But her brain argued her heart was wrong. Nothing had changed. This small trip to Briarcliff—for she recognized the path they took—an interlude only, a brief dream before waking. Likely, this was all an apology, a request for forgiveness before she took her leave.

Briarcliff rose before them—pretty from afar, troubled up close—and he slowed the horse, stopped it entirely, flung himself down, then reached up to help her dismount as well.

When he wrapped his hands around her waist, she felt light as a cloud, and when he brought her back down to earth, he did not release her. He'd not released her, in fact, since first wrapping his arm around her shoulders in the inn.

Now he pulled her warm against him, placed his lips to her temple, and said, "You're cold." An exhale that warmed her to her toes. "Come home and let me warm you." He bundled her under one arm and guided her into Briarcliff, up the stairs, and shuffled them through a door and into a large bedchamber with massive windows that looked out onto the garden. The room was stripped empty, a hollow space, bare and echoing. No rugs, no curtains, no bedclothes, no adornments. Even the wardrobe door hung open and empty. Nothing that made a house a home. Except the toy theatre on the trunk in one corner.

She looked up at him, shaking her head. "I am afraid your paintings make more sense than this."

He tugged her farther into the room, ignored the insult. "It's my bedroom. But I would like it to be ours. And I want you to make it *yours*. I want your music box here." He left her, rushing across the room to run his hand across the fireplace mantel. Then he darted the other direction. "And the watercolors Maggie made for you here. The bed is for your blankets and you may have whatever rug you desire." He grimaced. "Within reason." He ran for the windows. "And your curtains can go here. Naturally. Where else would curtains go. And I ... if you wish me to sleep elsewhere I will, but I certainly hope my wife will let me in her bed. Her room. Her heart. But I leave that up to you, too—where you place me within your home."

Words jumped frantically out of reach, rushed into sand, and slipped between her fingers. When she finally grasped on, she almost laughed. His favored phrase ... bollocks.

Bollocks because he'd hurt her. And bollocks because she

did not want to trust him. But also bollocks because she knew she was going to anyway. Because—bollocks—she loved him.

She stuffed her chin in the air. "I'll paint the room pink."

He turned her, stiff, as if waiting for her to flee, waiting to see which way he should run in order to chase after her. "As you wish. Tobias knows of an excellent shade. Quite soothing."

"And I'll put gold tassels everywhere."

"If it pleases you."

"I do not jest. I went through a phase five or so years back and procured pillows with tassels."

"If you come with the tassels, I'll welcome them with open arms." He took three halting steps toward her, grasped her hands, and hit his knees before her. "I cannot apologize enough. I have not been a gentleman. And I have not listened to the truth of my heart."

"And what is that truth?"

"That I need Matilda. That I'll take on any hardship to have her."

"Even if it means more hard years like the ones that came before?"

"I think they will be better. I have long feared bringing a woman into this disaster—"

"I don't care about any of that. I have often lived without, and—"

"And I have decided to be selfish for a change. You know what you walk into." He squeezed her hands. "And if you'll stay, if you'll marry me, I'll never betray your trust again. I'll give you everything I have, everything I am, little as it is—"

"No, Raph." She tugged him to his feet. "It is not little." She pulled their bodies closer together, and his large hands wrapped around her, a perfect fit as he bent over her, a cold man leaning toward the heat, his face a portrait of fear. She swept her thumb into the little bend of his elbow, nestled it in, let it find a home. "It is not little. I would stay. As you see, I have not left. Jane left days ago, but I've been sitting here still, unable to put any more distance between us. Unable, also, to leave this place."

"Don't then." He pulsed closer, their noses almost touching. "I know I do not deserve you, but I need you, and—"

She quieted his doubt with a kiss.

And like a ravenous man, he swept her into his arms, held her tight, and consumed her. Lips, tongue, soul and all, a series of clashing hard kisses that made her pant and made her grateful for the bed so nearby as well.

But she placed a hand on his chest and pushed just a bit, finding breathing space between them but holding tight. "You are in luck," she managed to say.

"Oh?" More shallow breath than word.

"Yes, I had decided, more or less, to visit you today."

He kissed her temple. "For what purpose?" He kissed the upper tip of her ear.

She shivered. "To propose marriage to you."

"Ha!"

She pushed away, arched a brow at him.

"Oh, you're serious?"

"Quite," she assured him. "You see, I realized I have a dowry. Of sorts."

He went oddly still and light for a moment, as if a breeze could topple him, then he bent low over her again, as muscular intention and heat in his eyes. "I don't want it. Just want you." He kissed her jaw.

She sighed, leaned into the caress. "Then I shall have to do what I wish with it."

He wrapped his arms around her waist and reared back a bit to peer down at her, brows knitting together. "Just out of curiosity ..."

"My cottage. I realized if I married and lived with my

husband, I would no longer have practical use for it, so I might as well, oh, rent it or sell it outright or—"

His brows leaped into arches high on his forehead. "Clever woman." He nipped her lips. "You may dispose of it how you wish."

"I think I might wish to find Molly's sister a position at Briarcliff. So her mother has both daughters nearby."

"Excellent idea," he mumbled against her ear. He nipped her earlobe with sharp teeth. "Yes, by the by."

"Yes?"

"Yes, I will marry you. And thank you for the proposal."

She laughed, threw her head back, and joy like she'd never felt rose up out of her but settled deep down in her at the same time. He kissed up the column of her arched throat and chuckled, adding his mirth to her own. He wrapped her tight in his arms and whirled her, waltzing their bodies through blurring space and tilting them. They fell through air and onto the bed, side by side, with a bounce. He covered her body quickly, so quickly, his lips laying claim to hers, and—

A knock on the door.

"We saw you both enter, Raphael," his mother said. "Please do tell—have you need of this yet?" The almost silent swish of paper over wood.

They both lifted their heads and looked toward the door where a bright square of paper glowed on the dark wood of the floor.

Raphael groaned and stood, and Matilda propped herself up on an elbow.

"You know," Franny said, her voice muffled behind the closed door, "I did a reading this morning and saw success for you, Raphael. And for Matilda. And for us all. I'm quite pleased. My dreams last night were encouraging as well. What were yours?"

Raph knelt to grab the paper. "Bollocks is what they were. Couldn't sleep."

A tsking sound from behind the door.

Raph caught Matilda's gaze. "But I expect them to improve tonight."

"Excellent," his mother said. "And you, Matilda dear?"

"As you well know, Franny, I am not in the habit of sharing my dreams with others." But they had been bollocks as well. And she, too, expected them to improve this eve. She nodded at the paper in Raph's hand. "What is that?"

Raph shook his head, unfolded the paper. "Bloody hell. That woman."

Matilda bounced from the bed to rush to his side. "What is it?"

He handed the paper to her. "A special license."

Franny cleared her voice so loud they heard it as if there wasn't a wall of oak between them and her. "I am quite good friends with the Archbishop of Canterbury. He has a fondness for Anthony van Dyck, and I happen to have one in my personal collection. We made a trade."

Raph flung the door open, blinked down at his mother. "When?"

Matilda had to admit, the timing was perplexing.

"Oh, as soon as she arrived." Franny grinned smugly. "The cards, dear, they do not lie, and they showed me that Matilda would stay. And the only way she could stay would be to marry one of my sons, and I saw she did not quite fit Atlas, so ..." She shrugged. "It is my wedding present to the both of you." She backed away from them and winked. "Now I shall leave the two of you to celebrate in the way lovers celebrate best." She winked and bustled away.

Raph shut the door quietly, throwing the lock in place. He nodded at the paper Matilda held gently between her fingers.

"You're the one who proposed. What shall we do with it? Use it? Or have the banns read?"

"Me? You painted me an entire gallery and hung it where everyone could see. You stripped your room bare so I could fill it and make it my home. Was that not a proposal?"

He nodded. "It was. But I want to know what you want. So I can give it to you."

She came to him with soft but eager steps, placing the license flat on a table as she joined him near the door. "Give me you. All I want is you. You are my home. It's why I could not leave." She wrapped her arms around his waist and rested her cheek on his chest. "I say we use it. As soon as can be because I plan to make good use of that bed behind us. "And I've recently realized I rather like babies. May very well wish to have one of my own."

"You too? Sneaky devils, aren't they? Stinky and loud until you find them squishy and cute."

"Precisely."

He tipped her chin up. "Matilda, I love you. There's no color or line to explain it. Only my soul reaching out for yours when it's not near. Only the shape of you calming me, giving me hope. You are everything that is soft and strong and beautiful at the same time, and I will ... I must have you."

She turned her head and placed a kiss, soft and slow, on his chest. "Well." She put space between their bodies and reached for his hand, traced the contours of his knuckles and kissed them. "You will be pleased to learn." Another kiss. "How well I love you." She laughed, a small huff of air across the top of his hand, and he drew her close again. "I may have for quite a long time. At the very least, you enchanted me somewhat. You were a very charming young man all those years ago."

"Telling truths now are we? Fine. I admit. After a few months of you living here the first time, I wanted to tup you senseless. After you helped me that day in the study, I wanted to marry you outright. Then I couldn't of course. If I couldn't afford a governess, I certainly could not afford a wife." He nuzzled the top of her head, and she could hear his heart beating wildly. "All those years lost."

"The wrong perspective. Instead see how many years before us." She burrowed against him, a worry entering her heart. "You ... you won't regret it, will you? Marrying me?"

"No." A stout word, strong and final. "Never. I know regret. I know what makes it scream. Sending you away. That's what angered it. Tore me apart, it did, and I poured it into every damn one of those paintings the people of Fairworth are laughing at right now. All my regret and love and determination to bring you home. Where you belong. With me."

Sweet words. She'd never heard sweeter, so she kissed him to taste the sweetness, and they found the bed once more, their bodies falling together in a tangle of limbs and clothing slipping off to reveal needy skin.

They would use the license later to bind their names forever.

Now, they would bind their bodies and hearts, reassure their souls they would not be pulled asunder, and through the binding, be stronger than before, a home for each other, and a home for everyone they loved.

Epilogue

April 1822

Somewhere above the London smog, stars must have blinked brightly, but below it, and ensconced in a carriage trundling toward Mayfair, Raph had other worries and his mind filled with a different type of brightness. He said nothing to his wife when they left the old earl's home and climbed into Tobias's carriage. He'd said nothing at all for several bouncing minutes, but now he must speak or explode.

"There was a theatre in that man's ballroom."

"Wasn't it marvelous?" Matilda leaned into his shoulder, twined her arm with his, and threaded their fingers together.

"It was ... fascinating." The only word that would come to the tip of his tongue. Though it wasn't quite the right one. "How did you discover that an earl lives on Drury Lane, and that he sponsors amateur theatrical productions in his ballroom?"

"Jane heard of it. And then I asked Tobias about it, and he'd heard of it as well."

"They charged us," Raph grumbled, "for whatever it was we just witnessed."

"Yes, and every penny of the ticket price goes to the performers. Lord Hellwater told me as much. The earl is a talkative fellow. Quite agreeable."

"Does he never stop speaking? He even had loud interjections during the play." And since it was Raph's first theater experience in almost two decades, excluding the one Matilda had performed for him, he'd rather hoped to experience it in some somber state of gratitude and contemplation.

"I thought his interjections quite fitting. Went with the spirit of things. And what a spirit. Kings and queens with cockney accents improvising their lines. Best play I've seen in ages."

"Not the best." He lifted her hand to his lips for a kiss, then he pulled her in closer and kissed her temple, too. "Your play was better."

She laughed. "You're only saying that because you got to see me in breeches."

"I've come to the conclusion that a fine woman fitted in a fine pair of breeches is an essential part of any theatrical seduction."

"Raph!"

"Pardon me." He grinned wide. "I mean theatrical *production*. Naturally."

"Did you enjoy it?" she asked.

"I am a bit dumbfounded, but yes, I did. I enjoy even more that you found such an oddity for me."

"We cannot afford to spend lavishly, but there's no need to deny ourselves the little pleasures." She bounced up and kissed his cheek.

"I'm coming to learn the truth of that." He tipped her chin slightly up and took her mouth. "*This* is no *little* pleasure, though."

"Yet it's one you take advantage of quite often," she said between kisses.

They did not part until the coach rolled to a stop, then Raph helped his wife out and into Maggie and Tobias's townhouse. They greeted the butler at the door, and as they strode for the parlor where he knew Maggie and Tobias would be reading or writing or designing or what have you with the baby nearby, he said, "Bring my wife some tea."

Matilda laughed and wrapped her arms around his waist as they found their way down the hall together. "You do not have to continue calling me 'my wife' every day, all day, every chance you get. Everyone knows."

"I like it, though." He tickled her ribs.

They burst into the parlor on a laughing fit.

"Good evening," Raph said. "Have you all met my wife?"

Tobias rolled his eyes and returned to his work. "I'm supposed to be the ridiculous one. What is this topsy-turvy world we find ourselves in?"

Maggie grinned. "I like it."

"How was the play, old man?" Tobias asked.

"Never seen anything like it before," Raph said. "I think I might go again next week."

The door opened as he settled himself onto a couch, Matilda by his side.

But the housekeeper with the tea cart did not enter.

"Zander!" Maggie gasped. "What are you doing here?"

"I found him!" Zander leaned against the doorframe and rubbed at this eyes. "The painter. He's here in London. I have an address and everything. But I'm dead tired and don't want to face the fiend until I've had a nap. Can I borrow a bed or couch or something? Somewhere to rest my weary bones?"

"Yes of course," Maggie said. "It will have to be a couch, though. Matilda and Raph have the only other bed."

Zander snorted and stumbled farther into the room.

"You'd think Mr. Silk Master over there"—he nodded at Tobias—"would have a bigger house. Can afford it, can't you?"

"The size hardly signifies," Tobias drawled. "It's how you use it that matters."

Lysander dropped into a chair slinging one arm over his eyes. The skin beneath them was bruised blue, shadowed gray.

"Zander," Raph said, "We've told you the painter doesn't matter. He doesn't have the originals."

"But he might know the location of the buyer. They are partners of a sort, after all." Zander yawned. "Mr. Duck Lips had me all up and down England looking for a rare vase."

"Duck lips?" Tobias inquired, the corners of his lips quirked up.

"Oh his name's Duckington," Zander said, "or something like that, but you should see his lips, Toby—just like a duck's. An aptly named fellow, I tell you."

"The painter?" Raph pressed. "The forger?"

"Oh, yes." Zander sat upright with a groan and braced his elbows on his knees. "I've had the address for a week or so now, but that damn vase has kept me busy. Finally found it, brought it home to Duckworth, collected my wages, and hied it here."

The tea cart came rumbling in and Zander pounced on it.

"Into a cup first, please," Matilda said.

Lysander lowered the teapot from a position precariously close to his lips, snagged a cup, and poured the steaming beverage into that instead. "Sorry. Raph, why'd you have to marry someone who orders me about? Now I'm ordered about by two people—three if you count my employers."

"Not that you do what any of us ask you to do," Raph said. "Except of course Matilda."

"How am I to say no to her?" Zander rolled his eyes. "If I

do, you'll smash me into the ground. Plant me in the fields as excellent fertilizer for the corn."

Matilda grinned. "A fact I'm well aware of and quite use to my advantage."

"We don't grow corn," Raph grumbled.

Zander threw the rest of the tea down his throat, cringed. "Burns, it does." Then he slapped his thighs and jumped to his feet. "Well, I'm off to find the painter. I'll return for that bed later, Mags."

"Don't you think you should rest first?" Matilda asked, using the tone that suggested it was not truly a question.

"It really does not matter anymore," Raph said, and meant it. "What is done is done, and to buy the paintings simply to sell them once more or to switch them out with the fakes ... it makes no sense. They served the purpose well when you sold them the first time, and we are the only ones with the copies. No harm done."

Zander, Maggie, and Tobias blinked at him, identical pictures of mystification.

Zander scrubbed his hands across his face. "All the harm done. But I'll fix it. I'll fix all of it, don't you worry." With a dangerous sort of determination glinting in his eyes, he strolled through the door then popped back in and grabbed a biscuit. With a wink, while biting into the biscuit, he disappeared once more.

Matilda worried her lip and stared at the empty doorway. "You don't think he's in danger with this painter fellow, do you Raph?"

"I can't say. I've never met a painter who would prefer to use his brush to stab rather than to create."

"Wouldn't the handle break," Tobias drawled, "before it pierced the muscle? Not asking out of insensitivity to our dear brother's situation, you understand. Merely out of the scientific curiosity."

"I mean it metaphorically," Raph said.

"Well," Tobias grumbled, "it was a rather bad metaphor. Sounded literal to me."

Raph stood. "I think I'd like to take my evening whiskey in our room. Matilda?" He held out a hand to her.

"I am rather tired." Matilda took his hand and stood at his side, a warm presence strong and soothing. "But I leave not because of any annoyance with Tobias." She smiled at the man. "I have entirely other reasons for wishing to retire for the evening."

Maggie snorted. "Go. We shall see you in the morning."

Raph and Matilda kissed all the way up the stairs, soft little sounds that promised much and gave even more. And as soon as they entered their room, the door snicked shut behind them, and their bodies fell onto the bed while they fell into each other.

When they lay sated and sweaty in one another's arms, counting heartbeats as a measure of happiness, Raph said, "Do you wish some days for the solitude of your cottage?"

"No, actually. It is still there if I need it. It is being put to much better use now. Who knew we could earn so much from renting it to travelers. It has inspired me." She pressed a kiss into his bare chest.

He grinned. He loved it when her brain whirred round, could almost hear the cogs working. He kissed the top of her head, her temple.

She slapped his shoulder, a playful tap as she leaned into him. "No distractions. I think we should put some of the funds from the cottage toward renovating the dower house. We could rent that out, too."

"We'll consider it. The dower house may be too damaged."

"Hmm. Perhaps. But damaged does not mean unfixable."

He knew that well now, gave daily thanks for it. "We can try, then."

She walked her fingers up his abdomen until her palm rested against his heart. "Or ... we can ask Lysander to create more copies of valuable paintings and sell the originals. Especially now that he's cornered the painter. I'll never understand why your father did that. Leaving the forgeries to you. He *must* have known."

Neither would Raph, but he'd let go of the question and let go of his anger in a wave of forgiveness that had opened his eyes. His father had toppled a marquessate, but he'd shown Raph the correct way to build it back up. He needed money, yes, but he needed love more. Because without it, the rest had no worth.

"I think," Matilda said, kissing his chest, "he was saying that things we think are most valuable are not. They're fake. The real priceless bits of art are in the people we love." She tilted her head, considered him. "Would you like to paint me again, Marquess?"

Raph rolled, pinned her to the bed and nipped her neck. "Vixen. God, I love you." He touched the tip of his nose to hers then placed his cheek against hers and whispered against her skin so close to her ear, again but softer, "I love you."

He would say the words over and over, as many times as it took for her to know that his heart would always be her home.

Afterword

I mention the names of many different Regency-era artists in this novel, but none of the references are terribly factual. While these artists existed and worked during this time period, or their work was popular and valuable during the era, they never attended a house party at the fictional Marquess of Waneborough's country estate. I briefly mention JMW Turner painting porcelain cups under the influence of two whiskies. This never happened outside of my imagination, so far as I know. And the man, apparently, preferred rum. However, the word whisky had better rhythm in the sentence. I mean no offense to Turner or his fans (of which I am one).

But he may haunt me now.

And, likely, I'll deserve it.

If you'd like to know more about the type of research I did for this and other books, check out my website!

Acknowledgments

There are so many people to thank all the time when writing a book that it's impossible to know where to start. First, as always, major gratitude to Anna Volkin, Chris Hall, and Krista Dapkey. Without them there would be no editing and no pretty covers. And they make the polishing end of putting a book together wonderfully fun and easy.

Thank you Rachel Ann Smith and Rebecca Paula, my author writing buddies who are always there to lift my spirits or perfect my blurb or tell me when my ideas make no sense.

Many MANY thanks to my ARC team and especially those with eagle eyes who spot those final typos so I can eradicate them. You are invaluable, and I am impressed.

Also, the Brazen Belles are a constant source of positivity and inspiration. I'm so lucky to be a part of that community of authors and readers.

Finally, thank you, THANK YOU to my husband and kiddos who have to live with me when I'm two feet away from them but also living in a different century and country.

Also by Charlie Lane

The Cavendish Family

Leave a Widow Wanting More

Teach a Rogue New Tricks

Bring a Boxer to His Knees

Love a Lady at Midnight

Scandalizing the Scoundrel (May 2023)

London Secrets

The Secret Seduction

A Secret Desire

Sinning in Secret

Keep No Secrets

Secrets Between Lovers

The Debutante Dares (with WOLF Press)

Daring the Duke

A Dare Too Far

Kiss or Dare

Don't You Dare, My Dear

Only Rakes Would Dare

Daring Done Right

About the Author

CHARLIE LANE traded in academic databases and scholarly journals for writing steamy Regency romcoms like the ones she's always loved to read. When she's not writing humorous conversations, dramatic confrontations, or sexy times, she's flying high in the air as a circus-obsessed acrobat.

Visit my website with the QR code and your phone!

Made in the USA
Monee, IL
04 December 2023